CAUSE OF DEATH

Praise for Sheri Lewis Wohl

She Wolf

"I really enjoyed this book—I couldn't put it down once I started it. The author's style of writing was very good and engaging. All characters, including the supporting characters, were multi-layered and interesting."—*Melina Bickard, Librarian, Waterloo Library (UK)*

The Talebearer

"As a crime story, it is a good read that had me turning pages quickly…The book is well-written and the characters are well-developed."—*Reviews by Amos Lassen*

Twisted Echoes

"A very unusual blend of lesbian romance and horror…[W]oven throughout this modern romance is a neatly plotted horror story from the past, which bleeds ever increasingly into the present of the two main characters. Lorna and Renee are well matched and face ever-increasing danger from spirits from the past. An unusual story that gets tenser and more interesting as it progresses."
—*Pippa Wischer, Manager at Berkelouw Books, Armadale*

Twisted Screams

"[A] cast of well-developed characters leads you through a maze of complex emotions."—*Lunar Rainbow Reviewz*

Vermilion Justice

"[T]he characters are so dynamic and well-written that this becomes more than just another vampire story. It's probably impossible to read this book and not come across a character who reminds you of someone you actually know. Wohl takes something as fictional as vampires and makes them feel real. Highly recommended."
—*GLBT Reviews: The ALA's GLBT Round Table*

By the Author

Crimson Vengeance

Burgundy Betrayal

Scarlet Revenge

Vermilion Justice

Twisted Echoes

Twisted Whispers

Twisted Screams

Necromantia

She Wolf

Walking Through Shadows

The Talebearer

Drawing Down the Mist

Cause of Death

Visit us at www.boldstrokesbooks.com

CAUSE OF DEATH

by
Sheri Lewis Wohl

2019

CAUSE OF DEATH
© 2019 BY SHERI LEWIS WOHL. ALL RIGHTS RESERVED.

ISBN 13: 978-1-63555-441-0

THIS TRADE PAPERBACK ORIGINAL IS PUBLISHED BY
BOLD STROKES BOOKS, INC.
P.O. BOX 249
VALLEY FALLS, NY 12185

FIRST EDITION: AUGUST 2019

THIS IS A WORK OF FICTION. NAMES, CHARACTERS, PLACES, AND INCIDENTS ARE THE PRODUCT OF THE AUTHOR'S IMAGINATION OR ARE USED FICTITIOUSLY. ANY RESEMBLANCE TO ACTUAL PERSONS, LIVING OR DEAD, BUSINESS ESTABLISHMENTS, EVENTS, OR LOCALES IS ENTIRELY COINCIDENTAL.

THIS BOOK, OR PARTS THEREOF, MAY NOT BE REPRODUCED IN ANY FORM WITHOUT PERMISSION.

CREDITS
EDITOR: SHELLEY THRASHER
PRODUCTION DESIGN: STACIA SEAMAN
COVER DESIGN BY TAMMY SEIDICK

Acknowledgments

I can't say thank you enough to my editor and friend, Shelley Thrasher. A beautiful person, a wonderful writer, and a world-class editor. She makes my life better.

To Jeni. I still can't believe you're gone. I miss your laugh. I miss your magic. I miss you. Rest easy with the angels, my beautiful friend. I will see you on the other side.

For God shall bring every work into judgment,
with every secret thing,
whether it be good,
or whether it be evil.

    Ecclesiastes 12:14 (King James Version)

Prologue

It began and ended with the eyes. His mother had taken her last breath to show him the way, and while he'd understood her message, even as young as he'd been at the time, he'd also known his quest would require much work. When the time was right, he began in earnest. Years of study and experiments had now confirmed for the Seeker one critical thing. He could find what he had dedicated his life's work to only in the organ of sight. That discovery had been a game changer.

Part of the journey had taught him to look at everyone in a different way. Like right now. The young man with him was handsome, maybe eighteen or nineteen, with curly blond hair and lashes that women would spend hundreds of dollars to achieve. Regular people would see only a tall, attractive man with model potential. The Seeker couldn't care less about his glossy hair or chiseled cheekbones. He zeroed in on the man's incredible blue eyes and the thick lashes he'd apparently been born with. They perfectly framed the ice-blue eyes that stared up at the night sky and the twinkling stars.

This subject, as well as all the others, confirmed the truth behind the trite saying that the eyes are windows to the soul. Until the one special day with his mother, he'd been unaware. The surprising gift he'd received at his mother's side had remained the guiding force behind his current spate of trials. He sought knowledge, and with each successive trial, he understood more clearly that the saying that sounded so stupid contained the truth he had long searched for. The joy that success brought was, at first, indescribable. He had expected the feeling to last.

It hadn't, which had been brought home only two months earlier. Like the young man with him now, the pretty woman with the chocolate-brown eyes had been special. He'd waited a long time for her, and when he'd completed his work without the expected rush of satisfaction, he'd been crushed. Then as he'd stood next to her and stared at the treasured jar holding her precious gift, a new realization gave birth to a revised and wonderful course. He'd returned home, added the jar to his collection, and started planning for the next phase.

As it began and the power it brought with it revealed itself, he couldn't stop. No other way to describe it beyond intoxicating and far better than any ingested, mood-altering substance. Who needed drugs or booze when this existed? One simply had to have skills and a bountiful supply of subjects. One had to be as smart as he just happened to be.

The Seeker reached for his shiny new scalpel and smiled as he completed tonight's work, his hand rock steady. Blue was one of his favorite colors, and tonight's treasure would fit in very nicely with the rest. As he stood and slipped the jar into his pocket, his smile grew, the joy of it flooding him. He walked away with a light step and didn't look back.

Chapter One

Vi gazed down at the newly minted identification card and grinned. Her full name, Bavilla Akiak, was printed right below the picture. Not her best photographic moment, but then again, she'd driven directly to the medical examiner's office, as instructed by her friend and former boss, Shirley Yarno. Shirley, the chief medical examiner in Anchorage, had been instrumental in securing her a position here in Spokane. Her direction to Vi as she'd left to head south had been crystal clear: go meet the ME before she even *thought* about going anywhere else. From Alaska through Canada and across Washington State, she'd kept those marching orders in mind. Like always, Dr. Yarno had been right. It took about two seconds for her to grasp that her new direct report, Dana Kelsey, MD, appreciated a prompt appearance at the office. One gold star and she wasn't even officially on the payroll yet.

Back out at her car, she stood for a while staring at the driver's side door. The journey from Anchorage to Spokane had been thousands of miles long, and she felt beyond ready to be out of the car for a good long while. She wouldn't object to never getting behind the wheel and driving again. Given that she'd rented a little home in a small bedroom community north of the city, where all the houses were situated on acreage and near enough to nature to make her feel somewhat like she was back home, she didn't have a choice about another stretch of travel. She hoped the compact house turned out to be as good in reality as it had looked in the pictures. Even if it was half as pretty, she'd be happy.

The adventure of coming here had been, and remained, nerve-wracking. It represented a dream coming true, but that didn't mean she wasn't terrified by the prospect of a complete change. To move away from the only home she'd ever known to achieve her goal held a certain amount of thrill. To leave behind her friends, her hometown, and everything she knew—well, that wasn't quite as thrilling. Her friends were generous with their encouragement and, more than that, with the push she needed to follow through. They understood why she wanted to become a doctor and, more specifically, a forensic pathologist in a medical examiner's office.

The figurative road to get here hadn't been quick or easy. It had taken her far longer than she liked to be accepted into medical school. She'd never given up, even when her application had been rejected not once or twice, but three times. The fourth submission turned out to be the charm, and her exhilaration to be starting school at the Spokane-based Washington State University School of Medicine needed no explanation.

So here she stood, gratefully employed, a fledgling medical student and a brand-new resident of eastern Washington. Once she'd located the place she'd signed a one-year lease on, sight unseen, she'd be, as her grandmother liked to say, in fat city. That turned out to be easier than she thought. The commute from the medical examiner's office just north of downtown Spokane to Highway 291 took her out to the area a road sign declared to be Nine Mile Falls. Her navigation app directed her to a lovely home on the Little Spokane River. As she drove down the long driveway, bordered on both sides by well-maintained fences, she saw llamas or alpacas inside the pastures, though she wasn't quite sure which was which. After her long drive, the beauty of it projected a calming effect that had her relaxing already.

A nice house sat at the end of the driveway. Not big. Not small either. A one-story painted beige with dark-brown trim and a railed porch that spanned the entire length of the front. Shrubs lined the outside of the porch and provided a pleasant spot of color. Double doors with leaded-glass inserts graced the entrance. She hoped her little rental house would have the same homey vibe as this lovely, welcoming one.

Vi got out of the car and walked up the few steps to the front doors. She had just reached out to ring the doorbell, when the sound of pounding feet made her turn around. Racing toward her sped a dog, medium-sized, with a mostly blue-gray coat and black hair around its eyes that made it look as though it were wearing a mask. Its deep, dark eyes were intent on her. She backed up, not because dogs scared her, but because by the looks of this one, in about five seconds, she'd be flat on her behind. She braced for impact.

"Lucy, sit!" A woman's voice came from somewhere around the corner of the house.

To Vi's astonishment, the dog stopped immediately and sat down at the bottom of the steps. Its tail continued to wag, and its whole body wiggled as if unable to contain its excitement. It was cute and impressive. Vi relaxed now that she wasn't about to be knocked down.

"I'm so sorry." A woman rounded the corner and headed up the steps in Vi's direction. "Lucy gets really excited when anyone shows up. Some kind of guard dog, eh?" She recognized the voice as the same one she'd heard on the phone as she'd arranged for the lease. Kate Renard.

She was medium height, with long, purposeful strides, but the red hair captured Vi's interest the most. Short and wild, it made her want to reach out and touch it. She kept her hands to herself, not wanting to make that kind of first impression. When she got close, she could see that her eyes were deep green and, well, gorgeous. She held out her hand. "I'm Vi Akiak."

The other woman took her hand, her grip sure and firm. Nice too. "I was pretty sure it was you." She winked, which made Vi smile. "I'm Kate, but everyone calls me Kat. How was your drive?"

She'd been right. Kate Renard, her landlord. So far, so good. Things were going well with this move. She'd been impressed with her boss in the ME's office, and now she had to say, her first impression of her landlord came off positive too. If she hadn't been exhausted, she'd be anxious to take time to get to know her new home. "Long."

Kat laughed. "No shit. I did that drive a million years ago, and you couldn't pay me enough to do it again. I think my butt still hurts from all those hours in the driver's seat. These days I'm about alternate and much quicker modes of transportation. Can you say airplane?"

Amen to that idea and yes, her butt felt fairly numb too. Vi would have loved to fly and bypass all the days on the road. If it had been a simple trip, she would have jumped on a plane in a heartbeat with a suitcase or two. Simple hadn't been in the cards. To move an entire life in a couple of suitcases would have been impossible. In a single vehicle it hadn't been much easier. She'd done it, though she never wanted to have to do it again.

She'd had to make some hard choices about what to keep and what to let go of. Some of her friends had suggested that she move the things she didn't need in the immediate future into storage and bypass a complete downsizing. Tempting as the idea had been, she'd had to go a different direction. Everything she still owned was in her car because she didn't know if or when she'd be back in Alaska. It would be years before she became a full-fledged doctor, and even more before she finished her specialty of forensic pathology. She would have to go where life took her from here on out. Planning for this life-altering experience had been stressful while home in Anchorage. Now here with her whole life boxed up in the car, it was even scarier. She was up to it. She hoped.

"Too much stuff to fly." She inclined her head toward her car, unsure if it looked like she was relocating or homeless.

Kat glanced at her vehicle, with the boxes stacked in the back, and nodded. "Gotcha. Come on. I'm sure you'd like to see your new home. I'm confident you'll find it comfortable here. We sure do."

We? Vi glanced toward the house and then back at Kat. None of her business who else lived here. "I'm liking things already." And she was. It was pretty here and, even better, quiet. Sleep and peacefulness were both treasured in her world and would be even more so once school began.

Kat smiled as she looked around. "Appreciate the vote of approval. I've loved this place since the first day I laid eyes on it." She returned her gaze to Vi. "I bet you're tired, so let's get you settled in. You can put your feet up and enjoy some serious R&R."

"That would be nice." What she didn't say was that she was less concerned about settling in and more about the bed. She'd like to sleep for about a month, not that rest would be on the agenda in any measurable amount. With her first full day of work scheduled to start at eight tomorrow morning, and school beginning in three weeks, she wouldn't have much time to relax. The way she figured it, she'd have about enough time to unpack, check in at the school, and get her sea legs at work before the insanity of her new life began in earnest. It was daunting and exciting all at the same time.

"Come on, I'll show you *su casa*." Kat turned and looked at the still-sitting dog, her tail moving back and forth as if she could barely contain her excitement. "Free dog."

Lucy sprang up and ran to Vi. Her tail picked up speed. Vi laughed as she reached down and ran a hand over her head. "You're a pretty girl."

Kat laughed too. "Don't tell her that. Trust me, it'll go right to her head. She already thinks she's the best thing since sliced bread. Don't you, my little girlfriend?" Lucy barked as if agreeing with Kat.

"She's awfully pretty." Vi liked the way the black hair around her eyes gave her character and how infectious energy rolled off her.

"Pretty talented too. She's a search dog and certified in multiple disciplines." The pride in Kat's voice shone through, and Vi could understand why. She was acquainted with several of the K9 officers back home, and the work they put in was nothing short of insane.

Vi squatted to be at Lucy's level and held out her hand. Lucy sniffed and seemed to smile. She ran a hand over her head. "So you're a working dog."

Lucy licked her face as if to say, "Absolutely."

"She's quite the worker," Kat said. "In more ways than one. She will work to find you if you're lost or work you until she gets half your hamburger."

Still squatting next to Lucy, Vi rubbed her head as she looked up at Kat. "Let me get this straight. You're a dog handler, but your name is Kat?"

Her hearty laughter lit up her face in a really nice way. "You hit that oxymoron right square on the head. Blame my brothers. They started calling me Kat when I was a baby, and it stuck. When I turned out to be a dog person, everyone in my family found it hilarious, but by then it was too late to change a thing."

"I love it." Vi laughed too, and Lucy gave her another big lick.

"Well, I'll be damned." Kat had her hands on her hips.

Vi looked up again into Kat's eyes. "What? Was that wrong to let her lick me? I'm sorry. I should have asked first if it was okay to pet her. I'm not usually this rude. I'll blame it on the fatigue." She dropped her hands away from Lucy.

Kat shook her head. "No. It's fine to pet her. Lucy's a very social girl and likes to greet people when they come here. The thing is, she doesn't lick anyone. She's not that kind of dog."

"Is that bad?" Despite Kat's assurance about petting Lucy, Vi couldn't shake the feeling she'd done something wrong.

"On the contrary, it means she likes you, a lot. She reserves that kind of affection for a very few. Only one thing to say about it: welcome to the pack."

Vi smiled and felt a twinge of something like hope. Her grandmother had been a big believer in signs, and she had a hunch she'd just been given one. "Well, thanks for the invite." She ran her hand over Lucy's head again. The softness and warmth beneath her hand sent a wave of comfort through her body. She stood and directed her smile at Kat. "I like her too."

❖

Two things struck Kat at once. First, her new tenant possessed something very special, or Lucy never would have taken to her immediately. Second, Vi Akiak looked enough like her teammate Circe to be a blood relation. How freaky was that?

Kinda cool though. Things had been a bit boring lately, and Kat felt ready for something new and exciting. It had just arrived in the form of this medical student. Like Circe, she was pretty, with her long, dark hair and dark eyes that shone with intelligence. She had that same light about her that Circe did too. Even freakier. She'd have to make a point of calling her pal to find out if she had some secret little sister she'd never mentioned.

She almost laughed out loud and caught herself. Didn't want to run Vi off by making her think she was a nut job. Well, some, like some of her own family, might call her a bit of a nut. After all, how many single women preferred hanging out at their farm rather than going on a romantic date? She couldn't help it. The animals never let her down. People weren't quite as reliable. She preferred the old better-safe-than-sorry. She'd done sorry enough times already to be way over it.

"Come, Lucy. Let's show Vi where she's going to live." She turned to look at Vi. "Lucy and I will walk, and you can follow in your car. That way you'll have all your stuff close. It's straight down that way." She pointed.

The wide gravel driveway snaked around scattered pines as it led back to the rental. She'd thinned out the trees a few years back to protect against the fire danger summer brought to this area and to give the place more light. When she'd first bought it, the entire parcel had been loaded with the pines. It wasn't that she didn't like them. She did. But sometimes less could definitely be more, particularly when they created a safety hazard. It turned out to be a perfect blending of light and shade.

She and Lucy started jogging along the side of the driveway, and in a minute or so, Vi followed right behind them in her car. The little house came into view, and they continued to jog until they'd made it up the three steps to the small porch. Vi pulled in front of the one-car garage and parked. "Home sweet home," Kat announced. "Hope you like it."

Vi stood next to the car, scanning the house and yard. Kat moved from foot to foot as she watched her, wondering what she was thinking. The house was the original dwelling on the place. It wasn't fancy—a one-bedroom, one-bath with a single-car garage and a swath of grass that went all the way around it. Kat had lived in it for the first five years while she built a larger home and a barn on the south end of the property. She kept it nice and hoped her newest tenant would like it.

A smile turned up the corners of Vi's mouth, and Kat couldn't help but think about what a nice thing the smile did for her face. She really was a lovely woman, and no doubt someday she'd break the heart of a patient or two. "This is beautiful and perfect."

Kat stopped shifting her feet. "It's nice and quiet, and I'm confident you'll find it very comfortable. It's also far enough away from the barn and pastures that the animals shouldn't bother you."

"I don't have a problem with any animal."

Kat liked her easy acceptance of her little farm. "We're pretty quiet by and large, and if we do bother you, please speak up. I promise not to take it personally. I want you to be comfortable here."

"It reminds me of home. One of our neighbors was a musher and always had a dozen or so sled dogs. I'll tell you what. Get a couple of teams of dogs howling at the same time, and that's noisy."

"You're gonna have to tell me about that. I find sled dogs fascinating. Always wanted to visit a sled-dog ranch."

Vi turned and studied her. "I can introduce you if you ever make it up to Alaska."

Only if you come with me. Well, where the hell did that come from? She was getting sappy over a woman she'd known for about ten minutes. Maybe she did need to rethink her self-imposed isolation and go on a date or two just to make sure she didn't embarrass herself whenever a pretty woman showed up. "That would be nice."

"Can I look inside?"

"Of course." She held out a set of keys she'd been holding so tight they left dents in the palm of her hand. "It's all yours for the next year." She glanced around and wondered if her excitement was all about her own delight rather than what might be best for Vi. A little shallow even on the best of days. "Are you sure you want to live this far out instead of in town closer to the school? The roads can get slick in the winters, and that hill up into Suncrest can be a real bitch with cars going sideways, if they can even make it up."

The laughter lit up her face even more. She really was lovely. "You do remember I'm a native Alaskan, right?"

Heat stung Kat's cheeks. "Ah yeah. I guess you have some experience with snowy winters."

"A bit, yes."

Kat held up her hands. "In my defense, you'd be surprised how many people fail to realize that eastern Washington has four seasons, and one of them includes a crap load of snow. Everybody thinks if you live in Washington it's all rain and coffee, aka Seattle-style. We have a whole lot more experience with bad roads on this side of the state, although our coffee is just as good as any you'll find in Seattle."

Vi turned and studied the house again. "I think I'll like here just fine. It's enough like where I came from I shouldn't feel homesick, or not too much anyway. I don't think I'll totally escape being homesick, considering this is the first time I've ever been away from Alaska."

"You've never traveled in the States?"

Vi raised an eyebrow, and Kat had the feeling she'd just made a faux pas. "You mean the lower forty-eight? I was born and raised in the States, technically speaking."

"Crap." She slapped a hand over her mouth and felt her cheeks get even hotter. If she wanted to look like a dunce, she couldn't do a better job than she'd managed to right at the moment.

Vi broke the momentary tension with a hearty laugh. "It's all right, Kat. People do that all the time, and we have to remind them that Alaska is a state."

"I won't do it again."

"Not to worry and I'm happy to remind you." Her smile took any sting out of the promise. "To answer your question, yes, I've traveled a fair amount. It's just that I've never lived anywhere except Alaska, so this is going to be an adventure for me in several different ways."

"Come on. Let's take a look at your new home." Kat's nervousness returned as she opened the door. It wasn't like Vi was the first renter she'd had in the little house. By far she held the title of the most attractive and alluring. Not to mention the first one she'd ever really wanted to impress.

❖

This one was different, and he found it acceptable. At times it became important to shake things up, and now was one of them. The opportunity presented itself, and only someone very foolish would squander it. The old woman on the bed represented a subject far from one the Seeker would have chosen, and yet, strange as it was, everything about her was perfect. Her eyes, the color of milk chocolate, were clear and aware, and not what would be expected from someone of her advanced age. Her skin, unaccountably smooth, with only a hint of the wrinkles that by rights should line her face, fascinated him. Seventy-six years old, she was the kind of woman anyone in their eighth decade of life would love to be.

Decade number nine would not be in her future. Her remarkable physical state became the very thing that had caught the Seeker's attention. That and the fact that she was a slight woman and easy to control jumped her right to the top of his list. All he had to do was follow her home and wait. After a mere sixty-five minutes watching from the shelter of a large hedge, he'd let himself inside the house and rendered her immobile on the bed in her tidy bedroom. Her small running shoes and athletic apparel were in a jumbled pile on the floor. It wasn't like she would need to use them again.

Now, he pulled the cell phone from his jacket pocket and tapped the voice-memo app to begin recording. He set the phone, still recording, on the nightstand next to her bed. He hadn't planned to add her to his list of subjects, so he wasn't sure about everything that might happen in this room.

He swept his gaze over her naked body, taking in every nuance of her physical state. "Subject is approximately five feet three inches tall, with short silver hair and brown eyes. She reports her age at seventy-six. Upon placing the gag in subject's mouth, it was noted that all teeth appear to be original models. No body markings or piercings noted. No major scars or evidence of surgical procedures."

The Seeker always did a thorough inventory of the subjects. It was important to collect the empirical data, or what would be the purpose of the experiments? He had nothing to compare against, no way to quantify the results of the work. That wasn't acceptable. Someday they would see and understand the true nature of the mission and how it had opened up an avenue of true knowledge that had never before been seen. Yes, everything must be done methodically and scientifically. She became his oldest subject yet, a characteristic that excited him. As much as he wanted to hurry through the process to see what he could learn from her, he reined in his anticipation. He had to do everything in its proper sequence.

"Subject is well-nourished but not overweight. Body mass appears to be within normal ranges. Muscle tone is exceptional for a woman in her seventies. Subject reports that she runs five miles three to five days per week. Overall, this subject is an excellent, if not above-average, representation for an elderly female."

Her eyes, the lids taped to her forehead, telegraphed the fear that her body could not react to thanks to his precise methods. There were no wounds, at least not the physical kind. Undoubtedly there would be psychological wounds, that is, if she were to survive what was coming. An odor of urine drifted up into the air. The first time it happened, it had almost ruined the experiment. Now, understanding the physical responses to fear, he welcomed the odoriferous evidence of success.

"Now, now, Lily." He brushed the fine silver hair off her forehead. "Don't you worry. I'm not going to hurt you."

It wasn't a complete lie. Gratuitous violence wasn't necessary. Or it wasn't any longer. When it had all started, perhaps some of the early experiments, especially with his first one, had involved a level of violence that the Seeker ultimately determined to be unwarranted. With time and practice, the process became far more refined. He achieved success with cleaner and simpler techniques. It was better for all involved. The subjects expired in a smoother and more predictable manner. For the Seeker, the orderly process allowed him to track the results of the experiments much easier.

Gazing at her, he saw the signs he waited for. She was ready. Her chest was rising and falling quickly, and her heart hammered beneath the hand he laid on her left breast. He liked that. It got the blood flowing, which was important. Her eyes were moving back and forth as if she searched for the help that would only arrive in time to take her body to the morgue. The Seeker would be long gone before the ME's van arrived. He always timed everything with an expert touch.

He glanced over at the phone on the nightstand, confirming that it remained in record mode. Then from the inside pocket of the bag he'd brought with him, he pulled out a small black, zippered case. From inside it he removed the scalpel with his latex-gloved hand and laid it next to her. Then he took out the second syringe, filled and ready for use. The first syringe, already administered, had been dropped back into the bag. He did all of it in front of her taped-open eyes, anticipating the fright that filled them. The enjoyment it brought defied description.

"Lily, Lily, Lily," he cooed. "It won't be long now. You and I will do this together."

He leaned in close and brought the syringe to her neck. Again her eyes rolled. "No, my sweet, look at me." When she didn't, he pressed the syringe hard enough against her flesh to pierce it. "I said," his voice turned hard, "look at me."

This time she obeyed and her terrified eyes met his. "That's better. Now, just focus on me and don't look away again. This will be over soon." He pressed the needle deep into her neck.

Chapter Two

Vi couldn't help but be impressed with both her landlord and her dog. She'd always loved dogs and, if not for her insane schedule, would have one or two or three. Once she got through med school, and residency, and her specialization training, well, yes, then she'd get one. Of course, by the time she finished all that she might be eighty. Still, it was never too late to get a dog, right? In the meantime, she could appreciate and be content with the canines that belonged to those in her orbit.

She dropped the last of the boxes from her car onto the kitchen floor. Even though she'd downsized to the capacity of her vehicle, it still seemed like she'd unpacked boxes for hours. In reality it had taken less than one to empty the car and get the boxes piled up in the living room. It seemed a little sad that she could move her whole life in about fifty minutes. How boring was she?

Yet moving like that also made her feel free. Opportunity stretched out before her, nothing holding her back. Oh, she would miss her hometown and the people who made it so special. But with her mother gone for years and her grandmother dead for almost a year, her ties to Alaska had become so thin they were near to breaking.

That wasn't exactly right. She would always feel connected to the mountains, the rivers, and the glaciers that were her birthright. Being part Yupik would forever tie her to the land and the people of Alaska, and she would never forget her heritage no matter how far away she traveled. Her grandmother had made sure she knew who and what she was, and encouraged her to be proud of it.

Despite all that, she'd been compelled to leave. The lure had been there even before grandmother had been called home to the great beyond. If she considered it very long, she'd admit that even before

Mom passed away, she'd known that she would someday follow her destiny into the world beyond the forty-ninth state. It hadn't been difficult to decide because she'd felt the draw for a long time, or rather the shove. Hard to ignore, especially when no one remained in her life to talk her out of leaving or give her a reason to stay. In the back of her mind she'd hoped that the thing—the sight—that had been with her since childhood would go away once she left Alaska. She'd held on to the belief since she was a child.

Grandmother had been different. She'd rejoiced in Vi's unique ability and looked at it as a gift. She'd spent the rest of her life trying to make Vi see it that way. Her attempts to sway her granddaughter's aversion to her so-called gift had never quite been successful, although they weren't totally unsuccessful either. Thanks to her grandmother, she'd become far more comfortable with it than she might otherwise have been. Together they'd figured out a powerful way to make it work for not only Vi, but for others as well. Her grandmother had been one smart woman. How she missed her.

Vi's move to Spokane and enrollment at Washington State University's medical school had initially been her grandmother's idea. It hadn't taken much persuasion to get Vi to realize it was a great one and exactly what she needed and wanted. It had set her on a path that spoke to her heart and soul. She'd done her undergraduate work at the University of Alaska and now finally had the opportunity to continue her studies here. Anxious to get started, she was also excited to see what she could do for those who could no longer speak for themselves. Leave it to her grandmother to come up with a way to make something so unwelcome, such as seeing the dead, become a positive part of her world.

After her grandmother died, her life took a dramatic shift. Only then had she realized how unusual she really was. All her life, the community had been polite and welcoming, and she had accepted their attitude with the innocence of a child. After the funeral the changes had been subtle but noticeable. The warmth she'd felt, or imagined she felt, faded, and far too many eyes looked away from her. Even as she made her plans to move away so she could become a doctor, she'd also continued to imagine herself returning home, where she would be welcomed as one of their own. She had a few close friends, and their friendship remained as strong and supportive as ever. The rest of the community was a different story.

One night as she had been driving home from a late shift at the

ME's office, the streets quiet and the homes dark, she'd realized it would never happen the way she imagined. The way she hoped. She would always be the odd little girl with the too-light skin, the dead mother and no father, and that was only part of what made her different. If her friends and neighbors had known that the dead came to her, she'd have been lucky to get even the little period of sympathy they'd afforded her after her grandmother's death. She feared that even her close friends who always seemed to have her back would also turn away. She didn't want to test that theory, and so leaving the area became the only thing she could do.

Now as Vi looked around at the small house, she smiled. For the first time since standing in the cemetery and staring at her grandmother's grave, she felt something like hope. This change would be a good one, and having people around her like Kat would make it all the more exciting. That Lucy had apparently welcomed her into the pack made it even better.

Outside a dog barked. She went to the door and smiled when she saw Lucy. She opened the door. "Hey, girl, miss me already?"

If she didn't know better, she'd swear that Lucy nodded before she pranced into the house. "Make yourself at home," Vi said with a laugh, and Lucy did exactly that by leaping onto the sofa, turning a full circle three times, and then lying down.

She watched her for a minute or so, expecting Lucy to jump up and want back outside. It didn't happen, and rather than wanting to leave, she appeared to be settled in for the proverbial long winter's nap. She didn't mind the company at all.

Worn out from unpacking, she thought Lucy's nap idea was brilliant. Before she could join her on the sofa though, a soft knock at that same front door made her retrace her steps. The pup opened an eye but didn't move.

"You don't happen to have a spare blue heeler around, do you?"

Vi smiled. "Funny you should ask." She waved Kat in. "My first official guest. You're now number two."

"Lucy!" Kat shook her head. "I don't know what to say. She's not usually a pest, but for whatever reason, you're her new best friend."

Kat would have no idea how happy that comment made Vi. Since her grandmother had gone on, she'd been adrift, without roots or connection. Something as simple as being inducted into this spirited dog's pack brought back a whisper of what she'd been missing, or maybe it was more like a whisper of what she'd always been missing.

❖

Kat should be furious with Lucy. She'd waited until she figured Kat wasn't looking and then made a beeline for the guesthouse or, as she called it these days, the rental. That dog was too damn smart for her own good, just one of the reasons she loved her with all her heart and why she'd evolved into such a damned fine search dog.

Of course, she had to follow Lucy and get her out of Vi's hair. The poor woman had driven all the way from Alaska, by herself, and no doubt was exhausted. Not only that, but Kat knew she already had a job at the Spokane County Medical Examiner's office as an assistant or investigator or something along those lines anyway. And if that wasn't enough, she was a student at the new medical school down in the U-District. The last thing a woman with that much on her plate needed was a pesky dog bugging the crap out of her.

Yeah, she should be furious with Lucy. She wasn't. A good excuse to visit with Vi again was not unpleasant. At least not for her. From the very first call, she'd liked the sound of her voice when they'd talked on the phone. Now that she was here, she liked the look of her even better. Once Vi got going with work and school, chances were they'd rarely see each other, which made her a little sad. It might be nice to have this tiny bit of time before everything got rolling to get to know each other.

Vi sat down next to Lucy and began to rub the top of her head. "She's a beauty."

She wasn't wrong. For a pup she'd rescued from a cage at the humane society, she was beautiful and, Kat was pretty certain, a purebred. Whoever had abandoned her was a total dumbass. Lucy had grown into an awesome dog. As if she'd known that Kat had wanted to spend more time with Vi, she'd taken it upon herself to make it happen. Talk about being in sync with her partner.

"I'm decidedly prejudiced but can't argue; she's pretty cute. Say, would you like to come over for dinner? I mean, I know you've got to be exhausted and all. I have some stew in the slow cooker and thought I'd toss some biscuits into the oven. Nothing fancy, but warm and tasty, and best of all you don't have to cook."

"I don't want to intrude on my first day here. I usually save that for after people get to know me." Vi smiled, and her whole face lit up. Kat didn't know much about the folks who made their living working with the dead, but she had to think they didn't look anything like the beautiful woman in front of her.

"Trust me, I'm not the kind who extends an invitation if I think it'll be an imposition. I really do have plenty of food, and I'd love to get to know you better. I'm pretty sure Lucy would insist, if she could talk."

Vi smiled and rubbed Lucy's head again. "Well, I don't want Lucy to kick me out of the pack on my first day here."

"Pretty sure that's not going to happen today or any day. Once you're in, you're in. She's a mighty loyal girl and picks the members of her pack wisely."

"So who's in it?"

"Counting you and me? That would be two."

"Seriously?"

"When it comes to my dog, I never joke."

"Then I'd love to have dinner with you two."

The easy acceptance of her invitation pleased her way more than it should. It worried her as well. She'd just invited this beautiful woman to her house for dinner, and other than the stew, it was slim pickings for food and drink. What the hell was she thinking? Dumb question there. She'd been thinking beautiful woman. But wait, there's more... beautiful woman that her dog likes. What was it that Bill Murray said one time? "I'm suspicious of people who don't like dogs, but I trust a dog when it doesn't like a person." The opposite also held true. She trusted her dog when she liked a person, and well, her dog really, really liked this person. Dinner it was going to be.

She needed to run to Rosauers and pretty damned quick. She hadn't lied when she said she had a stew going because it had been in the slow cooker all day. The biscuits? That might have been a stretch. A baker she was not, though she could toss brown-and-serves into the oven like nobody's business and she had a brand-new package of Irish butter in the fridge.

"So hey, I'll let you get back to unpacking, and I'm going to feed the animals before I dish us up. How does seven sound?" She might not have a whole lot of people food in the house, but her animals did not suffer the same fate. They were always first on her mind. It was just her own sustenance that she dropped the ball on.

Vi's smile did something quite nice to her face again. "Seven is perfect. I'll be sick of unpacking by then and, I suspect, pretty hungry."

❖

The Seeker had a problem. While the pace of his work had stepped up by design, the acceleration brought new logistical challenges with it. When things were slower and more deliberate, he had time to dispose of bodies and clean up messes. Every "i" was dotted and every "t" was crossed. As the work increased and the time between each project grew shorter, the challenge to keep things tight increased.

Not that he planned to change anything. He liked the way things were picking up. It was fun. In fact, it was exhilarating, and he was completely up to the challenge. All he had to do was look at things with clear eyes and a logical mind. If he did that, everything would fall into its proper place, just as it always had.

Despite the success he'd achieved and all the knowledge he'd gained, his extracurricular work seemed to have also become more personal. It had always been personal, in a way. In a strange way, the last one had reminded him of Mother, and it took him back decades to that little boy he really thought he'd left behind. He found it disconcerting. He leaned back in the chair and closed his eyes, allowing his mind to return to a time he rarely thought about.

The acrid smell defined the room, as always. The combination of stale air, stained sheets, and medical salves filled his senses, and even at nine he knew he'd never be able to erase the odor from his memory. Tears stung at the back of his eyes. He knew better than to let them fall.

"Sit, boy." His father put a hand the size of a dinner plate on his shoulder and shoved him into the chair permanently situated at the right side of the bed. The valuable antique wooden chair was hard, the force of the push sending vibrations up his back. He didn't cry out.

Her body so frail and faded, it was hard to discern that she even lay beneath the quilt that someone had told him his grandmother had made years earlier. It stood out in the room with the white walls, carpet, and furniture. He didn't know if the story about the quilt was true. He wasn't sure he had a grandmother. If he did, she'd never stepped foot inside the house.

His gaze lit for only a moment on the bed. Only the sound of labored breathing hinted that something, someone, lay beneath the colorful patchwork. He didn't want to look at her or hear the rattle of her breathing.

"Yes, Father." His voice was as bodiless as his mother was. He looked over the bed, his focus on the window that took up a large part of the far wall. The drapes were open, as if letting in the sunshine would breathe life into her failing body. Nothing would bring her back. That was the one thing he knew, and these days he did not believe he knew very much.

In the last three months his world had been turned upside down. His mother, once smiling and happy, had changed into the coughing thing beneath the blanket. When he walked down the hall, her cries carried through the closed bedroom door. His father, never the kind of dad his friends talked about, became a stranger who would drag him into this room day after day to pray over his mother. His dying mother. He knew that death would come for her soon, even though his father wouldn't say the words.

Beneath the sleeves of his shirt, bruises, the shape of big, thick fingers ringed his arm. No matter how hard he tried to flee, he failed every time. He was dragged to the room of sickness over and over again. His father might not think much of him, but he wasn't stupid, and his heart told him she wouldn't be around much longer. His prayers were not for her to hold on. Maybe then it would all stop.

"We will pray, boy."

He'd heard the words every night and day. Praying did no good. She didn't get better. Every day she disappeared a little more, the rattle of her breath deeper and more frightening. One day when he came from school, would he find nothing beneath the quilt?

"No."

He snapped his head around, settling his gaze on his mother's sunken face. She was pale enough to be a ghost, like the ones he read about in the comic books he snuck into his room. Her eyes, once alive with laughter, were the scary kind of black that looked just like those of the monsters on TV. He didn't like what he saw. He couldn't look away. How he wanted to.

"We must pray for you." His father took his mother's hand and kissed it. "We will pray away this sickness. You will come back to me."

"No," she said again, her voice a hollow rattle. Maybe she was a ghost already. "Your prayers fail. Don't make him do this anymore." She pulled her hand free, and that surprised him.

"God will not forsake you."

"There is no God."

"Do not speak that way." His hands balled into fists at his sides.

He sucked in his breath, his body tensing. He hoped he didn't pee his pants again. Would Father hit her for voicing the truth? If he did raise his hand to her, no amount of praying would fix her broken body. She would be like the birds that flew into the windows so hard he thought the glass would break. Outside, he would find them on the grass, their heads flopped to the side. Yes, she would be just like that, her body still, her head hanging to the side. He wanted to tell Father to leave her alone. He stayed silent.

"Take my hand." Her gaze now fell on him as she ignored the angry words of his father and the hands that seemed ready to rise in fury. She gave him the same kind of look that she would when she demanded he do his homework or clean his room or take his dishes to the kitchen. The look told him to do as he was told with no talking back.

He stood up from the hard chair and took two steps closer. His legs pressed against the side of the bed. The smell grew stronger and his stomach did a flip. He wanted to run outside, where fresh air would fill him and everything was alive. He closed his fingers around her hand. It was cold and felt weak like the bones of the Thanksgiving turkey hours after dinner was over and done with. Shivers shook him.

With surprising strength, she yanked him down until his face nearly collided with hers. "Look into my eyes."

He started to turn away, but she squeezed his hand in a grip even tighter than his father's. "Look into my eyes!"

Tears blurred his vision, and he worried that this time he wouldn't be able to hold them back. "I'm sorry, Mama." He wasn't sure what he was sorry about. Her getting sick? Or that he wanted to be anywhere else in the world but here.

"Do not look away. Only you can capture my soul. If you don't, I'll be lost, and you don't want your mama to be lost, do you?"

He shook his head, and as he did, his tears splattered her face. Her dark eyes almost seemed to glow. "No."

"Stay with me. Save me," she said. "Do not let the devil take my soul."

As he watched, something flashed, and then the light in her eyes faded. Her hand dropped away from his. His pant legs stuck to his inner thighs, warm and wet.

Chapter Three

"Rain check?" Only a minute before, Kat had come knocking on the front door. Vi had barely taken time to change her clothes in anticipation of heading up to the main house for the promised stew before Kat had returned.

That didn't last long, she thought as she stood in the open doorway. It wouldn't be the first time her aura of weirdness scared someone off. The vibes that rolled off her weren't anything blatant or explainable. Some people simply picked up on her unique aura, and it put them off. Not that she blamed anyone. She was weird—one of the reasons she'd chosen pathology as her specialization area. The patients she would serve didn't have to like her, and scaring them wasn't possible.

Besides, death investigation provided a place her brand of strange found a home. She could use it for the greater good, and wasn't that what it was all about? God, she hoped so, because if it wasn't, she might be tempted to follow in her mother's footsteps with heavy self-medication. Of course Mom had her own reasons for that road, but when it came right down to it, everyone could find some kind of justification for taking the easy way.

"Of course." She didn't bother to ask for an explanation. No point. The last thing she had time or energy for anyway was making friends. Between work and school she'd be lucky if she found time to sleep.

"No, no, no, it's not like that."

"You don't have to explain."

Kat laughed. "Oh, I so need to explain. Girl, your face is a telegraph, and I'm making a hideous first impression. I really need to minimize my damages. Here's the truth. I just got a call out."

"A call out?" The woman ran a small farm. What kind of call out could she possibly be talking about?

"Lost hiker up on Mt. Spokane. Remember earlier when I told you about Lucy being a working search dog? We're members of a search-and-rescue team in both Stevens and Spokane Counties. Got a call ten minutes ago that the air-scent dogs have been requested, and as it happens, one of Lucy's specialties is air scent."

Something like relief flooded through her. Pathetic. Like she was in the third grade again and was hoping Sue Simons would be her friend. "Well, that's not good."

"True enough but it's what we train for. We'll find the hiker."

"I bet you will."

"Look, I left the back door open because I really do have that pot of stew cooking, though I'll have to give you another rain check on the biscuits. I have no idea how long this will take. It could be two hours. It could be ten. You go grab some dinner, and I'll catch up with you tomorrow. Okay?" She didn't wait for Vi to answer. "Gotta run."

She meant it literally too. Kat sprinted across the yard and down the driveway. She jumped into an extended-cab pickup with a full canopy on the back and drove off. Vi presumed Lucy was already in the truck.

Part of her was disappointed that she wouldn't have a chance to hang out with Kat and Lucy this evening. Another part of her was grateful. The whole journey, not just the driving, but the relocation of her entire life, had left her drained. Hard to imagine she'd ever feel whole again. Too many changes. Too many losses. Witty conversation might be asking more of her than she could produce at the moment.

The thought of the stew, on the other hand, made her stomach rumble. Thinking back over the last eight hours or so, she tried to recall when and where she'd last stopped for something to eat. In particular, something decent. The convenience-store sandwich she'd picked up just after crossing from Canada into the US did not fall into the category of decent. Food on the road left a lot to be desired. She fully intended to take Kat up on her offer of sustenance.

Kat's kitchen presented a surprise. From the outside, the house appeared to be a moderate-sized farmhouse, very nice and well maintained though not anything that screamed high-end. The kitchen looked straight out of a recent home-remodel magazine, right up to the latest appliances and sparkling countertops. Someone had spent a fair chunk of change on this room.

"Wow," she muttered. The lady apparently liked to cook, a skill Vi sorely lacked. "But can she field dress a sucking chest wound?" she muttered to herself. Everybody had their strengths. The smell of the cooking stew filled the room with a scent that reminded her of home. Her grandmother had loved to simmer stews on the stove all day long during the cold winter months.

On the counter next to the slow cooker sat two bowls and two spoons. Napkins were in a stand-up holder, and a note directed her to the refrigerator for her beverage of choice. She took the lid off the cooker and breathed in the heavenly aroma. After she ate two servings of what turned out to be a fabulous beef stew filled with big chunks of meat and vegetables, and drank a large glass of milk, she cleaned up her dishes and returned everything to the same spot. Now that she'd eaten more than she had for a week, weariness weighed heavy on her. The stress of the move and the drive to the lower forty-eight crashed down, and she wondered if she had enough strength left to make it back to her new little home. Her arms and legs felt like they weighed a hundred pounds each. As much as she'd like to just lie down right here, she pushed herself out the door and down the driveway. A bed with her name on it waited for her.

The sun was starting to dip behind the mountains as she trekked from Kat's house to hers. A little bit of energy came back to her as she walked down the drive. Outside with the cool, refreshing air and the sky overhead turning deep red, it was pretty spectacular. Not quite the northern lights, but impressive just the same.

When she reached her house, she took one step toward the front door and stopped. All she really wanted to do was blast through the door and drop into that beautiful, soft bed. Her feet refused to move. A familiar buzz went through her, and she wrapped her arms around herself. She shouldn't be surprised, and yet she was.

"They need your help."

She lifted her gaze to where her grandmother sat in one of the two bright-red wooden deck chairs that decorated the lovely full-length front porch. Not surprisingly, she was wearing the same blue dress Vi had buried her in, and her white hair was in a tidy braid that hung down her back. "Who needs my help?"

"You will know."

Even after passing on, Grandmother was still full of mystery. She had been like that Vi's whole life, and why she expected her to be different now was anybody's guess.

"Help me." She was way too tired for mystery and puzzles.

Her grandmother shook her head slowly from side to side. "You never needed my help."

Oh, how off base her brilliant and intuitive grandmother was on that score. "I always needed it."

The braid swung back and forth as she shook her head. "No, child, you only needed my love, and that you always had. Now, rest up and ready yourself. They need you."

Tears slid down her cheeks as she stared at an empty chair. "I loved you too," she whispered. "And you're wrong. I always needed you."

Talk about piss-poor timing. This search put a serious crimp in her plans for the night. She finally meets an interesting, attractive woman who makes her think she might be ready to risk again, and boom, here comes the call. Sure, she could have declined to respond to the search, but that would have been wrong. She had no solid reason for not showing up except for dinner plans. Those could always be changed. Saving somebody's life, however, was a different story. In this kind of scenario, time wasn't their friend, and the sooner Lucy got out on that mountain using her incredible nose, the sooner they could bring the lost hiker home. Dinner with Vi would have to wait.

After all, Vi had signed a one-year lease, so at the very least they had twelve months to become friends and share who knows how many dinners. Many, she hoped. It wasn't like tonight was a one-and-done deal. She clung to that thought for the next three hours as she, Lucy, and their team searched their assigned area in a north-south grid pattern. She was confident in Lucy's skill, and the fact that she hadn't so much as twitched told her their missing hiker was not in their area. They were on their last grid when the call came in over the radio. Another team had found the hiker with what was reported as a possible broken leg or ankle. The ATV units were dispatched for extraction. For Lucy and Kat, the search was over.

It took another hour and a half to hike back to the command post, download track logs, sign out, and get on the road toward home. Lucy slept in the back seat all the way there. Kat would have liked to join her. The search had been a hard one. Rain had rolled in about an hour into their deployment and made everything on the mountain slick as ice, so with the steep terrain, it had become exhausting. Yet none of the searchers or the dogs gave up. It's what they all trained for. It was why they trained so hard. Every life was important, and each and every time they were called out, they prayed to bring the lost home, alive or dead. No one deserved to be left out there alone.

Now that she and Lucy were back at the house, she stripped off her wet clothes and stepped into the shower. God, the hot water felt like magic on her sore muscles. Going up and down the mountain with a pack that weighed at least twenty-five pounds would have been a workout any day of the week. Toss in rain, cold, and darkness, and every muscle protested. Good thing she worked out fairly regularly, or she'd be one hurting puppy.

Lucy didn't seem any more worn out than usual. Amazing didn't even begin to describe her. She'd search for hours without ever slowing down regardless of the weather or difficult terrain. Of course, she'd gotten the hour-plus nap in the truck and was currently passed out on her bed, so it was a little different for her. She'd pop up in the morning and look at Kat with an expression that said, what are we doing today? Lucy would search every single day if she could.

After her shower Kat went to the kitchen, and Lucy surprised her by jumping up and going to the door. She opened the back door to let her out into the darkness, presumably to do her business, although she wasn't sure she didn't race to the guesthouse to check on Vi. The immediate bond Lucy had formed with Vi was pretty telling. The one thing she knew without question was that the woman had a true and honest heart. Lucy would never invite someone into her pack who didn't. She was particular that way.

Despite the late hour and her fatigue, Kat wouldn't mind meandering down the driveway herself. She didn't. It would be rude and, well, yeah, inappropriate. No way to explain skulking around in the wee hours of the morning just because. That was the kind of thing stalkers would do, and she should know. Knowledge gained firsthand sometimes really sucked. Nobody ever thinks something like that will happen to them, and when it does, it's horrible.

That thought made her sober. Not somewhere she wanted to go at the moment. She gave a short whistle, and as expected, Lucy came zipping back quick enough for Kat to be confident she hadn't gone down to bug Vi. "Good girl," she said as she patted her on the head. "Let's call it a night and get a little sleep."

Her heart sank a little as she looked around the kitchen. Everything appeared to be exactly as she'd left it. Until this second, she hadn't realized how she'd hoped Vi would come and eat her food. Not that she could blame her. Who would feel comfortable walking into a relative stranger's home to grab a solitary dinner? Her kitchen might be lacking in bounty, her own fault for failing to stock up recently, but she could cook, and she'd wanted to show off, plain and simple. That she'd failed to make a good impression made her a little sad. That is, until she peered through the glass lid and realized the pot wasn't as full as when she'd left for the search. A smile turned up the corners of her mouth. Vi had been here.

"You're a sap," she said to herself. *A sap who doesn't care* is what she didn't mutter out loud. The fact that Vi had come over and eaten her stew had made her night. Correction, the fact that they'd recovered the missing hiker alive, and relatively well, topped her night. This came in a close second. She smiled as she put the leftovers into the refrigerator, turned out the light, and headed to her bed for a few hours of sleep.

A good eight hours is what she'd really like. But living on a working farm meant the animals didn't adjust their schedules for hers. They didn't care if she was up until the middle of the night trying to find the lost and bring them home. Nope, all they cared about was that the water was running in their troughs and they had food in the feeders first thing in the morning. Two hours of sleep or eight made no difference to them at all.

As her dad liked to say, she slept fast and got up by five thirty. Despite the fatigue that made her feel as though she had to drag her feet through mud, she made her rounds and got it all done by seven. Everyone fed and watered. Not for the first time, and it definitely wouldn't be the last, she contemplated seeking qualified help. She'd been running her farm by herself since Dad bought it for her. Dad's good luck had been life-changing for his whole family. She thanked him every day for the bit of paradise he had gifted her with and wished terribly that he could still be here to see all that she'd accomplished. He'd be proud of what she'd done here. She smiled at that thought. Dad was always proud of her, whether she was writing industry-changing programs or spinning wool or training search dogs. If she was happy, he was happy.

As if sensing her thoughts had turned to family, her phone rang. It was her brother, James. "What's up, little bro?" She smiled, thinking how funny it was to a call a six-foot-six, two-eighty-pound man little.

His bad luck in the birth department. At four years younger, he would always be her little bro.

"He's out."

It had taken the Seeker all night to figure out the solution. He'd done it though, as he always did. He had yet to encounter a problem he couldn't resolve. Certainly it would have been nicer not to have to sit up an entire night in order to formulate a plan, but sometimes things just worked out that way. When he encountered an obstacle, even if he tried to go to sleep without a resolution, it didn't work. His mind would not shut off no matter what he tried. He'd learned a long time ago just to roll with it and forgo sleep when necessary. As long as the end result turned positive and in his favor, everything was golden.

Now he stood in the local Lowe's picking out a stand-up freezer. He liked the chest freezers because of the capacity. The storage space they offered held a certain amount of enticement. The stand-up style, he ultimately decided, best fit his purposes. Once he made that decision, he moved to the aisle with the organizing racks. Several boxes of spice racks were perfect for what he had in mind. They would fit nicely into the freezer.

By the time he made it to the checkout counter, the new plan had come together. The only thing left to coordinate was delivery. That's where things went contrary to his plans. The delivery schedule was disheartening. He wanted immediate delivery. The clerk almost laughed in his face, which would have been the wrong thing to do. The customer was always right.

"Thursday is the soonest we can get to you, Mr..." He looked down at the paperwork. "Smith."

"I need it immediately."

His face remained impassive. "The schedule is completely booked until Thursday."

"Fine," he snapped. "Just make certain it is first thing on Thursday." He wanted to permanently wipe the smirk off the asshole's face.

"We'll do our best."

"Do better than that. First thing Thursday morning or I'll be making calls." He glanced at the name tag pinned to the man's shirt. "Roger."

He didn't miss the clerk's eye roll. What a prick. "On your Lowe's card?"

His fingers flexed as he held his hands down at his side, silently telling himself to remain calm. At the same time, he studied Roger's face and thought about his next experiment. "Cash." Brown eyes, a little muddy, filled with arrogance. Potential. Definite potential.

He left the store, stopping just before he walked out the door to use the hand sanitizer. The racks were the only part of his project he had available to him now. Disappointing to have his plans changed. He'd have to make the best of it until the freezer could be delivered. At least he could assemble the racks and have them ready for immediate installation.

He glanced down at his watch and grimaced. It had taken more time than he anticipated to complete his shopping. He'd hoped to put the racks together, and it wouldn't happen now. If that cashier hadn't been such an ass, he might have been able to work on them. Instead, he'd have to take his treasures home, change clothes, and head to work. The last thing he wanted to do this morning was go to the day job. Then again, he needed to get in to the office and have his schedule changed. Someone else in the office would have to handle Thursday. When Lowe's delivered his freezer, he would be there, and then he would take the rest of the day to create his masterpiece.

Chapter Four

Despite being in new surroundings, Vi slept. A good thing too, as she started her new job in earnest today. Before she'd ever left Alaska, she'd been warned that the two medical examiners could be difficult bosses. She'd already met her primary contact, Dr. Kelsey, and so far she liked him. He didn't come across as thorny, though they hadn't actually done any official work together. If he and the other ME turned out to be hard to work with, she could live with that. She didn't mind difficult. Often that was another way of saying they cared, and she was all on board for that.

Her mother's death had taught her one important lesson: excellent work produces excellent results. Unfortunately, for her mother, the work she'd received in solving her murder had fallen far short. Vi had entered the field as an angry survivor of violence who planned to do better. Her impression of the shoddy way her mother's case had been handled morphed into something different once she got on the inside. When she'd been younger and on the outside, she'd believed that the police lacked interest in her mother's case because she'd been a nurse suspended for a dependency on prescription drugs. She'd been under review at the time for drugs missing at the hospital she worked in. Vi had loved her mother. She also got her and didn't blame her for falling victim to escape. She'd been angrier with the police for not treating her case as a high priority. Her mother had been a very good person who had made a bad choice about how to handle emotional distress.

Her dissatisfaction with law enforcement and the investigators who'd been assigned the case had faded when she became involved in the process and increasingly knowledgeable about the work from their side. The truth became clear to her: they had tried to resolve her mother's case. They simply failed even when they declared the murder solved. A man sat in prison. They said he killed her, and they might even believe it. She didn't at the time and she didn't now. He wasn't the guy.

Her goals in life were twofold. First, she planned to find the man who really killed her mother and do whatever she could to make sure he got the death penalty. Grandmother would chastise her for wanting that result. She would say it was never appropriate to wish death on another being regardless of their sins. It meant dropping to their level, and in her house that was never acceptable. She would also remind Vi that her goal of becoming a doctor involved taking an oath to do no harm. Didn't change how she felt deep in her heart. She wished that man dead. She wished him erased from the face of the earth, and if that made her a bad person, she could live with that.

Second, she intended to use her gift to promote justice for those whose lives were taken against their will. If she couldn't escape the dead coming to her, she might as well use their appearance for some greater good. Nobody had to know, and nobody alive now did know. That state of affairs was perfectly okay with her. In a way it kind of made her feel normal. Mom and Grandma would be proud.

Enough of the journey into the past. Today, she headed in the direction her life was destined to be going. Of that she felt certain. She was where she was supposed to be. She would be one hell of a doctor and an amazing medical examiner. She could use her mind and her gift to bring answers and peace to those who deserved it.

The traffic wasn't bad from her new home to the ME's office on the north side. In a lot of ways it reminded her of Anchorage, and she found that comforting. The moment she'd driven out of the place she'd lived her entire life, the feeling she'd never return washed over her. This morning as she pulled her car between two yellow lines and stopped in front of the sign reading "ME Assistant Parking Only," she experienced a paradigm shift. She wondered if she'd leave this place once she held her medical license in her hand. Then again, she might not have any choice in the matter. She'd have to go where the job took her if she wanted to achieve her ultimate goal. Vi took a deep breath, stepped out of her car, and walked toward the doors that opened onto her new life.

Her orientation went fast. Of course, she'd been doing the same job in Alaska, and all they really had to show her were the particulars of local procedures. Her certifications were national and fit right in with the requirements of this office. By ten, she stood in the autopsy suite assisting Dr. Kelsey with a case. She had liked him yesterday when they'd first met and liked him even more as they worked together. He came across somewhat curt and very focused, and that she didn't mind at all. In fact, she appreciated the way he worked and his acute attention to the woman who lay on the table. He presented as the consummate professional who used his skill and knowledge to bring understanding where darkness descended.

When she returned the woman whose body had been discovered during a welfare check to the cooler, she gave a silent thank you for the uneventful autopsy. The woman had not come to her, which meant one thing: she'd died of natural causes. That conclusion echoed the finding Dr. Kelsey wrote on the death certificate.

"Nice work." Dr. Kelsey looked up from his computer as she came into the office. Though he didn't smile, she felt the warmth in his words.

"Thank you." She appreciated the validation. She'd been very close to Shirley Yarno, the ME in Anchorage, and had experienced an incredible education working at her side. Shirley had been her biggest champion, besides her grandmother, when it came to going on to medical school. If she'd told her once, she'd told Vi a hundred times, she had the right stuff to be an outstanding pathologist. Despite trusting Shirley with her life, she'd never shared with her why it was so important to her to take this step. Shirley thought it was all about her mother, and Vi let her believe that. It wasn't a total lie.

"No, I mean it. It's not every day we get someone new who can work in seamlessly right from the get-go. You know your stuff, and it's clear you have potential. Dr. Yarno didn't steer us wrong with her recommendation that we bring you on board. You're going to do well here and in med school."

"Dr. Yarno was a great mentor. She taught me everything." Credit given where it was due.

"I've no doubt. Still, I know talent when I see it, and you're going to excel in this field. When do your studies begin? I'm always grateful to be able to assist the next generation. Sit, sit. Let's take a few minutes to get to know each other."

Vi smiled as she sat in the chair in front of his desk. "Do we have time?" More cases had to be waiting for them. Then again, he was her supervising doctor, so should she question him?

"I say we make time. Now, tell me a little about yourself."

The benign inquiries he lobbed at her were soothing. As she talked, she realized she'd been wound up since she stepped inside. Her expectation of being bombarded by the dead once inside the building seeped away. Four hours and counting and not a single incident. Instead, she had the chance to simply do her job and gain respect. She had the ME interested in her not just as an employee, but as a person and a future doctor. Not bad for her first morning.

❖

Kat had just made a pot of coffee when her phone went off. An incoming text. She picked it up, read the message, and shook her head. Two call-outs in less than twenty-four hours, while not unheard of, weren't exactly normal either. They could go for months without a single incident. Right now it was like a case of when it rains, it pours.

This call differed a little. Last night it had been a missing hiker. Today they were asking for the nationally certified HRD, human-remains detection, dogs, of which Lucy was one. She was multi-talented, as were several of the dogs on the team, certified to do either live find or human remains. As the lead dog handler, Circe had sent the text requesting her availability. Kat sent a quick text back: *we're available*. Just as quickly, Circe responded with the location.

Despite having been out less then twelve hours ago, she and Lucy were back in the truck and on their way to the address Circe had texted to her within half an hour. As was true with the rest of her teammates, she kept her truck packed with gear and enough spare clothes to cover half a dozen searches before she had to do laundry. Lucy, always ready to go any day, anytime, anywhere, didn't require a second invitation to jump back into the truck. All she needed was her vest, a bottle of water, and her reward toy.

Circe and her German shepherd, Zelda, were already on-site when Kat and Lucy arrived. Nothing unusual about that. In the seven years she'd been on the team, she'd never beaten Circe to a command post. Today, the CP consisted of one deputy sheriff, who happened to be the lead for the SAR unit, and a detective. Three dog teams were responding. Kat and Lucy were number two, and they were waiting for team number three—Dion and his black Lab, Hercules.

Dion drove up in his black SUV five minutes later, Hercules with his head out the window, made his excitement clear long before Dion put the vehicle in park. That dog was a bundle of energy that Kat wasn't sure ever turned off. People looked at Lucy and commented on her drive and power. Hercules made her look like a slug. It was all good though. The dogs were very different and brought varied strengths to every mission. They also worked together in a way truly amazing to watch. They knew their jobs and did them well. Their K9 unit, through hard work and dedication, had become one of the best in the Pacific Northwest.

Today, they were parked in a gravel lot on the far north of the massive state park enjoyed by thousands in the area every year. Kat and Lucy loved to run trails here, and often the K9 team did their routine trainings in the park. They were fortunate that the state parks graciously allowed them to use their land and work their dogs off-lead while they trained.

Now, she was looking at the familiar parking area and the various trails that led off in completely different directions. She knew them all. As a team they'd trained on them. She and Lucy had hiked on them. They were beautiful and peaceful—*were* being the operative word.

Law enforcement, while not giving them many details, had reason to believe a missing young man would be found somewhere in the forty acres, give or take, in this part of the large park. It seemed a stretch to her that they would be able to narrow down a search area given the young man had gone missing only two nights ago, or at least that's what they were told during their briefing. Nineteen years old, six feet tall, with longish blond hair and bright-blue eyes. The last thing his family had mentioned that made this location feel off: he wasn't a hiker.

It seemed a stretch that he'd be here until the detective filled in the blanks. His cold car remained in the parking lot, his keys found on the ground near the driver's side door. A light spray of blood on the side window didn't suggest a friendly meet-up. But what came next really put it all into context. An early morning jogger had found a jacket on the trail, covered in blood…wet blood. That jogger had called 911, and the cop who responded happened to be the same one who'd talked to the family the night before. He checked with the family. The jacket turned out to be the same color and style the missing man had reportedly been wearing the last time anyone saw him.

The deputy gave Kat her coordinates, and she loaded her search area into her GPS, then went back to her truck to get everything else ready. She buckled a GPS collar around Lucy's neck, which would track Lucy's progress on the handheld device that also tracked Kat. When they were done, the GPS would show the deputy all the ground covered by both the dog and the human. It was an amazing piece of technology that helped her and the sheriff's office.

Sometimes navigators supported the dog team in a search, but not today. It meant that she would have to watch Lucy and navigate for herself. Not ideal and yet something they were trained to deal with. She got everything ready, slipping the GPS unit, compass, and FRS radio into the chest harness she wore. She kept Lucy on lead as they started walking. When she stopped at the corner of their assigned search area, so did Lucy. She sat next to Kat and waited not quite patiently. Her whole body vibrated with anticipation of what they were about to begin. She set the track logs for both herself and Lucy, unclipped the lead, and as soon as Kat gave Lucy the command, she jumped up and took off. Watching the enthusiasm Lucy had for the work never failed to make her smile. She loved what she did, whether it was getting a lost hiker to safety or finding an Alzheimer's sufferer who wandered away and lost the battle against the elements. As long as she could help in the effort to bring them home, Lucy was a happy dog.

The air was warm today, clear and clean, and a great change from a month earlier when wildfire smoke filled the air to levels so hazardous it drove everyone inside. When she'd looked out the window, it had been as if a curtain of gray dropped over all eastern Washington. At one point, the area had the worst air quality in the nation. A sad note for a part of the state area that showcased the best that nature had to offer on just about every front. She supposed that with the good always came a little bad too. In any event, she was grateful that clear and wonderful air surrounded them today. If she had to be both dog handler and navigator, this was the day to do it. Perfect conditions for a search.

Lucy raced ahead of her with her head down and her focus intent. As she followed, Kat too scanned the area in a sweep that attempted to take in a three-hundred-and-sixty-degree view. She looked for anything and everything that might tell her if someone had gone this way. She also kept a keen eye on Lucy to catch any change in her behavior, always the first sign that she was in a scent pool. Lucy didn't look for an actual body. No, she was trained to detect the odor of human decomposition, and thus her nose did the work and her body told the tale.

The change Kat watched for came thirty minutes into their search. The loud and distinctive snort made her focus on Lucy, and the change in her body obvious. Her own focus grew sharper, and she scanned as she followed Lucy, looking for any clue that something was amiss. It could be anything from discarded clothing to broken tree branches to smashed vegetation. Anything that indicated someone had come this way. It was a short wait, less than a minute. Lucy let her know their job was done.

Unlike the pride Lucy displayed at having successfully completed her job, Kat nearly tossed her breakfast. She wasn't expecting this.

In this part of the country with its mountains and forest, rivers and lakes, wanderers getting lost was not unusual. Nor was it unheard of for those people who went missing to fail in their battle against the elements, particularly if they were part of an at-risk population. That wasn't the case with the subject of today's search. He'd been young, healthy, and with no cognitive difficulties. The search teams were well-trained on lost-person behavior, including those of at-risk populations, and the science behind their training gave them a good understanding of needs and patterns and average distance of travel.

Everything here went against all that training, and the message being transmitted to her brain told her this man hadn't gone out for a leisurely stroll in nature. No. What she saw in front of her now needed only one word to describe it: murder.

The Seeker was pissed off at himself. He'd gone into the office solely to change his schedule in order to accommodate the Lowe's delivery and the subsequent time he would need to put it all together. He'd been able to schedule the leave without incident. What pissed him off was the sight of the new employee.

He hadn't seen a vacancy announcement go out, and it bothered him that he had missed it. That wasn't like him. He monitored what went on around here at all times and who and what were on staff at any given moment. All critical information to maintain the order of his world and to keep his secrets safe. That something this important had slipped by him was unacceptable, and his cheeks grew warm as he thought about it. He was less angry with himself as he was on guard. This oversight made one thing quite clear: someone had managed to keep things from him.

That a single new person had come on board wasn't a problem in the big picture. He would train this individual just as he had everyone else. They would see only what he wanted them to, and everything would be fine. What made the tic in his eye jump was the reality of being caught unawares. Not coming into this new dynamic fully prepared bothered him. In every other instance, he had a game plan in place long before a new pair of shoes ever stepped through the metal doors. Now he would have to plan on the fly, and despite his spontaneous adventure the other night, he really didn't care to do things that way.

With casualness he didn't feel, he sat at his desk and put his phone receiver to his ear. The light on the receiver indicated at least one voice-mail message. He punched in his access code and only vaguely listened to the voice on the message requesting his notes from yesterday. He quickly filed it away as unimportant. The notes could wait. He kept the receiver to his ear long after the message ended, in order to watch the interactions between the brand-new and the established employees in his office. Other than a fleeting hello, no one paid him any attention. He wasn't technically on shift, and those around him focused on what they were tasked with accomplishing. As far as everyone around him was concerned, it was business as usual.

By the time he pushed away from his desk, pieces were falling into place, and he had a pretty good idea of how to proceed. Again, his plan wasn't perfect, but it would have to do, and it made him feel better to have a clear direction. He promised himself not to get caught off guard again, and he wouldn't. He made few mistakes, and he certainly didn't make them twice. As he left, he smiled and waved, the happy-go-lucky guy they all knew and loved.

Chapter Five

"Frank, did you see this?" Vi turned just as a woman, maybe mid-fifties, wearing green scrubs and a multicolored cap, came in holding a stack of printouts. "The bastard has done it again. First this woman," she held out the papers, "and now we have number two on his way in."

Dr. Kelsey took the pages and flipped through them one at a time. His eyes narrowed and his brow furrowed. Whatever he was looking at wasn't making him happy. "Where is he?"

The woman pointed toward the back of the office. "They're bringing him in. Thirty minutes out. A search-and-rescue dog found him a couple of hours ago."

Vi didn't know if she should stay here or go. She wanted to hurry back to her cubicle and call Kat. Her truck had been in the driveway when she'd left this morning, although that didn't mean she and Lucy hadn't been called out or running errands after she got on the road.

Ignoring the urge to run to her phone, Vi stayed put and waited. Though they hadn't met yet, she recognized the woman who had just arrived as the other half of the medical examiner team. The photos she'd seen on the ME's website captured her very well. Right now, it felt like the two doctors were in a private conversation and she was an interloper. They talked as if she wasn't in the room, and while it made her a little uncomfortable, intrigue kept her rooted to her chair. Then Dr. Kelsey handed her the stack. The move surprised her enough that she almost dropped it.

"Vi, this is Dr. Ailene Durze. Ailene, this is our new assistant."

Dr. Durze held out her hand. "Glad to have you on staff. I've heard nice things about you." A second ago both of the doctors acted as though she didn't exist. To keep up with these two, she'd have to stay on her toes.

"Take a look at those." Dr. Kelsey nodded toward the papers she was holding. "Give us your first impression."

When Dr. Kelsey handed Vi the printout of an autopsy file, she tried to conceal her shock. She'd been given broad duties and responsibilities in Alaska, all of which she'd earned through her work and attitude. It wasn't uncommon for her and Dr. Yarno to discuss cases in detail. Her former boss was the epitome of a practitioner-teacher. This she didn't expect. She'd been here less than a day, and to say it surprised her to find herself opining on an open case was an understatement.

More than professional curiosity drove her to flip through the pages. Her fingers had started to buzz the second she touched the first page. The fact that Dr. Durze had taken the time to print out the whole thing on paper seemed out of standard to her. Records were all digital these days. That alone made whatever the pages held more interesting than anything that had happened thus far. That her body was telling her "beware" was a lure she couldn't resist. Her grandmother's words kept pinging around in her head: "They need you."

The stack included copies of photographs printed on a color multifunction machine. They were time- and date-stamped and gruesome. Far more than the standard autopsy file. Granted, she'd seen worse, yet something about the photos hit her heart hard. They showed an old woman lying on a bed in a tidy, colorful bedroom. Her arms were spread as if she were laid out on a cross, naked, her clothes in a pile on the light-green carpet. The bed was still made, its flowered green comforter smooth and tidy. Clearly someone had taken great pains to position her just so. That wasn't what hit her hard. It was her eyes… they were gone.

"Your thoughts, Vi?" Dr. Kelsey studied her as she sank into the nearest chair. A million thoughts raced through her mind, and one stood out among them: her first impression wasn't possible. She didn't know how to articulate anything plausible.

Vi took a breath and looked up. Rather than try to put her thoughts into words, she went a different direction. "I don't understand. Why are you sharing this with me? I'm the newest person here. You must have others far more qualified to review it."

Dr. Kelsey shrugged. "You came with stellar recommendations, along with the warning that you would surpass all of us someday with your skills and knowledge. Personally, I'm good with that, and if I can mentor you along the way, I'm happy to do it. Think of this as a mentoring moment."

Next to him, Dr. Durze shook her head. "I disagree, and I don't think passing along confidential information to the help is necessary."

That comment shook Vi out of her trance. The help? Well, nothing too condescending about that. What about women pulling up other women? Clearly Dr. Durze hadn't received that memo. As much as she already appreciated Dr. Kelsey, she wasn't sure it would be the same with Dr. Durze.

"Don't mind her," Dr. Kelsey said. "She doesn't like the idea that someone might actually be better than she is. She's easily threatened."

"Screw you," Dr. Durze shot back.

"Not today, my dear, not today. Now, Vi, tell me what you see." He had a twinkle in his eyes as he spoke and evidently enjoyed sparring with Dr. Durze.

She glanced down at the folder again and then looked up to meet Dr. Kelsey's eyes. "Murder." The single word came out a whisper because her voice felt as though it had died right beside the woman in the photo.

"A fairly obvious first observation."

She held his gaze. "True, but it would be the first thing I'd note."

He held up a finger. "Our job, particularly initially, is not to decide based on appearances. We are doctors, and we use our science to make the call on cause of death. You need to read the file and all the facts."

"I understand." She appreciated the way he spoke to her. No judgment. No condescension. He talked to her like an equal. She hurried to explain. "That's not why I make that leap to murder before studying the facts."

He crossed his arms and stared at her. Behind him Dr. Durze still wore a sour expression, yet Vi could also see that a flicker of interest had appeared behind her eyes. She wanted to know what Vi was getting at even if she wouldn't admit it.

"Explain."

She took a deep breath and began to tell them a story she rarely shared. "This elderly woman was posed, and it was done after her death. Two things tell me that fact. First, livor mortis, the pooling of blood caused by gravity, and secondly, the absence of her eyes. The livor mortis tells me that her arms were not spread in the cross-like position from the moment of death. The pristine nature of her bed also tells me that her eyes were not removed there because it's clear of blood or other body fluids. Someone put her on that bed and in that position after she expired. She might have been killed in her home and even in her bedroom, but not directly on that bed."

"Excellent, and I have to say I agree with your observations. Dr. Durze, are you on board with us here too?"

"Yes." The one word sounded grudging. Vi thought that Dr. Kelsey wasn't far off in his characterization of the woman not liking anyone to be better than she was.

"There's more to your theory, isn't there?"

This is where it got hard. She kept her gaze on Dr. Kelsey and nodded. "I've seen this before."

"Murder?"

"Yes, murder, but more than that, I've seen a murder victim positioned exactly like this."

"Ah, someone you processed through the Anchorage ME's office." Dr. Kelsey looked very interested, and he should be because it was about to get personal.

She shook her head slowly and told herself that she would not cry. "No, my mother."

❖

Kat took a bunch of deep breaths. Lucy, who had done her job admirably, held a down stay twenty feet away from the body. She watched Kat with intense eyes, waiting to hear what they were to do next. Her mind raced, and not because they'd just discovered a deceased person. She had trained with Lucy for the possibility of discovering a body for years and had even taken classes on crime-scene protocol in the unlikely event they came across one. Her focus had always been on finding the lost. In her mind that meant someone who had died as a result of inclement weather or because of an illness. In other words, a natural passing. She hadn't anticipated that she might actually find someone who'd clearly been a victim of homicide. This was not a hiker who had lost his way in the woods and succumbed to hypothermia.

If that had been the case, while she might expect to find them without their clothes, a common result of the effects of hypothermia, she most assuredly would not expect to find them posed as though they'd been impaled upon a cross as Jesus had been. Nor would she expect to see eyelids duct-taped to a forehead or eye sockets blood-smeared and empty. No, indeed, she would not expect to see any of those things.

Thank God for the muscle memory created by realistic practice over and over again. One of her favorite search-and-rescue teachers always told her, "Train like you search and search like you train." That advice had never rung more true than it did right now. She moved on autopilot while making the radio calls, securing the location, taking notes, and marking her GPS. It also helped that not more than a minute after Lucy let her know the location of the body, both Circe and Zelda rushed in to assist. Actually, as Circe told it, Zelda had caught scent, and even though it took them out of their assigned search area, she followed her dog. Any good handler learned this lesson early on: trust your dog.

It took a little more than an hour to complete her part of the recovery. She and Circe gave their verbal reports to the deputy and the detective at the scene before making their way back to the CP. Once they were there, they turned in their GPS units for download. Then they had to stand around and wait for the deputy to return and debrief them. By the time it was all done, she was wiped out. She'd been on much longer searches in the past, but none had hit her this hard emotionally.

"Are you okay to drive home?" Circe came over as she pushed up the tailgate, its click as loud as cannon fire. A result like this turned everyone somber whether they were part of the recovery team or not. Search-and-rescue really was an "all for one and one for all" type of community. Everyone shared the emotions, good and bad.

She started to blurt out how fine she felt and then thought about it. Was she okay? Truthfully, no. "I'll be all right," she finally said. Her hands were quivering like she'd downed a dozen cups of coffee, and her stomach rolled. Both were the physical indications of a traumatic experience. Given a little time, this would pass. She peeked through the window of her truck. Lucy already lay crashed on the back seat. The poor dog had to be exhausted after working so hard both last night and today. She'd earned a great dinner and a good, long sleep. Not for the first time or the hundredth she silently thanked the universe for bringing them together. She couldn't ask for a better partner or one she loved more.

Circe patted her shoulder and Kat turned to look at her. "You will be. You know I'm here for you anytime if you want to talk after you get home."

Since the moment she'd met Circe, she'd been a true friend. Now was no different. "I know and thank you. Hey, how did you get to us so fast?" Circe had mentioned earlier that Zelda had caught scent, and that made sense, sort of. Given the wind direction at the time they made the find, Zelda should have been a fair distance away. Unquestionably a phenomenal dog, she and Circe had an impressive track record. Even so, it struck Kat now that it had to be quite the moment of chance for Zelda, given the location of their assigned search area and the direction of the wind.

Circe's answer seemed to echo her thoughts. "It was a quirk for sure. I don't know how my girl caught it. Right place, right time, I guess. You know how it is. You just follow your dog."

It could happen, she acknowledged in silence, too tired to give it more thought. Besides, how or why they ended up in her search area didn't matter. Circe's presence in that surreal moment had been welcome. "At least we know that between our girls, they can bring the lost home regardless of what the wind is doing, and that's the only thing that's important."

"It certainly is, and Lucy and Zelda can rock it. Now, take this chance to get out of here before anybody thinks of more questions to ask you. Trust me, if they get going again, you'll get stuck here for at least another hour. I've learned to bail at the first opportunity." Circe gave her a quick hug.

Circe didn't need to make that suggestion twice. Too wiped out to consider standing around talking with the deputy for even a minute longer, Kat pulled her key from her pocket. She hopped into her truck and left, the cadres of lights, uniforms, and crime-scene techs fading in her rearview mirror as she drove north.

❖

The Seeker didn't think they would ever clear out enough that he could get a look at the files. He'd waited until the day shift left and then made a casual entrance for the second time in the last eight hours. The security logs would show he'd entered and exited twice on his day off. That is, if anyone actually looked at the logs. That only happened in the event of a breach, and since there wasn't one, he had no worries. He had other, more important things, on his mind. To stay armed with information, he had to see what was what. After sitting in his workstation for an hour that felt more like a day, he finally found himself alone in his part of the office. The evening folks had clocked in and were in another part of the building doing whatever they did this time of night. They wouldn't come over here unless they needed something specific, which was a rare occurrence. He'd be safely by himself for as long as he needed.

With a few keystrokes, he logged on and accessed the files he needed to read. He could have tried while everyone milled about, but that would have been taking an unnecessary risk, and he wasn't that guy. If anyone looked over his shoulder, they would wonder why he cared, and they wouldn't hesitate to ask. People paid attention around here because they were trained to. Not that he blamed them. Bad press had visited their office on an occasion or two, and no one wanted that to happen again. An abundance of caution became their creed, and share nothing the unofficial office motto.

Not a single surprising fact came out of the files that had been dictated earlier, which pleased him. Good to know that things were interpreted exactly as he'd intended. He did like to sail a tidy ship, and from what he read here, that's exactly how things were. Tidy. Tidy. Tidy.

And perfect. His work was progressing nicely, his vision coming together, and nobody the wiser. It paid to be both smart and talented. Being in the right place at the right time also had its advantages. His choice of a career put him in an ideal position to always be in the know. The access it gave him into different worlds that might touch his work was unparalleled. It wasn't by chance either. Nothing he did was. Oh, except for a couple of his projects. He'd be lying if he said he had planned those well. No, they had been cases of right time, right place, and why would he question what fate put in front of him? He took what was presented to him and said thank you to the universe.

Besides, those instances had been infinitely satisfying. He loved the game, the preparation, the stalking, and ultimately the killing. At the same time, impromptu situations were a thrill all unto themselves, and he appreciated both the planned and the unplanned. Particularly the one nearest and dearest to his heart. It had been spontaneous and at the same time anticipated for a long time without him even realizing it. Later he could see how the seeds had been planted.

"I said on your knees, boy." His father slapped the back of his head so hard he was seeing stars.

He dropped to the floor with a bang, the impact sending a jolt of pain up through his still-growing knees. He didn't dare cry out. Always best to keep his head low and his eyes downcast. Never, ever make eye contact. Never, ever make a sound.

"It's your fault."

"I prayed," he protested, though it was a lie. He'd given up on prayers. If God existed, he'd abandoned everyone in this house.

"You didn't pray hard enough, or worse, you have been sinning when I'm not here to watch you. The Lord took her away because of you, and now I'm left alone to feed and clothe you. It is not right. It is not holy. She should never have been put through that pain. It should have been you."

"I'm not a sinner." That wasn't a lie. His thoughts might be dark. His actions were not.

Again his father's open palm connected with the back of his head. The blow hurt enough to make his stomach lurch. "We are all sinners!" His roar was so loud that if they had close neighbors, they'd surely hear him. Not that it would make any difference for him. Now that his mother was gone, none of them would even glance his way. If they saw his father, they would turn and hurry to him, shake his hand and tell him how sorry they were about his loss. They all loved to be close to the rich and powerful. No one noticed him. No one told him how sorry they were he no longer had a mother.

"Pray that God redeems your soul."

His gaze settled on a soiled napkin lying on the floor. He focused his energy on the piece of trash so that the anger roiling inside him did not spill out. It wasn't his fault that his mother had died. The cancer had started the process, and his father had finished it.

Though no one ever noticed, he held the top spot in his class. He was beyond the average smart kid and knew that his father's belief that God would save his mother had been wrong. Never taking her to the doctor had killed her, and all he had left was the piece of her spirit he had caught from her eyes as she died. As much as he wanted to stand up now and rage against his father and his lies, he didn't dare. In time he would grow tall enough and strong enough to face him man-to-man, and when he did, nothing would be the same.

Chapter Six

It took every ounce of self-control Vi possessed not to throw up. The impossibility of what she was seeing was eclipsed only by the call that came in just as she scrolled to the last page of the file. One thing about the electronic age, the photos included in the file were brilliant and graphic. Dr. Durze had taken her printed copies with her when she left, and Vi understood. At the same time, she had to see more, so for at least half an hour she and Dr. Kelsey had holed up in his office, sitting in front of his computer and reading the original digital file together. Everyone else from the day shift had left, including Dr. Kelsey, and now she alone sat in her workstation staring at the computer. She didn't want to believe what she'd seen. Any doubt that this victim was an exact copy of her mother disappeared in a flash.

Twenty-four hundred miles from home and a serious case of déjà vu hit her hard. Talk about vindication. On the big flat-screen monitor in front of her, everything she believed about the person who had killed her mother proved to be 100 percent correct. It also brought back all the emotions attached to the murder like an incoming blizzard. The unreality of the coincidence defied explanation. It wasn't similar. It was exact, and she should know, because she'd studied the crime-scene photos at least a hundred times. All she had to do was close her eyes, and she'd see everything in minute detail.

Not just the duplicative nature of the crime scene bothered her. What she'd told law enforcement since the day they'd arrested Conroy Wolf had been on target. Nothing about the man had rung true to her from the minute he'd been taken into custody to the day they'd locked the door of his prison cell. The circumstantial evidence that had cemented him into a life sentence had never convinced her beyond a reasonable doubt. Unfortunately, a jury of his *peers* had viewed it differently. The fact that the killings had stopped after his arrest had only added substance to law enforcement's strongly held belief that Wolf was the killer. Anchorage PD had closed the file and refused to listen to her argument to the contrary.

Would they listen now?

Of course, how did she explain the two-thousand-plus-mile move and the five-year hiatus between the last murder in Alaska and what she looked at now? The bigger question: why did she have to explain it at all? This evidence clearly showed that a mistake had been made, and now it was up to the APD to figure it out. Her sole job, as an ME's assistant with knowledge of a similar case, was to bring it to the attention of the Spokane police.

"Tell me about your mother." Vi looked up to see Dr. Kelsey standing in the opening to her workstation. She hadn't heard him. In fact, she'd thought he'd vacated the building like the rest of the day staff. She motioned to the empty chair in her small space, and he sat.

All she'd told him earlier when Dr. Durze remained in the room with them was that her mother had been murdered in Anchorage and left in a position identical to the elderly victim here in Spokane. Now she gave him a more detailed explanation, even if it had a CliffsNotes feel to it. She could share a million details with him if she wanted. At the moment she didn't, so a quick synopsis would have to do. It appeared to be enough to pique his interest.

"The other one is being brought in," Dr. Kelsey said. "It seems to be just like the one you're reviewing, and from what you told me, exactly like your mother. Dr. Durze went to check him in, and I'll be doing the autopsy in the morning." So both the docs were still here. A little surprising, though it gave her a hint of how seriously they were taking the spate of murders.

"Same MO?" A dumb question, given what she'd just read. It still fell out of her mouth.

He nodded and frowned. "It appears so, and I don't like the look of this. The body coming in makes number two here and, with your mother, number three. I hesitate to say it out loud, but it looks much like we have another serial killer in our midst. We had Robert Yates some years ago, and that deeply disturbed man put our fair city on the global map—not in a good way. Then not too long ago we had the woman suffering from dissociative identity disorder, and she killed quite a few before a search-and-rescue K9 handler, of all people, stopped her reign of terror. I think the worst one showed up in the form of a deputy who killed women and buried them on the perimeter of the historic Wild Rose cemetery north of the city. It's sad that one of our own turned out to be a depraved killer, and even worse that it took a so-called psychic to catch him rather than one of our highly skilled law-enforcement officers. We have good folks here, Vi, and they do a good job. In that last case, it simply took more."

She didn't care who caught the killer, as long as he or she got caught. If a cop had tracked them down, great. If it took a psychic, so be it. In the case of this killer, this was the first time she hoped her own special powers could shine and show her exactly who the bastard was. But if it did play out that way, she feared she'd mete out justice with her own two hands.

Kat looked down to see her hands shaking. It didn't matter that they trained for all types of situations in which they might encounter a deceased individual, including those that could be part of a criminal investigation. She knew the correct protocol to follow, and that's exactly what she'd done. She took pride in their work and was grateful they could bring that young man home to his family. At the same time, emotions rolled through her with surprising strength.

Since she'd gotten home, the sheriff's deputy in charge of the K9 unit and two of her teammates had called to check on her and Lucy. Circe went so far as to send her a text telling her she was on the way out. Of all the members of the dog team, Circe understood more than anyone about the emotional toll a recovery takes on both the dog and the handler. She also understood the ramifications of finding a murder victim, which wasn't a routine occurrence for anyone in SAR. Hard for her to wrap her head around a murder, and in a way all she really wanted to do was sit here and decompress.

In another way, she really wanted Circe to get her ass out here. She was cold, she was sad, and she was alone. Except for Lucy, that is, and all the other animals she'd had to make sure to feed and water before she could plop down on the sofa. Lucy hadn't been much interested in food and had eaten only a few bites of kibble before promptly jumping on the sofa and closing her eyes. She'd done her job and wanted nothing more than a snooze. Kat wished it could be that easy for her.

The doorbell chimed, and a rush of relief flowed over her. Emotional support had arrived as promised. Lucy jumped up and ran to the door barking. It wasn't her stranger-danger alert bark, though. It sounded more like my-friend-is-here bark. Given what Lucy did for a living, it wasn't hard for her to catch Circe and Zelda's scent through the closed door. Kat also didn't have to look out the window to know if Zelda came with Circe. Again, a given. She never left home without her.

Circe didn't say a word when Kat opened the door. Instead she stepped in and wrapped her arms around Kat. The unexpectedness of the gesture brought tears to her eyes. Kat had no idea where they came from, yet the moment her teammate and friend hugged her, the dam broke. It took at least a full minute before she pulled herself together and morphed into a functioning adult again.

"Sorry." Kat stepped back and wiped her face with a sleeve-covered arm. Good grief. She had to look like the dumpee in the midst of a bad breakup instead of a professional HRD dog handler. She'd believed she'd steeled herself to be tough enough not to crumble. At least if she lost it enough to fall apart, she shared it with someone who made her feel safe. Circe had to be about the least judgmental person she'd ever met.

"No." Circe took her by the arm and walked with her to the living room. Lucy and Zelda had zoomed out to the backyard with the energy that belied the fact they'd both spent hours in the wilderness searching. "You have zero to be sorry for."

"I don't mean to break down. I mean, I've just never..."

"Here's a little secret." Circe sat on the low table in front of the sofa and took both of her hands. "It affects us all, and it doesn't matter if it's your first find or your fifth."

"But it's what we train for. I should be tougher."

"It is what we all work so hard to be able to do well, and you and Lucy did a good thing out there today. That doesn't take away from the fact that an individual lost a life. If you didn't feel overwhelming emotion after everything got quiet, I'd be really concerned about you. It means you're very much human and have empathy. That's good. Really good."

"It was so—"

"Unexpected."

"Yes, unexpected. We train to search for the dead all the time, yet out there today I saw much more than death."

Nodding, Circe let go of her hands and moved to the chair. "Way more."

Things suddenly clicked for Kat, and she realized why this situation bothered her so much. "It felt evil."

Circe squeezed her hands and held her gaze. "Because it was."

The Seeker made it home by the time the Lowe's delivery truck arrived. The call he'd received just as he walked out of the office had him hurrying out to his car and racing through the city. The delivery scheduled for Thursday had been bumped up, and while he would be the last drop-off on their route, it was coming tonight. That scenario made him very happy. Maybe that asshole who'd waited on him wasn't as bad as he believed.

When the truck backed into his drive, he didn't have them unload his purchase in the garage or bring it into the house. Instead he had them transfer the freezer, still in its protective box, to the back of his pickup truck. They seemed confused by his request, which he found annoying. His directions upon delivery had zero to do with their jobs and everything to do with respecting the customer's needs. That's what he paid them for—not to question how and where he wanted it unloaded once they brought it to his property.

He stood in the driveway and watched until the big-box truck was well out of sight. Only then did he locate several tie-down straps and set to work securing the freezer in the bed of his own truck. Finished, he climbed into the cab and started the vehicle. In less than half an hour, he would have the freezer at its forever home. In an ideal world he'd keep it at his house—close to his heart, in a manner of speaking. He'd considered the possibility briefly and then discarded it just as quickly. Too risky.

On the surface, his life appeared to be an open book. Friends, the few he had, and people he worked with knew that they could drop by his house any time. He wore his persona of a guy everybody liked and trusted like a favorite coat. Because of that, he did have occasional guests. Not that any of them wandered into rooms beyond the living room, kitchen, or bathroom. Even so, he wasn't foolish enough to believe it couldn't happen. Thus he exercised an abundance of caution when it came to his work. It wouldn't do for someone to stumble onto his secret. It had happened once before. He had taken care of it.

He'd rather not have a repeat performance of that one. Then again it had been kind of a self-fulfilling prophecy. He'd told that guy for years to back off or one day he'd go too far. That day had arrived, and well, he'd taken care of it in his own special way. The memory still made him smile even after all these years.

By the time he arrived at his destination, darkness had fallen. The wide driveway in front of the multi-bay garage made it easy to turn the truck around so that the bed faced one of the overhead doors. From the glove box he pulled a remote that he never put on his visor. The door in his rearview mirror rose, and once it was all the way up, he backed in. He put the truck in park, turned off the ignition, and jumped out. Time to get to work.

As he outfitted his new freezer with its beautiful racks that gave it a display quality, his joy grew. It had been a true bitch unloading the thing by himself, but asking for assistance was out of the question. The time it took him to get it out of the pickup bed and maneuver it into the storage space was well worth the effort and sweat in terms of his personal safety. Only he knew the location of his shiny, new stand-up freezer. Now plugged in and running with the racks in place, all it needed was, as he thought of it, the art.

He arranged by color. Blue first. Brown second. Green third. Perfect. He should have thought of this method earlier instead of hiding their beauty in the depths of the old man's chest freezer he'd been using for the last three years. This was so much better, and the interior light made everything glow. He loved it. When he closed and locked the big door, sadness filled him. He really wanted to just stand here for hours gazing at its contents, which told a visual story of most of his work. He had lost his first treasures to inexperience and lack of technique, which was a shame. An unfortunate part of the learning curve.

He sighed as he looked at the aging chest freezer. It had to go, and it had to be sooner rather than later. The leak that had resulted in a trail of water across the garage floor had caused him to buy the new one. It had been heading toward failure, and he'd acted because he didn't want to risk a total breakdown.

Once more, he pushed, pulled, and heaved until the ancient piece of crap sat in the back of the pickup. By the time he finished, sweat soaked his shirt, and his back would definitely hurt like a son of a bitch tomorrow. Nonetheless, managing to move it all by himself filled him with pride. Just went to show that when something was right, it was right.

After he used straps to secure it, he wiped down the exterior, making sure not to miss a single spot. He had plans for the disposal of the freezer, and it wouldn't do for anyone to find his fingerprints on it. He'd already cleaned the inside, and since then he'd touched nothing unless gloved up. As he drove away, he hummed a bright tune, and by the time he made it to Rutter White Parkway, he had switched to singing like a rock star.

Chapter Seven

Vi's first full day had turned into a marathon event. She was okay with the work. It was good practice for what was to come between school and work. Once school did begin, her days were going to be long. Might as well get used to it now. She also walked from Dr. Kelsey's office feeling like she'd been welcomed into the fold in a big way. That he'd felt confident enough in her abilities to seek her input on the most recent murders meant a lot. Their final chat in her workstation impressed her even more. She came away feeling as though she'd been a part of this office for a long time instead of one day.

A new car sat in the driveway when she drove past Kat's house. She shouldn't wonder or care that her landlord had company, yet oddly enough, a pang of what she recognized as envy passed through her. She ignored it, as well she should, and let herself into her own house. She dropped into a chair and kicked off her shoes. Closing her eyes, she relaxed for the first time in ten hours.

Her rest lasted all of about thirty seconds before insistent scratching at the front door announced that she had a visitor of the canine variety. She should be irritated. Funny enough, she wasn't, and instead of being angry, a smile warmed her as she walked to the door. Lucy raced in the second she opened it, and as she started to shut it, a German shepherd who had to weigh at least seventy pounds bumped the door back open. She gave Vi a brief glance before she trotted after Lucy.

"Well, and you would be?" she asked the dog sitting next to Lucy and staring at her with dark, intense eyes. She was a gorgeous dog, more black than tan, with hair so shiny it looked like it had product in it. Someone took phenomenal care of this girl.

Neither Lucy nor her friend gave up her name. After staring at Vi expectantly for a minute, Lucy ran behind her and pushed her toward the door. It might be more accurate to say, she herded her to the door. Good thing she wasn't a cow, or Lucy would most likely be nipping at her ankles. "Okay, okay," she said with a laugh. "Clearly you're on a mission so show me something, whatever that might be."

As if she understood what Vi had just told her, Lucy ran to the door and hit it with her paw until Vi opened it so she could run out onto the porch. Her pretty friend followed suit, and both turned their heads as if to make sure Vi stayed right behind them. "Coming." Things in her life really were changing. Now she conversed with a couple of dogs like they could talk back. First ghosts and now dogs. Were the zombies planning to show up next?

The path they wanted her to follow became clear. They were taking her back down the long driveway to Kat's house. Exhaustion aside, the thought of seeing Kat gave her a spark of energy. By the time she'd turned off her computer and walked out of the office, she'd been certain she'd get back here and collapse on her bed. Amazing what a couple of dogs could do to energize a very weary woman.

At the back door to Kat's house, both dogs scooted inside through a dog door, and while it was certainly big enough for her to crawl through, she had her limits. She did not crawl through dog doors to get into someone's house. A knock would have to suffice.

When Kat came to the door, immediately she sensed something was very wrong. Her face had the puffy look of someone who'd been crying, and suddenly she wished she'd ignored the dogs and stayed at her place. Nothing like making a good impression early in a friendship by intruding on a personal moment. For all she knew, the car out front of Kat's house might belong to her boyfriend or girlfriend. If it had to be one or the other, she hoped it was the latter.

"I'm sorry," she said when Kat opened the door. "The dogs came to the house and seemed to want me to come here. I'll leave you. I can see you're busy. I'm really sorry." She'd caught movement behind Kat, and her impression of being intrusive solidified.

"No." Kat put a hand on her arm as she started to turn away. "Please don't leave. I'm sorry for this." She waved a hand around her face. "Had a pretty traumatic find today, and this is the aftermath."

What had Dr. Kelsey said earlier? A body had been found by search-and-rescue. It clicked. "Not the..."

Kat nodded. "Yes. The body came to you, I presume."

"Well, into the ME's office, yes. One of the docs will be conducting an autopsy tomorrow." Poor Kat. If she'd found the guy, her heart ached for her. Nobody should have to witness something like that. Just seeing the photographs of murder scenes affected her, so she couldn't imagine the horror of experiencing one firsthand.

"Come on in." Kat opened the door wider and waved her in. "Come meet my friend and teammate, Circe Latham."

"And the German shepherd?"

Kat's smile banished some of the sadness in her face. "Oh, that would be the fabulous Zelda, search dog extraordinaire."

"She's a beauty."

"Thank you."

Vi looked up at the sound of another woman's voice. She glanced up to see a lovely woman with great hair and intense eyes. A compelling spirit seemed to swirl about her, and she immediately knew they'd be friends.

"I'm Vi." She held out a hand.

"Circe Latham, and you've met my Zelda." They clasped hands, and a charge of electricity shot up her arm. What the hell?

Vi stared into her eyes. "You felt that?"

Circe nodded. "Oh yeah. I totally felt that."

"You two don't see it, do you?" Kat looked from one face to the other. "Like you seriously don't see it?"

Vi took a step back from Circe and rubbed her still-tingling hand. "I don't know what you mean. See what?"

"Circe, come on. You gotta see it? You do, right?"

Circe's brow wrinkled. "What in the world are you talking about, Kat? What is there to see exactly?"

"You two could be related."

❖

Seriously, Kat couldn't believe the astonishing resemblance between the two women. Circe was a little taller and Vi's skin a little darker, but their eyes, their noses, their hands went beyond mere resemblance. They were identical. Totally freaky, and what were the odds?

Circe stared at her with a wrinkled brow. She could imagine her thoughts. Something along the lines of the search today had her so upset she now imagined things that weren't there. She'd be wrong. Kat was seeing exactly what was here, and she intended to prove it to both Circe and Vi.

"You're an Alaskan, right?" She looked at Vi, who stared at her with an expression that seemed to suggest Kat might be losing her mind. Good thing Vi's proposed specialty wasn't psychology.

"Born and raised," she confirmed. "To my knowledge, I have no close relatives. It was always just my mother, grandmother, and me. My grandfather died before I was born, and I never knew my father. Now, it's just me."

"I'm sorry. Well, you have us now, so it's not just you anymore," Kat told her. She couldn't imagine a life without family. Her own had always been tight even in the face of her parents' divorce. To their credit, they had accomplished co-parenting like professionals, and because of that, Kat liked to think she ended up pretty well adjusted for the proverbial kid from a broken home. She didn't really know what that even meant. As far as she was concerned, her family was far more functional than many where the parents stayed together "for the children." With Vi, it wasn't even a choice. Life had dealt her a crummy hand. Still, looking from face to face, Kat thought that even if they weren't related, they should be, and sometimes families of the heart were even stronger than those of blood. They might have just met, but she meant what she said. Vi wasn't alone anymore.

Circe had her hands on her hips and looked at Kat like she had, in fact, lost her mind. "As you well know, I'm from Spokane, also born and raised. I have relatives that don't live here, but nobody who's spent any time in Alaska that I'm aware of. Besides, I think you're nuts. We don't look alike. I just don't see it. Do you, Vi?"

Vi shook her head. "I'm with Circe. I don't think so."

"You sure about that?" Her previous sadness was fading as this new mystery unfolded in front of her eyes. When she'd first met Vi she'd thought she reminded her of Circe. Now that they stood side by side, the resemblance jumped up to uncanny. "Look at your hands. Come on, you two. Hold them out, side by side, and then you'll see what I'm talking about…"

They looked decidedly uncomfortable, though she got the sense that she'd reeled them in enough to have them at least a little intrigued. Both of them stared down at their hands. After a few seconds, Vi tentatively held out a hand. Circe shrugged and then followed.

Vindication was hers when Circe's brow wrinkled. "All right, I'll admit they're similar. Lots of people have hands that look alike."

"Bull." Kat almost laughed. "They're more than similar. Now, come on, ladies. Let's go take a little look in the mirror, and then you tell me if today's stress has me seeing things or if you two look like relatives. I'll bet you twenty bucks I'm right. Stay right here."

Before either of them could say a word, she rushed to her bedroom. On her wall hung a mirror about two and a half feet wide by at least three feet long. She grabbed the outside edges and lifted it off the hanger. Then she carried it back down the hallway and into the living room. Fortunately, it was fairly lightweight though somewhat awkward to handle.

"All righty, here's the wager. Twenty bucks says you two look enough alike to be long-lost sisters. Any takers?" Kat held the mirror with the glass side to her body. She could hardly wait to see the expressions on their faces when they got a good look of themselves side by side. They didn't see it yet, but they would.

Vi was shaking her head. "Did you get enough sleep last night?"

Kat smiled and raised an eyebrow. "Enough. You up for the bet, or are you going to wimp out?"

Before she answered, Vi turned and studied Circe. Her head tilted and a curious light filled her eyes. "Yes. I think I am."

Now Kat looked at Circe. "Come on, my friend, give it up. Vi's up to the challenge. Twenty bucks says I'm right."

Circe finally laughed and threw up her hands. "Fine, I give up. You're on. Now turn that thing around."

Twilight always unsettled him. It wasn't a mystery why. His father returned home every night as the sun began to set over the mountains and the rituals began. Thereafter followed two hours on his knees praying to a God that had done nothing for him but fill his life with misery. Even now, all these many years removed from that torture and the man who had orchestrated it, the mere memory made his knees ache.

At about thirteen years old, he'd tried running away. Anything, any place would have been better than in that mausoleum with him. He'd been old enough to come up with a plan though too young and naive to realize that it would never work. With his father's high visibility and connections of the type only those in the top of the social strata possess, he never had a chance. Outside the walls of their home, no one saw the monster. He'd been so well liked, admired even, that when his son went missing, it became a big deal. It took only a single call from his father.

The one time the Seeker summoned enough courage to try, he'd made it on foot as far as Liberty Lake when a sheriff's deputy spotted him. An hour later, he'd been delivered back into hell. It was the first and last time he tried to escape. The old man made sure he never had a chance to do it again. In his words, he was saving his soul. The Seeker didn't need his soul saved; he knew even back then where it had already been promised.

He shook his head and stared out into the growing darkness. He didn't want to think about his father or the years of captivity created by his twisted web of beliefs. He simply wanted to go out into the night and bring back a new contribution to his collection. Doing that would make him feel complete and banish the lingering memories that refused to go away no matter how hard he worked at it. His work—not useless prayers or painful memories—saved his soul.

The problem today was timing. The compulsion grew with each passing day, and he recognized that fact. He might be a lot of things, but a fool he wasn't. His work wasn't about evil intention or thrills; it embodied knowledge and understanding. He'd understood it the second he'd seen his mother's soul leave her eyes. His path had been set in that moment, and he'd never deviated. In a way, though, to say it wasn't about thrills wasn't exactly right. As the work progressed and he came closer and closer to complete understanding, it had evolved into thrill. How could it not? In any job, ultimate success always brought a high. There was no reason his success would result in anything different.

At his sides his hands clenched and unclenched. An ache began behind his right eye. "No," he said out loud. "No." Need pressed at him as if a giant invisible hand pushed him toward the door and out into the night. It reminded him of his father when he would put a hand on the Seeker's shoulder and shove him to the floor. That hateful image gave him exactly what he needed to find the energy to resist.

He breathed in and out with slow, steady breaths. Another technique he'd developed over the years to push away the pain. The agony behind his eye began to fade. In and out. In and out.

The Seeker turned away from the window and the beckoning darkness. "Not tonight."

Chapter Eight

Vi tossed and turned all night. The violence they'd witnessed in the body brought into the ME's office yesterday hadn't disturbed her as much as what she'd seen in the mirror. Kat had nailed it. When the two of them had stood together, not only did their hands look alike, but their faces did too. Staring down now at the picture on her phone, she shook her head. The whole thing boggled her mind.

She couldn't figure out how two women born thousands of miles apart could share such similarities. Disconcerting didn't even begin to describe it. Neither did infuriating, yet the clear evidence was unsettling and unbelievable. When it came to the subject of the identity of her father, her mother had kept her secret. As the old saying went, she literally took it to her grave. As she'd stood staring into the eyes that looked exactly like hers, she'd known in her heart that her mother, well intentioned and loving as she might have been, had withheld something she had the right to know.

Equally frustrating to be here stuck with this so-called gift, and she couldn't even make it work for her. She could use it to help people she'd never met, yet when it came to her own life, zippo. Sure, her grandmother would make periodic appearances to impart cryptic messages she expected Vi to decipher, and damn her, she always did, sooner or later. Not so with Mom. Her mother had left her all those years ago, and she'd never seen her since. It wasn't fair, especially right now. She wanted to know the explanation behind what she'd seen last night. It was her life, after all, and she deserved to know the identity of the man who had fathered her. That she most likely never would filled her with disappointment.

From the look on Circe's face, she was in the same place—as intrigued by the uncanny resemblance as Vi. Unlike Vi, Circe knew her parents because they lived right here in Spokane. No mystery for her to solve about who fathered her. Sometimes Vi envied people who grew up in those traditional families. One mom, one dad, a brother or sister or both. Most of the time, though, she was grateful for the home her mother and grandmother had made for her. Despite her silence about her father, her mother had been wonderful. Never once did Vi doubt the love she had for her only child, even when she'd been mired in the depths of her addiction.

Same for her grandmother. She ended up stuck raising a grandchild all on her own, and Vi strongly believed that hadn't been in her great life plan. Bless her heart. She spent every day giving Vi unconditional love, absolute acceptance, and the kind of security every child deserves. Hard to be bitter about family like that. It also explained why she missed both of them so much. She'd drawn a lucky hand to be blood kin of those two strong and amazing women. Who needed a father when she had them? Didn't, however, soften her irritation about the knowledge her mother denied her.

She was still thinking about the puzzle when she walked into the ME's office ready to begin day two. It had to be a calmer day than yesterday. What a way to start a new chapter in life—exciting and challenging all at the same time. In fact, being here helped her get her mind away from her doppelganger. She had so much work to do, she didn't have time to think about the weirdness of her own life. As soon as she got in, she checked the schedule. Today she was on tap to assist Dr. Durze.

"You were right."

Her head snapped up at the sound of Dr. Kelsey's voice. "Excuse me?"

Once again he stood next to her workspace. The man moved like a ninja. "About the similarities in your mother's murder and our victims. The MO is the same, the findings of the Alaskan ME's office and ours are identical. Looks like we have a serial killer on our hands, and he's covered a hell of a lot of ground."

Chills went down her spine. "You know they put a man in prison for my mother's murder."

He shrugged. "That might be true, but as you well know, the science doesn't lie. I'll take your word that a man is sitting in prison up there in Alaska, but facts are facts. That leaves us with two possibilities: either he's not the guy or we have a copycat."

Vi agreed with him. Science didn't lie, and she'd been banking on it to solve the mystery sooner or later. The answer to his theory was easy for her. In fact, not a single thread of doubt existed in her mind. "It's not a copycat."

He patted her shoulder. "As much as I hate to say it, I don't believe it is either. No copycat has the ability to do what this guy has done with the same degree of consistency and detail. I believe we're dealing with the same killer."

His words almost made her cry. She'd been trying for so long to get someone to listen to her, and finally someone got it. She wanted to jump up and hug him. "I tried to tell them in Alaska."

"They wouldn't listen to you, would they?"

She shook her head. "That's why I'm here, why I'm working so hard to be a forensic pathologist. I had to find a way to deal with finding truth however I could. I figured I'd have to do it on my own because no one would pay attention to what I tried to tell them."

"Trust me, I understand, Vi. We all find our way here for different reasons, yet oddly they're very similar when you get right down to it."

"You lost a loved one too?" She found it surprising that Dr. Yarno hadn't mentioned it earlier when they talked about her impending job in Spokane. At the time it had seemed as though she'd given her a pretty good background on her new bosses. Now she wondered.

He shook his head. "No, nothing that personal. It wasn't a family member or close friend. For me it's all about an eight-year-old neighborhood girl who disappeared when I was around fifteen. They found her body a week after she went missing, and it took until two years ago to track down her killer. Even as a teenager I kept thinking more could be done, and it pushed me to where I am today."

Her admiration for him grew. His experience might not have been as personal as hers, but clearly, he got it. "How did they find her killer?"

"A new autopsy and DNA. Things have come a long way in the decades since her murder. I was beginning to wonder if they'd ever find the guy."

"I get that. I'm here primarily because of my mother, and I still hope that someday I can find out who's really responsible for her death. It's not the man sitting in that prison."

He squeezed her shoulder lightly. "I like your attitude, and keep that goal in mind. It worked for me. I got to see justice in action for that neighbor girl."

She looked up at him. "You were the one to do the autopsy?"

"It took me decades to convince the family to exhume her body and let me do a new workup. Law enforcement was none too happy with me when I finally got the family to sign off. Not that they had a problem with closing a cold case. No, it was more about the push coming from outside their ranks. A little on the territorial side, those behind the thin blue line."

"Tell me about it."

He patted her shoulder in a way that let her know he understood. "My findings combined with the results of the DNA resulted in a match to a predator who'd already spent the better part of sixteen years in prison for the rape of a young girl. What I brought to the court put the bastard away for life. He's enjoying the perks of being a child killer in Walla Walla."

Vi understood that he was referring to the Washington State Penitentiary, located in the central Washington town of Walla Walla. It had a reputation for being one of the toughest prisons in the United States and, as far as she was concerned, was an appropriate place for someone like Dr. Kelsey described. Prison populations had their own code of conduct, and those who preyed on children historically did not fare well in that environment.

"Good place for him."

"It is, and the point I really want to drive home is don't give up. It may still take you years, but all things are possible with good science, good work, and tenacity."

He didn't know her well enough yet to understand that she would never stop until the person who had really killed her mother ended up behind bars. Given the way things were going already, she hoped that day would come very soon.

❖

Now that Kat had handled all her chores for the morning, she could sit at the kitchen bar drinking coffee and marveling over the freaky resemblance between Circe and Vi. She could still see their expressions as they'd also recognized it the moment she'd held the mirror up in front of their faces. Seriously, what were the odds that her new tenant, traveling all the way from Alaska, would be Circe's twin? She'd heard the old adage that everyone had a twin out there, but this was the first time she'd actually seen its truth for herself. Made her wonder if she had one somewhere too. Wouldn't that be a hoot? She hoped her twin also had a Lucy twin. Now that really would be a hoot.

At least the diversion of Circe and Vi's resemblance had taken her mind off yesterday's recovery. A good night's sleep didn't hurt either. When she had made it to bed after the two women left, she'd been certain she'd be restless all night. It not only didn't happen; the exact opposite did. She slept like the dead…no, that was a horrible way to think of it after what had happened. No, she had slept like an exhausted toddler. Much better. When she'd rolled out of bed, she'd been ready to face a new day.

The ring of her cell phone made her jump. Maybe she wasn't quite as rested as she thought. The display showed it was her older brother, Shane. She pressed the speaker button. "Hey."

"Was it you?"

"And good morning to you too."

"Yeah, good morning. Tell me about yesterday. Did you and Lucy find that dead guy?"

"Come on, Shane. You know I can't talk about it."

"I'm your favorite brother. Of course you can. Tell me all the details."

They'd had this same conversation a dozen times. Shane didn't get it. There were a lot of very good reasons why, even though she worked as a volunteer or, as the sheriff's office liked to categorize people like her, an unpaid professional, her work on missions remained confidential. She could talk to the sheriff's deputy who handled the search team, she could talk to the detectives, and she could talk to her teammates, but she could not discuss a case with anyone else. "No, I can't. We've been through this before."

"Well, that's messed up. I can't believe they bar you from talking to your family. I'm not convinced that's even legal."

"It's policy, for a whole lot of reasons."

"Name one."

She'd named one each and every time he'd called and pressed her for details on missions she and Lucy had deployed on. "You know them all. They haven't changed since the last time we had this conversation."

"Yeah, and I still think it's bull. They don't have the right to tell you that."

"Yes, Shane, they do. Now come on. Let's change the subject. I have some newly dyed yarn I think Cyn would like." Cynthia Elison was her brother's longtime girlfriend and an avid knitter. Cyn created amazing work and had a fine business designing knitting patterns. She'd actually been the one who'd first suggested that Kat raise alpaca and spin the yarn. Not less than a hundred times, Kat had thanked Cyn for the push. It had been the absolute right direction for her. She'd always needed to use both sides of her brain, and her corporate career hadn't allowed space for the artistic side. She'd remedied that since moving to her little farm.

"God, you and Cyn have one-track minds. I can't believe either one of you finds that crap exciting. Snoozer."

Bait and switch. It worked with her brother every time. She smiled. "Just tell her. I know she'll love it, and you can let her know I need a new favorite sweater."

"Oh, dear God, if I tell her that, she'll be head down and on a mission until she gets it done."

"That's what I'm hoping."

"Did James call you?"

Her mood darkened. "Yeah. I know. He's out."

"You need to be careful."

"I always am."

"I'm serious, Kat. You know he's crazy, and I'm betting he still sees you as the love of his life. He's a full-on nutbag, and I doubt prison time made him better. In fact, it gave him about a million more hours to obsess about you. You have to be careful."

"I know, I know. I'm not alone. I have my dog, and I've got a great new renter."

"Just promise you'll keep your eyes open and if he shows up, you'll call the cops ASAP. Don't mess around with him. Promise."

"I promise. Thanks for calling. Love you. Don't forget to tell Cyn about the yarn."

She ended the call, smiling despite being reminded about Scooter, the wild card in her life. She'd never been exactly sure how or why he'd latched onto her. Then again, mental illness didn't lend itself to easy understanding. If not for the stalker laws, she'd probably still find him peeking in her windows and following her car. Thank goodness for her brothers; they were always looking out for her.

She'd been lucky in the family department. Her divorced parents hadn't turned out to be the bitter ex-spouses that used their children to get back at each other. On the contrary, they had been happier apart and seemed to enjoy their children and their lives much more when they weren't together. Her mother had gone on to happily remarry, and Kat got along with her stepfather very well.

Dad took a far different path. He seemed to thrive as a single guy and had been more than happy to stay that way, despite a string of girlfriends. The last one had been a keeper, and had he lived, Kat felt confident he'd have married her. When they lost him to a fast-moving cancer that took him in three months, Kat's heart had been broken. He'd purchased this place for her when he'd won the lottery a month after his terminal diagnosis, and she thought of him every single day. He'd set them all up with their dreams, overjoyed to do it. He'd won millions and then lost his life. Sometimes the universe sucked.

Even so, her dad had been happy all the way to the end. In fact, both her parents had found love, whereas she was alone. Like her father, girlfriends had come and gone. She had certainly loved a few of them, though more in the love-ya style than the my-heart-aches-for-you style. Taking any of the relationships beyond dating had been out of her capacity to commit to anything long term. A casual girlfriend was fine. A meet-my-parents kind of girlfriend, not so much. A good therapist would probably say that because she was a child of a broken home she feared abandonment. She didn't believe it for a minute. Her parents' split had nothing to do with her inability to commit to another woman.

A therapist, good or otherwise, didn't need to tell her what she already knew. Simple fear held her back. She avoided being completely open. Always a little different, she'd been teased and bullied at school. Not horribly. Just enough to push her to build walls of self-protection. She'd convinced herself that walling herself off wasn't a sign of dysfunction. When the right woman came along, she'd know it, and she'd drop her defenses to let her in. That was the story she was sticking to.

Today, she didn't much care for that story and wasn't dumb enough not to know it had something to do with the alluring Vi. She couldn't find much to not like about her. Attractive, smart as hell, and best of all, she had received the seal of approval from Lucy. Her dog was the absolute best when it came to judging character. Lucy knew good and bad, and when she made the call on bad, chills ran up Kat's back. The only time she'd heard her growl was when they'd come face-to-face with a man in a hotel hallway. Lucy's body language had changed, and her low growl had been ominous in the small space. She and Lucy had made a hasty retreat. While she never knew what about the tall man in the dark business suit made Lucy react that way, she did know something about him gave off very bad vibes. She trusted Lucy's instincts without reservation.

Lucy's approval of Vi warmed her and also brought home how alone Kat was. She'd made this life and set all the ground rules, so she had no one to blame except herself. Suddenly, her unwritten rules sucked. Maybe the time had come to finally open up and give love a chance. Or maybe she'd finally met the person who made her want to. Kind of hard to admit that after knowing Vi for such a brief time, yet there it was.

All concerns about Scooter faded into the background, replaced by pleasant thoughts of Vi. Her new tenant was bringing an exciting light into Kat's world.

"So, what do we do about it?" she asked Lucy, who'd trotted in from the backyard and now sat next to the counter staring up at Kat. "You know, about Vi?"

Lucy gave a quick bark, which made Kat laugh. "Why, I couldn't agree more. We should ask her over for dinner again, and maybe this time we can actually eat together."

❖

Staying home last night and resisting both temptation and potential problems made the Seeker feel proud. Had he not been a strong man, he'd never have resisted the lure of the previous evening or survived his childhood or his early adventures. Despite the crappy hand he'd been dealt, he'd thrived. How far he had come from the broken and beaten boy who'd held his dying mother's hand. That moment had changed the course of his life, and for that he still harbored a great deal of gratitude in his heart.

Today he had to put on the mask that served him well and pretend to be as boring and uninformed as the masses. It amazed him how oblivious they were and how easy it was for him to do his special work and keep it his secret. If he were the one in charge, he'd see the messages in work like his. He'd be able to grasp the whole picture, while these fools missed the simplest missives.

In the larger scheme none of it mattered. While he could show them all up should he choose, he didn't, for quite a simple reason. To do so would take him away from what was most important to him. He excelled at making choices, and he always made the right ones.

"The usual?" The woman who waited on him behind the counter

in the popular coffee shop knew what he wanted because he came here every day. Part of it was the allure of this particular barista. Clearly a trans woman, she intrigued him. He would like her to be one of his subjects. Generally speaking, he had nothing against trans people. His interest was purely scientific. He wanted to know if he would capture the same thing in her eyes that he did from the cis population. Cis had been his testing group. She could be a control group of sorts. He would have to think this idea through and see if he could come up with a good plan.

The main problem boiled down to his appearance in this shop on a fairly regular basis. They knew him, knew his face and all about his coffee addiction. Still, the thought captured his imagination. Broadening his pool of subjects and adding a new section to his collection was too enticing not to act eventually upon. For the time being, however, he would admire her from afar while giving serious thought to what she might be able to teach him.

"Yes." He gave her his warmest smile. He used his expression like a butcher used a favorite knife. It was sharp and powerful. Best of all, it did the job each and every time.

She smiled back. "You got it, Rick." She wrote his name on a large cup, using a heart for the dot over the "i," marked the appropriate boxes for his drink, and pushed it toward the barista working behind the espresso machine. "Anything else I can get for you?" Her voice still had a touch of huskiness. He found it a bit of a turn-on.

His smile grew. Rick...it had a snappy ring to it, which was why he took it as his moniker whenever he came here. It also happened to be the name of the bastard who had returned him to his father all those years ago when he'd come close, relatively speaking, to escaping. If the impossible happened and they tracked him here, all these people would be able to give them was his name and a description of the light-haired man who always wore a cap and gloves, and ordered a sixteen-ounce latte, no flavor.

He almost laughed thinking about it. Rick, the blond-haired coffee addict. Little did any of them know that neither of those things existed. As he got within three blocks of the office, he slipped off the cap with the shaggy blond hair sewed into its brim and ran his hands over his head. He wasn't blond and he never wore a cap. Growing up, he hadn't even been allowed to play baseball, let alone wear a baseball cap. Far too common.

On his way through the back door of his office, he tossed the untouched cup labeled Rick into the trash can. His whistle melodic as he swiped his security card across the reader on the door marked B124, the Seeker felt more than ready to play the game of a normal guy at the office. He had a strong feeling today would be very interesting.

Chapter Nine

Vi didn't mind working with Dr. Durze for the day, although the woman had the personality of a doorknob. She realized five minutes in that she preferred Dr. Kelsey, with his lively, interesting banter. She'd felt his trust in her immediately, whereas she would have to prove herself to Dr. Durze, which wouldn't be a quick or easy test. The cases they worked on throughout the day were run-of-the-mill, unattended-death situations that revealed nothing suspicious or evil. Arteriosclerotic heart disease, ruptured cerebral aneurysm, and one sad case of complications brought on by chronic alcoholism. She had seen her share of the latter in her days in the Anchorage office, and sadness for those lives needlessly wasted always assailed her.

They completed their assigned cases around four. While she'd been assisting Dr. Durze, she had stayed busy with the details of learning the needs and preferences of a new doctor and thought of little else but the work. By the time she finished, she felt confident she grasped what Dr. Durze required of her. At the same time, her thoughts immediately turned to her conversations with Dr. Kelsey.

As soon as she had cleaned up and put the autopsy suite in order, she searched for him. When she found that he'd left for the day, her disappointment almost had her stomping her feet in a mini tantrum. Earlier she had felt as though she'd been making headway toward answers, grisly as they might be. Dr. Kelsey, as the senior ME, had assigned himself the case of the young man brought in yesterday— the same man Kat and Lucy had found and also the same man Vi was certain her mother's murderer had killed. She'd waited all day to talk to him about what he'd found when he performed the autopsy. To have to wait until tomorrow felt almost unbearable. For a minute she stood outside Dr. Kelsey's office with her hand on the door handle, as if her mere presence would bring him back.

Vi looked down at her hand as tremors rippled through her body like the currents that flowed beneath the calm surface of the Spokane River. She couldn't see anything, yet she felt something just the same. Memories flooded back into her mind, and she wanted to cry. She didn't, just as she hadn't in all the intervening years. She once again called on the strength of her mother and grandmother.

And of the spirit that stood next to her. The appearance of the spirit cleared up a lingering question about her move away from her birthplace. Her powers were not grounded in the lands of Alaska. Moving here had changed nothing. It was as it had always been, working in the world of the living and glimpsing the world of the dead.

Sometimes she could hear their voices, and in those instances, discovering the truth turned out to be much easier. Far more often, she heard only silence, and then finding the answers that the spirits demanded became like solving a mind-teasing puzzle. No words were coming to her now. Clearly another thousand-piece jigsaw exercise.

Vi turned and studied her. She recognized her, though in the pictures Vi had seen, she'd been posed to illicit horror in those who would come too late for rescue. The ghost of the elderly woman found slain on her bed stood next to her, and bony fingers kept touching her eye sockets as if she could bring back vision. That wasn't possible, because neither the body tucked away inside the cold room nor the ghost beside her had eyes. Her heart ached for the violence visited upon this weak and vulnerable victim. At the same time her resolve strengthened. This had to stop.

She'd never considered the man in prison for her mother's murder responsible because of the eyes. None of the victims he'd been convicted of killing had their eyes when they were discovered, and the police found none of them when they arrested him and searched his residence. A truly guilty suspect would have kept the missing orbs, and nobody would ever be able to convince her otherwise. The police maintained he either had an undiscovered second location where he stored his trophies or he had destroyed them. She didn't believe either to be a correct assumption. Not then and especially not now.

The true killer remained free out there somewhere. Rather, out *here* somewhere. He might have been in Alaska at one time, but he wasn't any longer. The killer, for whatever reason, had come here, and when they found him, they would also find the missing eyes. This woman's and her mother's. A chill slid down her back.

She pulled her hand away from the doorknob, and the vibrations vanished, as did the ghost. Time to call it a day. Usually, the appearance of a ghost filled her with angst. Not so today. The experience proved how right she'd been all along, and for that affirmation, a strange kind of gratitude filled her.

At the house, a note had been taped to her front door. Now what? She thought of last night's weirdness. She could do without that kind of thing tonight. Her resemblance to Circe didn't take the top spot in her mind. Murder did. Granted, she wanted to explore that coincidence more fully, and she would, once everything else had been resolved.

The brief note filled her with warmth. Kat wanted her to come over for dinner, again. Well, not just Kat. Lucy had also signed the note, with a paw print drawn beneath her name. She laughed. What could she do? It would be rude to refuse such a gracious invitation. Grandma would not be impressed if she declined. She had no choice but to accept.

The note said dinner was at six, and it was five thirty now. That gave her enough time to jump in the shower and wash off the lingering scent that tended to follow her from work. She prided herself on being a wash-and-wear kind of woman, and thus thirty minutes was plenty of time.

Once out of the shower, she surveyed her clothing, still in boxes she had to dig through. Jeans and a shirt would probably be more proper, except that right now she wanted to go for comfort. It had been a crazy couple of days, and she sensed that Kat wouldn't mind, so leggings and a long-tailed jersey shirt won. Once dressed, she felt clean, fresh, and comfortable, not to mention ready for dinner with an attractive woman and her beautiful dog.

If her casualness bothered Kat, it sure didn't show on her face when Vi arrived at her house at five minutes after six. In fact, her expression came across as incredibly welcoming. Clearly, they were destined to be good friends. "Come on in. I'm so glad you could make it. I hope you're hungry."

Vi went breathless for a moment. Last night Kat's face had been drawn and haggard. The effect of coming upon a murder scene had taken its toll, and understandably so. She'd been entitled to a physical and emotional response to the situation. The woman who opened the door tonight was alert and smiling and downright beautiful. Her heart jumped, which shocked the hell out of her. She couldn't remember the last time she'd actually noticed another woman, let alone felt an immediate attraction. With so much on her plate, feeling anything came as a surprise. She barely had time to sleep. Definitely no time for a relationship. Still, nice to know her insane schedule hadn't rendered her immune.

"Hi." For someone highly educated and on her way to a medical degree, she was quite the conversationalist, wasn't she? Perhaps she needed a little less time in the morgue and in the books, and a little more time out.

Kat held the door open wide, and pleasing scents wafted out. Her stomach growled, and she hoped Kat didn't hear it. "Come in, please. We're so glad you could make it."

"We?" Vi peeked around Kat, expecting to see someone sitting at the table. She'd hoped it would be just the two of them.

Kat laughed and waved her in. "No surprises tonight. Just me and my girl." Lucy must have heard their voices, because all of a sudden she appeared at Vi's feet, circling her with an energy that made her envious. If she had even a tenth of the dog's drive, she'd be done with medical school and her specialized training in record time.

"To be honest, I'm glad you invited me. I'm starving and still haven't made time to hit the grocery store. For that matter, I don't even know where the grocery store is."

Kat frowned. "You should have told me. I'd be happy to run to the store for you or go with you."

"I don't want to impose on you any more than I already am." She waved her hand toward the table set for the two of them. "You're two for two with dinner, and it's been only a couple of days."

Kat turned and looked at the table. "That isn't an imposition. That's fun. I love to cook, and it's a lot more fun to do it for someone other than just myself. Do you know the last time I actually ate at the table?" Her laugh sounded like sunshine.

"On the sofa with a plate and the television remote?"

"You got it. Me, a salad, and the six o'clock news. I'm an endlessly fascinating person." She laughed again. "You want something to drink? I've got wine, iced tea, water?"

Wine sounded heavenly, but with her schedule, a treat of the fermented-grape variety would have to wait. "Iced tea would be great."

"Iced tea it shall be. Have a seat and I'll be right back."

She pulled out one of the chairs at the table and sat. Lucy promptly jumped up on the chair next to her and stared. Vi couldn't help it. She started laughing, and God, it felt good.

At the sound of Vi's laughter, Kat stuck her head around the corner. Oh, for heaven's sake. That dog would be the death of her yet. "Lucy! Down."

Lucy glanced at her, turned her attention back to Vi, and stayed put. Seriously? Clearly they were slacking on their obedience skills. Tomorrow they were going to do some drills. A lot of drills.

Vi reached over and ran her hand over Lucy's head. "She's fine, if it's okay with you."

Kat shook her head. "It's embarrassing. She knows better than that and usually does what I tell her. I don't know what it is about you. She seems to be stuck like Super Glue. You sure you're not going to vet school rather than med school?"

"Definitely med school." Vi's smile was warm. "I'm flattered she wants to be my dinner mate. I hate to admit it, but it's been a long time since someone wanted to be my dinner date."

Kat shook her head and gave up. She'd work on Lucy's manners another time. She debated admitting that she would love to be Vi's dinner date and then decided it was a little too early for that. She took one last glance at Lucy and decided maybe her partner was playing wingman. Smart dog. "She wants to be something, that's for sure. I'll be right back."

After the glasses were filled, she picked them up at the same time her cell rang. She set them back down and grabbed the phone. The display showed Circe's number. Interesting. Probably just checking in on her again. All her teammates were thoughtful like that. She punched the Accept button and put the phone to her ear. "Hey."

Circe jumped right in. "Listen, can you get ahold of Vi?"

Unexpected and yet an easy request. "Sure. Why?"

"We need to talk."

Circe's voice held a grim tone. That wasn't like her. Her typical easy manner made her one of the most appreciated members of the dog team. "As a matter of fact, she's here at my house right now. We're just sitting down to dinner."

"Perfect. I'm on my way to the Seven Mile trailhead. Meet me there."

"I said we're just about to sit down for dinner. Can't this wait?"

"No. Put dinner in the oven to keep it warm."

Hard to impress Vi with her cooking if it got stuffed for hours in the oven only to get dried out and old? "Seriously? What is this about?"

"You opened a can of worms."

She hadn't done anything lately that could be considered a can of worms. "Me? What did I do? Does this have something to do with our recovery yesterday? I told the deputies everything I saw and did."

"Not a thing to do with that."

"Come on, Circe. Stop being mysterious. What do you mean I opened a can of worms?" She really didn't get where Circe might be headed.

"It would be more accurate to say your observation did that."

"My..." And then it hit her. "The fact that I picked up on how much you and Vi look alike?"

"That's the can I'm talking about."

"Holy crap." Her appetite vanished, and her curiosity took a giant leap. She could impress Vi with her cooking on another night.

"You have no idea. Grab Vi and meet me at the trailhead. I'll see you in thirty minutes."

"Why don't you just come here?"

Circe paused. "I need the air."

"I have air," Kat said.

"You do, but we can hike while we talk. This conversation will benefit from both fresh air and the release of endorphins, if you catch my drift."

If the intended conversation went in the direction she thought it might, she did catch her drift. Even so...she glanced out the window at the fading daylight. "It's getting a little dark for a hike."

"Bring a headlamp."

❖

The Seeker had been so proud of himself for the restraint he'd used last night. Restraint appeared to be fleeting, because things were different this evening. Wound up so tight, he needed to delve into his work to relax himself. His fingers twitched, and a pounding picked up strength behind his right eye. It always started like this.

Since he'd stared into his mother's eyes the last time, it had been this way. The impact had been physical, and despite his youth, he'd immediately and correctly interpreted the importance of their connection. His father had missed it all and been more the fool because of it. He didn't know the secret his mother had gifted to the Seeker. Her death had made him, and his love for his mother had grown beyond measure in that moment. As had his hatred for his father. Yin and yang.

To ignore the pain behind his eyes risked debilitating pain. The light would begin to feel like knives in his skull, and noise of any significant level would make his stomach roil. The one and only thing that eased it all was the work. When he was younger, his father had used his tried-and-true to heal his pain: prayer. Again, his father had failed in his bid to use faith to heal his son, just as he'd failed to save his wife from terminal illness. His inability to see his own shortcomings had cost his mother her life and ultimately his own. Even as he went along with his father's ridiculous reliance on prayer, the Seeker had found his own path to health and knowledge. It possessed mountains of power his father could only have dreamed of.

In some ways he wished his father was still around so he could prove to him how superior he'd become by using his science against his father's faith. Father had failed over and over again and ultimately earned a place in hell. Or at least that's where the Seeker hoped he'd ended up. He wasn't convinced heaven and hell actually existed, although he liked the idea of his father suffering in perpetual fire. His mother remained always with him, and thus he didn't have to worry about her well-being. With the Seeker she stayed forever safe.

He thought about what he could and should do tonight and worried that doing anything might be pushing it. As if sensing his thoughts, a female voice from the television caught his attention. He turned away from the window and to the screen. The young reporter with the ubiquitous blond hair and slim figure was, with a face appropriately serious, reporting on the recent homicides. She chose her somber words with care to convey just the right level of serious decorum.

"I beg to differ," he said to the pretty face of the six o'clock news. "Those were not homicides. They were volunteers."

He laughed, thinking about his subjects. Perhaps saying they were volunteers was slightly inaccurate. In actuality, he had pressed them into service, so in essence they were drafted. In his defense, he did try to make sure they understood the importance of their sacrifice. Even in a military draft, people knew why their service was required. The same applied to his work. They needed to know they were serving a higher purpose. It wasn't like he was some kind of psychopath. God, no. He had always been a seeker of knowledge with a divine purpose.

The newscaster droned on, and he pressed the remote's mute button. The sound of her voice and her clearly feigned concern got on his nerves. Underneath the somber expression, the carefully made-up face, and the perfect attire lurked a predator. People like her thrived on violence and destruction, and no matter how hard they tried to come across differently, not a single one of them fooled the Seeker. While he felt it important to keep an eye on the pulse of his community through news reports, he hated the task. He wanted to wipe each and every smug face off the planet.

That thought gave him an idea, and it made him smile. The more he did his work, the more he realized that to gain supreme knowledge, he shouldn't limit his pool of candidates. Just like with the trans barista, a good cross section of society would broaden his findings. Yes, a grand idea bloomed, and he didn't know why the particular type of subject hadn't occurred to him before. Not that he would dwell on why it hadn't. The fact that it had come to him now was enough.

The epiphany also gave him a plan for tonight, and the mere thought eased the tension in his shoulders. In the kitchen he pulled several bottles of water from the refrigerator, took a bag of chips from the cupboard, and then grabbed his keys from where he'd laid them in a bowl on the counter. He would reconnoiter tonight. The chips and water were his reward for the hours of watching and waiting he'd require to develop his next plan.

As he drove into the night he thought about blond hair and blue eyes. Especially the blue eyes.

Chapter Ten

Vi came into the kitchen and caught enough of the phone call to realize Kat was talking with Circe. Evidently they were in for another far-from-quiet night. She could say one thing about her move—so far it hadn't been boring.

After Kat ended the call, she told Vi what Circe wanted, and together they put the chicken enchiladas into the oven to keep them warm and the salad back into the refrigerator. Kat drove, with Vi riding shotgun and Lucy in the back seat. They made it to the Seven Mile trailhead in twenty-nine minutes. Though hungry, she felt excitement at the upcoming jaunt. Vi hadn't had time to do any exploring and had no idea this place existed.

The Seven Mile trailhead was beautiful, even in the growing darkness. Tucked off Highway 291, it lay sandwiched between the far north side of Spokane and the start of Nine Mile Falls. Vi never would have known it existed if Kat hadn't piloted them to the meeting place. A circular driveway also served as a parking area, and Kat pulled in and stopped. They were the only vehicle in the lot, which wasn't surprising considering the time.

Headlights came into view as another vehicle pulled in behind them. The moment Lucy saw it, she started whining and pacing in the back. It had to be Circe and Zelda, though it was a different car than she'd driven to Kat's when she'd first met her. "She knows their car?" She'd already picked up on the fact that Lucy was wicked smart, and she confirmed it every time they were together.

Kat laughed. "Oh, yeah. She knows their car and that her best friend is inside. It's always this way. Those two can never get enough of each other. They play together, they work together, and they even eat together." Kat got out, and Lucy jumped over the seat to follow her through the open driver's door.

Circe climbed from her vehicle, and just like Lucy had done, Zelda popped out right behind her. The two dogs met, tails wagging. It surprised Vi that neither of them took off running into the wilderness. Instead they stood, obviously excited, right next to Circe, as if waiting to find out what the plan was. Pretty impressive. She'd never been around dogs this highly trained before, and she wanted to learn more. In less than a week, a couple of working dogs had captured her heart and had her fascinated.

Not only the dogs captured her curiosity. She also wanted to know what was so important that they had to drop everything and meet Circe here at this time of night. To say it had been quite a day was playing down the intensity. From the moment she'd read the note on her door, she'd been anticipating dinner with Kat, and had anyone else interrupted them, she'd have been angry. Instead, the chance to hear Circe's news had her anxious. A hike wasn't exactly high on her list, given she'd been on her feet all day and could easily drop into her bed and sleep for days. Top that off with everything else that had happened over the last week, and it pressed down on her.

Kat spread her arms wide. "Okay, mystery woman, we're here. Tell us why?" Kat's words echoed the thoughts in her mind. She hoped Circe would get to the point. Her stomach growled again, and she crossed her arms over her midsection. She thought of the enchiladas waiting in the oven.

Circe ran her hands through her hair while taking long, even breaths. To Vi, she seemed nervous and nothing like the calm woman she'd met before. That woman had been confident and open. Even though they'd met only the night before, this behavior seemed out of character. Circe finally tipped her head, and when she did, her gaze met Vi's. The intense look she gave her sent a tingle of something unsettling flitting through her. "I have a story to share with you."

"A story? You brought us out here at this time of night to tell us a story? We could have done that from the comfort of my living room, you know." Kat was shaking her head. "Not to mention you interrupted dinner, and I, for one, am hungry. Endorphins? Really?"

Vi wasn't exactly sure what the endorphins comments meant. Before she could ask, Circe turned away while starting to talk at the same time.

"I know, and I'm sorry. It couldn't wait. Come, walk with me."

Circe clicked on a flashlight she'd been holding and started walking toward an asphalt path labeled "Centennial Trail." Zelda and Lucy took off running with glee.

Kat had slipped on a cap with a light attached to the brim. "Let's go," she told Vi as she too clicked on her light. "She hikes like a demon, so we don't want her to get too far ahead, or we'll be running to keep up. Hard to hear whatever she has to say if we're looking at her back."

She took Kat at her word and hustled until she walked beside Circe. With Lucy and Zelda taking the lead, the three of them walked in silence for probably ten minutes, though it seemed more like half an hour to Vi and her tired feet. Then Circe veered off the asphalt and onto a wilderness path that led through woods and down near the river. She couldn't see the river for the lush overgrowth, though it was easy enough to hear the rush of the water in the quiet, and the dirt path provided a welcomed change beneath her feet. She had the sense that, like her, Kat let Circe take the lead. She had a story to tell, and they were simply waiting to hear it. She hoped she got to it pretty soon.

Kat caved first. "Come on, Circe. We're out here, we're walking, we're tripping on branches and rocks, so now it's time to start talking before one of us face-plants in the dirt. What's this all about?"

Circe shoved her hands into her pockets and said quietly as she stared straight forward, "It's about the sister I never knew I had."

❖

Kat expected a good explanation for the impromptu hike, but that bombshell came as a complete surprise. "Did you just say sister?"

Circe had stopped and turned to stare at Vi, who likewise stood motionless in addition to being speechless. "Yes, I said sister."

"You mean me." Vi's words were soft on the evening breeze. Her words were filled with the same kind of amazement Kat was feeling. The insistence on a fresh air hike now made a lot more sense. Those endorphins didn't hurt either.

"Yes." If Kat wasn't so damned stunned, she might do the gracious thing and leave the two women to talk this out, but hell's bells. No way did she intend to miss out on this story. When she'd thought they looked enough alike to be sisters, she'd considered it nothing more than an interesting coincidence. The everybody's-got-a-twin-thing that had zero basis in genetics. This appeared to be going down way too real.

Vi sank to a downed tree. "Tell me." In the light of Kat's headlamp, her hands were trembling as she held them in front of her.

"You don't sound surprised." Circe sat next to her and took one of her hands between both of hers. "I sure was."

Vi stared down at the ground while shaking her head. "My mother was incredible, yet I always felt she had more to tell. She died before she became willing to reveal her secrets. How could she keep something like this from me?"

"What about the rest of your family?"

"It was only me and my grandmother, and neither of us knew anything about my father. We never knew why my mother didn't trust us enough to share. She had to know we never would have judged her. I guess she didn't." Her words trailed off to a whisper. The whisper couldn't hide the sadness Kat could still hear, and her heart ached for Vi.

At the same time her conscience started to get the better of her. "Would you like me to wait back at the car?" Not that Kat wanted to. She wanted to hear everything because it sounded like something incredible.

"Sit," Circe told her without looking at her. "If it's okay with you?" Her eyes were on Vi. "Is it?"

Vi nodded. "Stay with us. I've been through terrible times in my life, and having friends always made things better, not worse. Please stay."

Kat felt a rush of warmth to hear her use the word "friend." She rarely sought companionship or tried to make new friends. Though she had them, she allowed very few close. Life, her life, worked much easier that way. All of that aside, this affirmation held a weight that surprised her as much as it pleased her. She sat next to Vi, drawn close to her warmth. She took Vi's free hand and held it.

"Tell me," Vi asked Circe, squeezing Kat's hand as she said it.

Circe shifted so she looked at both Vi and Kat. In the filtered light of the headlamp Kat had pointed toward the ground rather than in the faces of the other women, Circe's expression appeared pinched. In all the years they'd known each other, in all the grueling searches they'd been through together, she'd never seen a look like this on her face before. Behind them twigs snapped, the sounds of paws running along the path they'd walked across moments before. Zelda and Lucy skidded into sight, stared at them for a moment, and then ran off into the darkness again. They were having a grand time playing together and were content to let the humans sit and talk. Kat sure hoped a park ranger didn't happen by and bust them for having their dogs off leash. She was willing to take that risk.

"I stopped by my parents' house and shared with them how much you and I look alike. In fact, I showed them the picture we took. Let's just say the reaction to that photo wasn't what I expected. I thought they'd laugh while finding it an amusing coincidence. They didn't do either. My mother started crying, and my father went white as a ghost. I've never seen my dad react like that before about anything."

"That doesn't make sense." Vi was shaking her head. "We lived thousands of miles apart. There's no way we can be related. Our resemblance to each other is a fluke and nothing more. It has to be."

"I was thinking the same thing when I showed them the picture, up until they shared with me something I never knew. When I was five years old my parents split up for just under a year. I was so young at the time of the separation I didn't remember any of it, although after they told me I had a vague recollection of Dad being gone for a long while. I was a little kid, and while it clicked with me that he'd been gone an extra-long time, it didn't register in my little-kid brain that anything was out of the ordinary."

Scenarios started to roll through Kat's mind as Circe talked. She was, as her brother liked to say, connecting the dots. Vi was sharp, or she'd never have made it into medical school, and she had to be connecting those same dots. "Holy shit," Kat murmured.

Circe took a breath. "They decided to put some distance between them. Dad spent most of that time working as a consultant in Alaska."

"Anchorage." Vi had pulled her hands free and looked down as she twisted them in her lap.

"Yes," Circe said as she nodded. "He returned home after eight months away, and my parents patched up their differences. As they explained it to me, counseling was involved, as was forgiveness on both sides. As far as I knew in my mature five-year-old world, we were a normal little nuclear family. Daddy had been gone. Daddy came home. End of story."

"Except there's more to the story, isn't there?" Now Vi looked Circe in the eye. Even though she no longer held Vi's hand, Kat could feel the vibrations rolling off her. She wished she could comfort her.

Circe nodded again. "Way more. Long story short, he had a serious romantic relationship during his time in Anchorage. This morning, Dad and I went for coffee without my mom. He wanted to be able to talk freely and didn't think he could do that in front of Mom. He told me that while she'd been aware of the relationship, she'd never held it against him because they'd been separated and most likely heading toward divorce at the time."

"Your dad and my mother had a romance."

"Yes."

"Why did he abandon me?" The break in Vi's voice made Kat take her hand again. She couldn't help it; she had to do something. The trembling had returned even stronger than before. Vi didn't pull away.

"He didn't know about you."

"Isn't that what they all say?" Zelda and Lucy took that moment to skid into the clearing again. Both were panting, and they dropped to the ground.

"If you'd seen his face when he looked at that picture of you and me, you'd believe him. I'd know if he was lying. I'm certain he told me the truth. Vi, he isn't the kind of guy who walks away from responsibility. It's one of the reasons he and my mother decided to work it out. Responsibility."

"I always thought I'd feel better when I knew. Why don't I?"

Circe put an arm around Vi's shoulders. "It's a lot to take in. I'm still blown away, and I can't imagine how all this is hitting you. I mean, think about it, Vi. We're sisters."

A tear slid down Vi's face, and Kat wanted to pull her into her arms and tell her it was all going to be great. Circe would be the best sister.

After shaking off Circe's arm and pulling her hands free from Kat's, Vi stood. "I need to walk." She started down the dark path, and Zelda and Lucy took off in front. They always had to be in the lead.

Kat jumped up and followed. Vi walked fast and didn't have a headlamp on. Kat worried she would trip over a downed tree or one of the ubiquitous rocks that stuck up out of the ground like a cruel obstacle course. Those rocks could cause a nasty gash if she fell on one. Nobody had a first-aid kit on them.

She caught up with her just as Vi stopped, and a cry escaped her lips. "Not now," Vi whispered. "Not flipping now."

Circe came up from behind and stopped next to Vi, putting a hand on her shoulder. For a good five seconds, neither of them said a word. Then Circe asked quietly, "You see her?" Kat had never heard such tension in Circe's voice before.

"Yes. You see her too?"

"Afraid so."

Kat swung her head right and left, spotting nothing. She didn't know where Lucy and Zelda were and figured that had to be who they were talking about. A second ago the two dogs were traipsing along in front of them, and then they both took off like lightning. She didn't see the dogs now, and she sure didn't see a *her*.

"See who?"

"The dead woman," Vi said quietly.

By nine the Seeker had gathered plenty of information, enough to begin his preliminary plan. He preferred to have all his ducks in a row before he started a new project. The process created his brand of fun and gave him a rush of anticipation like nothing else. Now he could take his photos and his notes and put together his timeline. This one would be really enjoyable and, of course, an excellent addition to his knowledge base and specimen collection.

At the same time, emptiness besieged him when he couldn't act. Spending time with his collection would ease that feeling, but to get to the collection would require a drive he didn't want to take right now. A closer alternative existed. Sometimes it came in the form of sending law enforcement on a wild-goose chase, and that's what he had done with a number of his subjects, like the beautiful young man with the silky blond hair. He had no doubt they were still puzzling over why he'd been left like Jesus out on the popular hiking trail. Others were different, and he preferred to keep those elite few to himself. They served a dual purpose: to further his mission and to keep him company at times like this.

She'd been a special one indeed—green eyes that had shown him heaven. She'd become the start of the green section. It hadn't taken more than a moment's consideration to determine she was a keeper, and given her slim, athletic body, he'd found easy to carry her to a secluded resting place. She deserved that beautiful spot because of her exceptional beauty. He liked visiting her, talking with her, remembering their time together.

He parked his car near the old airstrip, where he could tuck it away from sight should anyone else decide to go for an evening stroll. A second parking area existed just south of the airstrip, and most visitors preferred the ease and convenience of that one. On the occasions he came to visit in the evenings, he rarely ran into others, as theoretically the park closed at dusk. The posted closing time didn't stop the truly dedicated, and once in a while he did have to fade into the darkness to avoid being seen. Not a difficult task considering how skilled he'd become at wrapping the shadows around himself, kind of like a vampire who became one with the night. He'd always been good at it, except when it came to his father. That bastard could find him anywhere. His father would attribute his own ability to the grace God had bestowed upon him, a sign of his divinity. The Seeker considered it more a curse of Satan. The two of them never looked at anything the same way.

The Seeker cut down toward the river and hiked along the trees and brush. The night turned cool though it remained comfortable. The moon rose high, the sky filling with stars. He liked the solitude and peace this place captured, and that's why he'd brought her here. Her resting place had been decided on long before they met on this very path. He'd seen her run the same route many times, even though she'd never noticed him. Another of his gifts. He could blend into the background anywhere. Given his calling, a very valuable trait.

Anticipation swept over him as he moved without error across the rocky path bordered on both sides by heavy vegetation. In the winter it was more wide open, but once spring came, the vegetation flourished and created a shady oasis. Only a little farther to go and he could spend some time with her as the moon grew brighter and the sky darker. A sort of romantic visit under the stars that would feed his soul.

He stilled when a sudden noise broke the soothing silence. He stopped and listened. A dog? No, wait, two dogs. Damn it. That meant he wasn't alone. Maybe a late runner had brought the dogs along for protection and company. It also wasn't unheard of in this area to see cougars, deer, and moose. Yes, that's what it must be, wildlife. All he had to do was wait for them to pass and he could continue.

As quietly as he could, he shifted off the path and into the brush. He moved slowly and quietly, inching closer to his date. He stopped again at the sound of voices and, seconds later, saw the movement of light. Damn, damn, damn. He'd hoped for a couple of deer, maybe a coyote. Definitely not humans. The presence of other people would mess up his visitation plans. Then he saw something that made him want to scream. The flashlight held by one of the intruders was trained on two dogs, but that wasn't what made him want to throw up. Both dogs were sitting right on top of her, not that they could know that, for she had been buried deep enough that no one could or would find her. Yet a sick feeling in the pit of his stomach told him they just had.

"Oh, crap." It was a woman's voice.

"I'll call it in." A second woman's voice.

"That's amazing." It was a third woman.

What in the hell? Had an entire coven showed up to destroy his night? With his impeccable work, this could not be happening. He knew how to do things right. She should stay hidden, with only one person alive knowing where she rested.

"It's what the human-remains detection dogs do, and yeah, they are amazing."

He swallowed the bile that rose in his throat. In what kind of messed-up universe did cadaver dogs show up to uncover one of his secrets? It wasn't fair, and calling on all the self-control he possessed, he managed not to scream. A good thing he didn't have a gun because he'd shoot them all. As he stood in the shadows and worked to even his breath, the Seeker realized he had only one choice—to play like a ninja and get out of here undiscovered. Nothing he could do at this point. She was lost to him forever, and he would have to find a way to reconcile with that fact. It wasn't fair, but then again, hadn't he learned a very long time ago that little in life was?

He threw one final glance toward the three woman and the two dogs before moving away in silence. As he did, he decided to up his current schedule. If he lost one of his precious, another must take her place. Simple mathematics, and he always did like math.

Chapter Eleven

Vi stared at Circe. "You can see her. Seriously, you can?" They were waiting for the sheriff's department to respond after Kat made the call. Both the HRD dogs had made it clear they detected the odor of human decomposition, both in the same place. Not that Vi needed their confirmation. The woman who had been standing in the path told her the truth of what lay beneath the soil where Zelda and Lucy were in a down without her ever having to say a word. The dead didn't tease or lie or pretend.

"Yes. I can see her."

"What are you two talking about?" Kat sounded frustrated and Vi couldn't blame her. It had to be confusing.

Kat's call to the sheriff's department came in direct response to what the dogs were telling them. Kat couldn't see the spirit of the woman Vi stared at. But she'd just discovered that Circe could, and that reality blew her mind. For the first time in her life, Vi wasn't alone in the space between life and death. Her mother and her grandmother had both known what she could do and had tried their best to make her not feel like a freak. Until right now she'd never told another person outside of her family, and it seemed right to share it with Circe. She felt like she was talking to family, more specifically, a sister, and if what Circe had told her earlier ended up being correct, then she was talking to family.

"I'll take this one," Circe told her at the same time she squeezed her hand. She turned to look at Kat. "You know how I told you my dad had a relationship with Vi's mother while he worked in Alaska? Well, he didn't know about Vi, because he left Anchorage with a clean split, and he never talked to her mother again. From what Dad told me, they mutually agreed on it being the best for both of them. They'd had fun, they sincerely cared about each other, but neither of them wanted it to be forever."

"She was protecting him." That explanation fit perfectly, because it was the kind of thing her mother would do. She always took care of those around her, even if she had to sacrifice herself. The realization of what her mother had done brought tears to her eyes.

Now Circe turned and looked at her. "I think so too, but he knew the second I showed him your picture. I could tell by looking at his face that he had no doubt you were his daughter. The timing fit, and he said your mother had been a good and honorable person who would do something like take on the responsibility of a child so he could try to repair his marriage."

Vi couldn't argue. "That's exactly what she'd do." Her heart ached. As she thought back, all the pieces fell into place, and shame filled her at how angry she'd become with her mother whenever she demanded to know her father's name. She felt sad that her mother's secrets had driven her to chemical dependency. How she wished she could talk to her now and make it right. To tell her how much she loved her.

Another thought crossed her mind, and she looked over at Circe. "This thing," she waved her hands in the direction of the ghost only she and Circe could see, "had to come from him."

"What the hell are you two talking about? What came from him? Who is *her*? Neither one of you is making sense at all."

Circe kept looking at Vi. "I don't need Zelda to tell me where a body is. The dead come to me."

"Me too," Vi admitted, loving how free it made her feel. "Me too."

For the first time since they'd met, Kat had apparently been rendered speechless. She stared from face to face and then finally found her voice. "No fucking way."

Circe shrugged. "Afraid so."

"Really? You both see bodies?"

"No, not bodies so much," Vi told her. "Their spirits. They come to me for help."

"Fucking awesome." Kat smiled and shook her head. She looked over at Circe and her eyebrows rose. "Well, that certainly explains a lot."

"I suppose it does." Circe smiled back at her.

"How does something like that even happen?" Kat's eyes still shone with excitement.

Circe shrugged. "Until right now, I never knew where this gift came from, only that it's been a part of me as long as I can remember."

"Me as well." Vi had assumed it came courtesy of her Native American heritage. It had never occurred to her that it might be from a father with a Euro lineage.

Circe took her hand, squeezing it lightly. "Now I think we can agree that we got it from our father."

"Our father." The words sounded strange on her tongue. She'd waited her whole life to know the name of the man who helped give her life. Now that the day had finally arrived, it had a very surreal feel to it.

"He wants to meet you."

A wave of emotion flowed over her with a power that nearly brought her to her knees. In all her fantasies, she'd only wished to know his name and where he came from. She'd never taken it beyond knowledge, and the reality that she might actually meet him stopped her. "This is all too much, too soon." Her heart beat wildly, and she wondered if this was how people felt when they experienced a panic attack.

Kat put a hand on her shoulder, and she was grateful for her touch. It grounded her in a way that shouldn't be possible, given that they'd met only recently. Yet there it was, just the same. She hoped she didn't take her hand away.

Circe nodded and squeezed her hand once more. "I really do understand. When you're ready, I'll set it up however you like. Dad really wants to meet you, but he understands. It's been a big surprise to him too, and he gets that it's an even bigger one for you. He's a good guy, Vi. Trust me. You're going to love him."

Given how panicked she felt at the moment, Vi wondered if she'd ever be ready to find out.

❖

By the time Kat got to her bed, exhaustion weighed on her like a hundred-pound ball. It had been three hours before the sheriff's department responded, questioned them, and then allowed them to leave the park. As soon as the initial team reached the body location, Kat, Vi, and Circe had walked back to their rigs to put up Zelda and Lucy. After that they spent a good two hours talking to the sheriff's deputies. Not a single one of the responding officers seemed particularly surprised that once again Circe and Zelda had stumbled across a crime scene, because it wasn't the first or second time it had happened. They'd been instrumental a while back in stopping a killer who had hidden bodies all over the county. Kat had been impressed at the time by Circe and Zelda's extraordinary skills. Now that she'd been brought in on the secret, she found herself even more impressed.

Kat hoped that tonight's find would turn out to be an isolated instance and not a repeat of what Circe had been drawn into before. Given what she and Lucy had found, combined with the news reports on another unsolved murder of an elderly woman, things were looking a bit dicey around town.

She didn't want to think about murder. Her concern fell squarely on Vi. Talk about getting hit with a two-by-four. She'd walked away from everything she'd ever known to move to a new city and start a new life. She'd overcome the murder of her mother and the loss of her grandmother. Now she finds out she has not only a father here in town but a sister who just happens to share an incredible secret with her. All that would be overwhelming and intense without anything else in the mix. The universe didn't seem to be siding with her because tonight's events put Vi, as well as Circe and Kat, right square in the middle of a series of murders.

The secret. Her mind remained blown over that one. Both Circe and Vi could see dead people? She thought that kind of thing happened only in the movies. If she hadn't been standing there and witnessed their reactions, she'd think they were messing with her head, not that it was the kind of thing Circe would do. She sensed that Vi wouldn't either.

Here alone with the world now quieted, she felt unanticipated emotions roll in. She'd expect to be shocked at finding a second victim. For any rational person, that would be the normal reaction. As much as Kat loathed to admit it, she felt excluded. Mentally she acknowledged that the exclusion had nothing to do with her, yet as Kat sat on the edge of the bed, her feelings were hurt. She'd always believed she and Circe were tight, yet if that were true, she would have been party to the secret, right? That she wasn't told Kat their friendship wasn't as close as she believed.

Clearly she possessed thin skin. She was a grown woman, and just because someone held something close didn't mean they weren't friends. Maybe not as good as she thought, but they were and still remained friends. It had to be enough.

Sure, and that's why she felt like the kid nobody chooses for kickball. She wanted to be the first kid picked, or the second at the very least. Not the one the team got stuck with when no one else remained, and that's the way it hit her. She ran her fingers through her hair and closed her eyes against the threatening tears. Fatigue, that's all it was. In the morning after she'd had a good night's sleep, she'd be back to her chipper self, and all these feelings of being an outsider would vanish.

"Right," she muttered to herself. It would be hard not to feel like an outsider when Circe and Vi shared such an intimate ability. She started to laugh. Crap. Not only did she feel left out. She was jealous too. Good Lord, she really did need to get some sleep and maybe some professional help while she was at it.

A soft knock on the front door caused the sleeping Lucy to jump up from the bed and run into the other room barking. Her heart started to beat wildly, and like Lucy, she leapt from the edge of the bed and headed toward the front door, the source of the knocking. Could it be Scooter? He'd tracked her down despite having moved since he'd been sent to prison? The fear that, if he'd found her, the circle of stalking would begin again made her sick to her stomach. *Please, God, don't let it be Scooter.*

She let out the breath she'd been holding when she stepped into the front hallway. The light on the front porch, always left on at night, reflected a familiar silhouette through the oval stained glass of the solid wood door. Not Scooter. Her fear faded, replaced by curiosity. What would bring Vi here, given she'd dropped her at her front door half an hour ago? Her schedule had been more hectic than Kat's, and she had to be close to dropping.

She opened the door. "What's wrong?" Something had to be wrong to bring her here.

"Nothing, and I'm so sorry to bug you."

All feelings of exclusion and jealousy evaporated in an instant. The fact that Vi felt comfortable enough to come to her without hesitation made everything okay again. "Don't be. Come on in. Tell me how I can help." She opened the door wide and motioned Vi inside. She glanced outside before shutting and locking the door.

Vi walked into the living room, though she didn't sit. She stood in front of the fireplace, twisting her hands. "This might sound strange and definitely needy, but the quiet of my place is too much tonight or," she glanced at the handcrafted wall clock Vi had picked up at a farmer's market, "this morning."

Kat's heart took a leap. She couldn't remember the last time someone had come to her seeking simple companionship. Or, she wondered, had anyone ever really come to her like this? Didn't matter because the fact that Vi had meant the world to her.

The thing was, she really did understand, particularly after the other day. Circe had been there for her, and she was ready to be there for Vi. "I get it, and that's one of the reasons I've always had a dog. You're never alone when you have one." As if on command, Lucy trotted in to lean against her legs. She rubbed her head and smiled at the warm, soft fur that met her fingers. "She never fails to soothe my soul."

Vi looked at Lucy and smiled. "Maybe I should borrow her."

Kat waited until Vi looked up and their eyes met. "Or maybe you should just stay here."

The Seeker couldn't help feeling pissed off. Those fucking women had taken away a precious possession of his, and while he knew he could soon replace her with another, it still wasn't the same. He controlled what did and didn't happen with his subjects, and only he had the right to say who would be returned to their friends and families and who wouldn't.

This wasn't, however, the time to let it bother him. He had too much on his plate to allow wrongs perpetuated against him to sidetrack his plans. Unfortunately, none of the usual distractions were working to get his mind away from the loss. He stared at his monitor and wished for the video he'd taken earlier to feed his soul and gift him with temporary peace. He couldn't concentrate no matter how hard he tried. Rather than longed-for peace, anxiety raged inside him. His right eye twitched like he suffered from some neurological condition, and that pissed him off. The spasm hadn't been this bad in years. Not since the day he said farewell to his father for the final time. Now that had been a very good day indeed.

A visit to the old man might help, or it could possibly make him more anxious. Confronting the dragon, so to speak. After all this time the Seeker would like to think he'd moved beyond his reach, but the mere thought of his father made his blood pressure rise and his muscles tense, as if waiting for the touch of that big hand against the back of his head. That his father could have such power over him despite the fact that the Seeker had been the one who made certain he'd never been able to lay a hand on him again came as a disappointment. The more he considered a visit, the more he realized it really would be a bad idea. Better to leave that dragon alone.

Just the same, the thought brought a smile to his face. Several decades had passed, and they were still trying to solve the high-profile case of the missing senator from eastern Washington. He'd seen programs on the subject no less than three times—the kind of shows that poked into unsolved mysteries, as if paid hosts, most of whom were actors, could actually solve real cold cases. The entire premise struck him as stupid, but that didn't stop producers from badgering him time and time again to appear and plead for the public's help in solving the mystery of his father's untimely disappearance. Each time they called, he refused. He wasn't worried they would stumble onto the secret. He took issue with having his name associated with the man who had put him through hell. Bad enough that folks around here still remembered that they were related. He didn't need to take that type of name recognition national, or international, the way television worked these days.

When they spoke of his father in this part of the state, people still revered him as the torchbearer for their region. He'd stood up to the powers that be in Washington DC and made things happen. They viewed him as a tragic soul who had lost his wife to the scourge of cancer far too soon, only to be left to raise a child by himself, all while doing his duty as an elected lawmaker. The saint.

In reality, he'd been a two-faced devil that none of them really knew. The sinner. Those in his inner circle believed they were intimates. How wrong they were. If anybody wondered how the Seeker could be so good at living two completely different lives, all they had to do was take a good long look at the man who'd sired him. He'd learned from the best. But the Seeker had turned out to be better. The pupil had become the master.

Tapping his fingers on the desktop, he embraced the truth of his mastery, and the pain behind his eye receded. He had performed everything surrounding his father's disappearance with absolute perfection. At the time, his sole purpose had been to get him out of his life once and for all. Once he'd accomplished that goal, he'd come to understand that its success brought him much more than freedom. It gave him the laser-focused purpose and direction he'd been seeking since the day his mother had passed. It gave him power and strength through release from the invisible bondage that had held him prisoner his whole life.

The best part. The very best part? His father's obscurity. He received no attention from the masses such as he'd enjoyed when standing on the Senate floor regaling the unsuspecting with his empty rhetoric. No hometown-hero status to sustain him if and when his bid for reelection finally fell short. No lovely middle-aged women vying to be the next woman on his arm at state dinners. Everything the bastard had hoped for vanished in less time than it took to brush his teeth. No other explanation for it beyond true beauty and divine inspiration.

Now a smile came back to his face. All of a sudden he felt much better, and once more he turned his attention to the computer and the video playing there. His fingers stilled on the keyboard, and as he watched, the rush of joy he'd been hoping for earlier flooded him. Focus returned. On his screen a lovely blond woman walked across a busy street, one hand brushing her hair away from her face. He only wished the shot had been with a telephoto lens so it would have captured the sparkling blue eyes.

His fingertips brushed the monitor. He'd planned to stretch this one out a bit and relish the sweet anticipation the process brought him. In light of tonight's turn of events, he decided it would be a good idea to up the schedule. Tonight would be optimal for his emotional needs, if less than prime for the necessary logistics. For that, he would have to wait one more night. Though he didn't like having to wait, he would. Working his plan through in his head, he realized it made sense. In less than twenty-four hours it would all come together, and he believed he could wait that long.

Leaning back in his chair, he put his hands on his head and blew out a long breath. In a few hours he would go to work and pretend to be just another working Joe. He would smile and engage in small talk with his coworkers and supervisors. How they all liked him. In fact, they often invited him out for drinks to unwind with the rest of the crew after a particularly stressful day. Once in a while he went. Keeping up appearances and all that. He didn't care to drink, in particular didn't care for the way alcohol dulled his senses.

He wanted to feel and experience everything, and he never knew exactly when an opportunity might present itself. If it turned out to be one of the nights when he'd stopped with them, he'd lose the sensory joys of the adventure if he imbibed. Still, he was smart enough to understand it wasn't wise to make himself stand out, and thus he made the occasional appearance. He'd have a beer, laugh at stupid jokes, and tell elaborate stories. He suspected the stories they shared with him were all true. His were not. They never caught on, but then again, why would they? His mastery had no bounds.

He took one last look at the face of his next project, sighed contentedly, and powered down his laptop. His mind and body had calmed enough now that he could rest. A few hours of sleep and the new day would be upon him. Pleasure awaited on the horizon.

Chapter Twelve

Until the invitation had been issued, Vi didn't realize that's exactly what she'd been hoping for as she'd made the walk over. Tonight had rocked her, and that was grossly understating things. She finds out that not only does she have an older sister, but said older sister also has the same gift she does. Top that off with a dead body, and the night rockets from shocking to bizarre in an eye blink.

Kat had driven her right to her own front door, a kindness that did not go unnoticed. She'd showered, put on comfortable clothes, and hoped. Whenever she felt lost, her grandmother chose those occasions to appear. She so wanted to see her and gain her help in understanding what was happening around her. More than that, she wanted to hug her grandmother and feel the strength that had always been in her, even as her last day drew near. The hug would never happen again no matter how hard she wished for it. While it was true that she could see the dead and sometimes even talk to them, she couldn't touch them, nor was she sure she really wanted to. Her grandmother had been warm and approachable while smelling faintly of the cinnamon she liked to sprinkle in her tea. To Vi it represented the scent of home and happiness.

Right now, she would give anything to grab that feeling and hold on. Her world reeled already in turmoil with the changes she'd freely charged after. What had occurred tonight never came up in any of the scenarios she'd imagined. Grandmother could make sense of it. That had been her gift, and now the time had arrived to share that information with Vi.

After half an hour, Vi gave up her hope that her grandmother would come to her and, even as unreasonable as her reaction was, felt as though she'd been abandoned. For the first time she'd been left alone when her spirit hurt. A flicker of fear went through her. As much as she'd always resented this thing she could do, at the same time she'd found immense comfort in her grandmother's occasional appearances. She refused to consider that she might not come to her again.

Two options presented themselves now. She could stay here and feel sorry for herself, or she could only reach out, and boy, looking to another for comfort sure wasn't her thing. Lessons learned in childhood were hard to shake. She'd been bullied because her hair was too dark and her skin too brown. Being different had been driven home time and time again in the cruel way that only children can accomplish. As she got older and grew into her looks, the boys no longer taunted her. Instead, they wanted to date her, and then she realized not just her heritage set her apart. She discovered another part of herself that made her even more unique. She liked women. In the end, she built walls for protection too strong and too high for anyone to break through. Those walls were like old trusted friends.

Like seeing the dead, only a very faithful few knew her second secret. Unlike her hair and her skin, she could hide the fact that she wanted to kiss Faye Uline instead of her football-star brother, Franklin. The kids in her world didn't need any more ammunition than they already had. For most of her school years, she remained isolated and introverted. A few movies with close friends here and there, an occasional football game. Enough to keep up the appearance of being a normal kid. Not enough to allow anyone to get too near the real girl.

Everything changed when murder entered her world. Her mother's death gave her an intense focus that effortlessly shut out everything and everyone else. She turned her attention to education and pursuit of the truth, and didn't care about fitting in or finding companionship. Given that kind of single-mindedness, no one stood a chance, man or woman, and they all quit trying. No more bullying. No more attempts at dates. It worked for her.

But it wasn't working for her now, which is why she stood in Kat's living room seriously considering her offer to stay the night. The invitation was most likely the platonic offer of a new friend, with nothing sexual about it. Not, if she was being honest, that she would be averse to the latter. Right from hello, she'd been drawn to Kat. Attractive, smart, and with an incredible dog, she had three checks in the awesome column right from the beginning. She also ran a farm by herself, did what she wanted, and seemed to be the happiest person Vi had met in a very long time. All of these factors combined to make Kat the kind of person who appealed to her. Like *really* appealed to her. She hadn't even been tempted by another woman since her senior year in undergrad, and even then, it had been a college fling never destined to go anywhere. This didn't feel like beginnings of a fling at all.

Silently she told herself to stand down. What she was interpreting as attraction could be as simple as stress expressing itself in inappropriate ways. Kat had done nothing except be kind to a tenant brand-new to the area. Her imagination had them jumping into bed together. Her college courses had included a minor in psychology, and she had a fair idea about projection. Pretty sure that's what she was doing right now. *Take it down a notch, girlfriend.*

She smiled at Kat. "That's really kind of you…"

"Kind, my ass. After the night you've had, you should be with friends, not out there in the north forty by yourself. That's the way my daddy taught me."

"Your father sounds kind."

"Oh, he had his moments."

"Had?"

"We lost him five years ago to colon cancer. Not pretty, but he was a fighter and gave that shit a run for its money."

"I'm sorry. I know what it feels like to lose a parent."

Kat put an arm around her shoulders. "I kind of sensed that earlier."

"Hard to talk about."

"Cancer?"

"No, murder."

Murder. That word would have rocked Kat under normal circumstances. Their night had been quite far from normal. As she'd put her arm around Vi's shoulders, she'd felt tension so tight Vi was almost brittle. On the outside, this woman seemed to have it all. Not what Kat would classify as beautiful in the traditional sense, but beautiful just the same. The color of her skin and the deep, dark hair that framed her face were gorgeous. And her eyes had captured Kat's attention from the moment they met. Dark and intense, they radiated intelligence no one could miss. The whole package made her as sexy as one woman could get.

Now it might be off-putting to some that this beauty made her living in a medical examiner's office and would soon head to school to become a pathologist, but not to Kat. She ran a human-remains-detection dog, for heaven's sake. Vi became infinitely more interesting to her because of her chosen path.

People often didn't understand Kat or what drove her. She was okay with it because only a few could do what she and Lucy did. She also understood that their actions were important in ways that most wouldn't get. That wasn't the case with Vi. Not only did she get it, but Kat didn't even have to explain any of her reasons for working in their particular discipline. Nor did Vi have to clarify why she chose her profession. Kat got it and admired it even before she heard the word "murder."

"I'm so sorry." She meant it too. Kat's heart had broken when cancer took her feisty, full-of-life father away. She couldn't even wrap her head around what it would have been like to lose a parent at the hands of another. "That's why you want to be a pathologist."

Vi nodded and sat down on the sofa as Kat kneeled in front of the fireplace and proceeded to build a fire. "A forensic pathologist, to be more precise, and yes, it is. The system put someone in prison for her murder, and no matter how hard I try, I've never believed he's the person who took her life."

"This is your way of seeking the truth."

"You have no idea," Vi murmured.

"Try me."

Kat sat on the floor with her back against the chair across from Vi. Firelight flickered over Vi's face. "It's never felt right. I've reread the police reports and trial transcripts over and over. My opinion hasn't changed no matter how many times I read the files. No other murders in Alaska with similar MOs happened after Mom. That turned out to be the biggest puzzle piece in the minds of law enforcement, proving they had their man. The case was closed, and the cops were satisfied they'd done their job."

"You don't agree." Kat wasn't asking a question because clearly Vi had a different opinion.

"Not at all. I don't disagree with the fact that no additional murders happened in Alaska after Mom was killed. Unlike the police, I think there's an alternative explanation. I always believed that he…or she… would someday show their hand, and I'd be in a position to know. I found my calling because of my mother's death."

"We all get to where we're supposed to be in odd and interesting ways. Sometimes it's tragedy that takes us there."

"Definitely tragedy in my case, and that's okay. As long as I bring justice to her, I'm fine with it."

"Have you made any progress in proving your theory? Like finding similar murders?"

"Again, like I said, nothing similar in Alaska ever came up after they put that man in prison. It's a mixed blessing. I'm glad no one else from my home state lost their life, but the downside of it resulted in zero inquiry into alternative suspects."

Something in the tone of her voice made her ask, "But you found one somewhere else?"

Vi looked into her eyes and nodded. "Yes."

The conversation got more interesting by the second. Could it get any better? She would remember this night with Vi for a long time. "Well, don't keep me in suspense. Where?"

"Here."

The Seeker couldn't believe how great he felt. Nothing that had occurred in the last few hours had been planned. Everything reeled out of whack and out of his normal style of work. The end result of the chaos was nothing short of magical. He didn't know why he hadn't done this earlier.

He threw his arms out as he walked back to his car, smiling broadly. He'd always thought that his father had been full of crap when it came to all his prayers to God. Tonight, he wasn't quite as certain. The years of praying on knees that screamed in agony from the hardwood floors, the pain that still lingered, might just have been worth it. No matter what he did or how he did it, he'd been protected—proof that when something was right, it was right.

He rested his hand on the small jar as he drove slowly through the quiet South Hill streets. Her house fell far behind him before he even passed another vehicle. Apparently, no one in this part of the city traveled in the wee hours of the morning. Good for him. The odds of anyone recalling his car leaving her neighborhood were, as his father liked to say, slim to none. Oh, how he liked his little sayings. The Seeker had hated every one of the trite plays on words, though he could never tell the old man, who thought everything he said imparted great knowledge to his progeny. He'd been sadly mistaken. The Seeker didn't miss listening to him drone on as he tried to make his son "a better man." Dumbass didn't realize that he'd never be able to make anyone a better man. How could such a hypocrite do anything worthwhile? Simple: he couldn't. As a child he'd understood his father's lack of integrity, and maturity hadn't changed his opinion. The community still referred to his father as a leader, an inspiration, a trailblazer, and the unsolved mystery a great national tragedy. They could think whatever they wanted, and he wouldn't bother to correct them. Too much effort for a man who wasn't worth wasting a single breath on. As for that great national tragedy? In a twisted way it actually gave his father what he desired most: immortality. That the old man hadn't gotten to glory in it made it a consequence both unintended and most satisfying.

"Rot in hell, you bag of bones," he muttered with a smile. It also amused him that people didn't remember his father for any of his so-called great works but for vanishing without the proverbial trace. His father would have been crushed to see how quickly someone filled his seat in Congress. The man who believed himself irreplaceable had been replaced in a nanosecond all because the Seeker had embraced his own destiny. Again, it struck him how much joy came from his work regardless of the circumstances. Just like tonight.

However, this project had taken most of the night, the sun would soon rise over the mountains, and he wouldn't have time to sit back and enjoy the fruits of his works. Earlier he'd talked himself into waiting to complete this task. He'd even gone to bed. When he couldn't sleep, he'd decided to go for it, schedule be damned. Fun didn't begin to describe how the mission had turned out. Now he needed to hurry.

The clock on the dashboard showed that he'd have just enough time to put away his latest addition in the freezer, run home to shower and change, and then get to work. He could call in ill, as he had plenty of sick time banked up. He didn't like to fall back on that ruse unless no other alternative became available. He should do the same thing he did every workday. Part of his successful toolkit included adherence to routine.

The neighborhood was quiet as he pulled into the driveway, stopped in front of the garage doors, and got out. Inside the garage, the Seeker placed the new jar into the blue section with reverence. His fingertips brushed the warm glass, and he thought of the moment he'd captured her spirit. Each subsequent event became easier. The years of work paid a benefit, and he now understood all the signs that told him when it must happen. Her soul resided inside him now, her energy infused with his own. This must be how gods feel.

The epiphany struck him. He was a god. If he wasn't, how could he capture the essence of another human being? That was what his mother had been trying to tell him with her last breath. Now that he understood fully, he also realized how his work would have to go on and on. He was truly unstoppable and untouchable.

He closed and locked the freezer, running his fingers lightly over the closed door. Back in the car, his earlier weariness vanished as he turned the key and started the engine. He turned around in the driveway and headed back toward the city. The decades-long pain in his knees vanished. A vision of the world spread out in front of him with brilliant clarity, full of color and light and power.

Chapter Thirteen

Vi shot up, her heart racing. Where was she? What was going on? She blinked and brought the room into focus. In a second it all came back to her. Walking from her house to Kat's. Getting comfortable on the sofa as a fire warmed the room. Quiet conversation. Peace. Then nothing.

The nothing turned out to be deep sleep like she hadn't experienced in quite a while. For her to drop off like that in someone else's house was about the last thing she would expect. She smiled and decided she would take it as the gift it was. Her mother's murder had pulled the foundation of her life right out from under her feet, and yesterday's experience had that same feel. When she'd come back after the sheriff's deputy had finished questioning them, she'd figured she would have another sleepless night. It probably would have been too, if not for that split-second decision. Reaching out to Kat had been the right one.

Kat lay curled up in front of the fire that had burned low and now put off only a thread of warmth. A blanket was pulled over her shoulders. Vi wondered how long she'd sat tending the fire before she too dropped off to sleep. She stretched and thought about how nice it would be to spend the morning here drinking coffee and talking with Kat. Her vibrant spirit made Vi feel comfortable in a way no other woman had. She wanted to ignore everything else and just be here with her.

Sounded like a good plan, except when she glanced down at the exercise tracker that also served as a watch. She had an hour and half before she needed to be at work, and it was a forty-minute drive to town. Sitting here watching Kat sleep or sharing a cup of coffee when she woke up wasn't an option. Darn.

As quietly as she could, Vi got up, folded the blanket Kat must have placed over her after she'd fallen asleep, and laid it on the end of the sofa. She was stepping toward the door when the click of Lucy's nails on the floor made her turn. A second later, Lucy leaned into her legs with deceptively strong pressure, given the size of the dog. She kneeled and began to rub Lucy's head.

"Good morning."

Her head snapped up. Kat, with her tousled hair and sleepy eyes, stood just inside the living room watching her pet Lucy.

Vi smiled. "Good morning. Sorry I woke you."

"I'd say I caught you in a walk of shame, but considering all we did was sleep, I'll give you a pass on that one."

Vi laughed, already becoming very fond of the way Kat used humor to make every situation lighter and more comfortable. With anyone else this could be awkward. Not with Kat. "No walk of shame. Just a mad dash to grab a shower and get to work. I don't want to make a bad impression by being late during my first week here."

Kat leaned against the door frame and raised one eyebrow. "Ah, well, then I won't take offense that I caught you trying to leave without a good-bye after I built an impressive fire and gave you the coziest blanket I own."

Vi straightened and raised her hands in mock surrender. "No offense intended, I swear. More like embarrassment. I kept you up way too late, and I know all the work you have to do first thing every morning. It wasn't very considerate of me, so I tried to be quiet to let you sleep as long as possible."

Kat laughed. "Apology accepted. It was quite a night, wasn't it?"

"Understatement."

"Yeah, I suppose it is. Blew my mind, and I can't imagine how you're feeling."

She didn't know either. She now had a sister and a fellow what? Psychic? Post-cognitive? She'd never come up with what to call herself, let alone someone else who had the same affliction. Or gift, if one believed her grandmother's take on the whole thing. She'd believed only she possessed the unique ability, despite her grandmother telling her a thousand times that there would be others. No matter what she heard, no matter how many times her grandmother tried to reassure her, until yesterday she didn't believe. To discover firsthand that someone else could see the dead rocked her.

Yes, mind blown. Not in a bad way either. "I'm in a little shock."

"A little? You're obviously stronger than me. I think I'd be ready for the straitjacket right about now."

She shrugged. "Close."

Kat laughed, a gentle, soothing sound. "Naw. I might not know you that well yet, but I can already tell you're solid. A straitjacket will never be in your future. You're going to be some kind of kick-ass doctor."

She'd like to believe that and appreciated Kat's vote of confidence. "I have to get through school first."

"It's gonna happen, trust me." She winked and patted her on the arm. "I'm an excellent judge of character."

Her words both warmed her heart and made her laugh. "I hope you're right."

"I'm always right."

"I'll hold you to it. Now if I don't run, I will be late, and I don't think my new employers will be very impressed."

"Do you think you'll be working on the body we found last night?"

She'd been thinking about the same thing since she woke up. "Possibly, though I doubt it, given my involvement. Then again, it depends on who I'm assigned to work with." Under normal circumstances, she would never be allowed to work such a case. But if Dr. Kelsey was assigned to the autopsy, he might well allow her to. He seemed less concerned with politics and more concerned with getting to the truth, however it happened. She really liked that about him. Down the road he would be a great ally.

"Tell you what. Swing back by tonight. I'll make you dinner and we can talk some more."

The invitation made her feel warm all over. "I can't eat here every night."

Kat shrugged. "Don't know why not."

"Are you like this with everyone who rents your property?"

Kat's smile grew mischievous. "No. Only cute doctors-to-be who my dog likes."

She couldn't help smiling in return. "And who likes your dog in return. I'll see you tonight."

❖

Kat did her chores, and the brisk morning air woke her up. Despite the horror of last night's discovery and having slept only a few hours, she felt great. Her heart had warmed when Vi showed up for companionship. Most of the time Kat enjoyed her solitude. In theory, she didn't have anything against relationships and had had her share of girlfriends through the years. In practice, it was a different story. The last four or five years, she'd been content with her status as a single woman. She couldn't even remember the last time she'd been on a date or even wanted to.

Given all the work her farm required, she didn't have much time to sit around and think. Throw in her search-and-rescue work, along with the phenomenal amount of training hours required to keep their skills sharp, and she had little time left for a serious involvement. Happy and busy, she didn't notice the loneliness the vast majority of the time. That's what she told herself right now as she watched Vi disappear down the driveway.

Too bad it was all a crock. Nothing like hanging out on a quiet night with a smart, beautiful woman and a roaring to fire to bring home the lie. She felt content, and that much was true. Happy? That was a lot more complicated. If pressed right now she'd have to admit that bliss wasn't exactly the state of her existence. Over the last few years she'd realized that contentment became an easy place to exist, and it was equally easy to rationalize it as being enough.

Yet it had taken one woman from thousands of miles away walking into her life, making her dormant emotions perk up, and impressing her dog, and bam! The game had just changed and blown her comfortable state of denial to hell.

Saved by the bell. In the kitchen, the ring of her cell had her trotting down the hallway. Right where she'd left it on the counter plugged into the charger, her phone vibrated on the marble as it played the popular song she'd downloaded for her ringtone. The display showed it was Circe. "Hey. More bombshells to drop?"

Circe's chuckle on the other end was soft. "No. I think we've all had enough of those for a very long time."

Kat thought about what had been revealed last night. For her it went far beyond the mere fact of a familial relationship between one of her close friends and her new tenant. That was freaky enough all by itself and, frankly, odd-defying in a way that made her want to go to the casino to place a big bet. The fact that she'd been working side by side with Circe as a human-remains-detection teammate for years without knowing that she possessed psychic abilities made her question everything she knew about everybody.

Circe, Zelda, Lucy, and Kat had traveled hundreds of miles together, slept in hotel rooms together, trained, and tested together. That she could be oblivious to something that huge shook her confidence. They were teammates, yet she didn't know the most important thing about her comrade. Was it possible that being a SAR K9 team wasn't her calling, and all this time she'd been fooling herself?

As if she could read her mind, Circe said, "Don't go there, Kat."

"Go where?" She could play dumb when she wanted to.

"You know what I'm talking about. I went out of my way to make sure you and everyone else were in the dark. It's not something I share. Ever. It had nothing to do with you and everything to do with me."

"You didn't trust me." Saying it out loud hurt more than she had imagined, and she recognized pain at the heart of her feelings. It had less to do with Kat not catching on to the skills the wonder team possessed and more about the fact that she believed them to be as close as sisters. Circe's revelation last night proved that her feelings had been one-sided. Trust, something so sacred to Kat, had been shattered.

She expected Circe to argue and wasn't prepared for what she actually said. "Initially, yes, that's absolutely true."

Tears built in her eyes, and she wished she hadn't said a thing. To hear it articulated was worse than she'd thought, and damn it, she hated crying. "That's pretty clear."

"Not really."

"You're serious?" No way could she make a case for anything other than distrust. She'd kept Kat in the dark for not an insignificant amount of time. All of a sudden anger displaced the tears and the hurt.

Kat's clear anger didn't seem to faze Circe. Her voice maintained its even, calm tone. "Initially I didn't trust anyone. Not you, not any other member of the team, or anyone else for that matter. Listen, you walk a mile in my shoes, Kat, and then tell me you'd have handled it differently. I didn't need people to think I was crazy. I suffered through enough of that as a child. I closed down a very long time ago to protect myself. You have no idea what it's like. Zelda is the only thing that gave me back some respect and sanity. She saved me, and I don't say that lightly."

Kat gave weight to her words. As hurt as she was by what she perceived as Circe's personal slight, the ring of truth to what she said helped. It also made sense, given she'd lived it in a way. She'd spent years hiding inside her closet so she wouldn't have to admit she wasn't like her friends. She could have cared less if Jon Vartum or Stan Lester asked her to the prom, because she really wanted Emily Highsmith to ask her. When none of them did, pretending heartbreak over Jon and Stan had been easy. All her friends, even her family, took her hurt feelings at face value because that's what they wanted to believe. Exactly like how she wanted to believe she and Circe were Krazy Glue tight.

"I understand." Perhaps not completely, but suddenly enough to allow some of the angst to fade away. The tightness in her chest eased.

"In time you will, and that's enough for me. You have been one of the best friends I've ever had, and believe me when I tell you that I didn't want to deceive you. Kat, I trust you with my life. I trust you with Zelda's life."

Tears came back into her eyes, this time spilling down her cheeks. Those magic words took away every ounce of her hurt feelings. The life of a K9 handler put them in a unique position when it came to their dogs. The relationship went beyond symbiotic. She didn't know a good handler who wouldn't sacrifice their own food and water to make certain their dog got everything it needed, even carry them for miles if they were injured. To say that she trusted Kat with Zelda's life went beyond huge.

"And I trust you with Lucy's."

"We're solid, then?"

"Yeah. We're solid."

❖

The Seeker hated paperwork more than anything. To sit behind a computer typing away at a report and filling in the blanks with all the nauseating details made him...well, nauseous. He excelled in fieldwork. It was fun, it was interesting, and he liked talking to people. On every employee evaluation he'd received top marks for his people skills.

After he'd made it home, he'd cleaned up and chugged an espresso before he headed into the office. All things considered, he felt pretty good, and he didn't look too bad either. No dark circles under his eyes, and a quick trim of his facial hair made him stay tight and tidy. He wasn't the guy who rocked the long-shaggy-beard look. Nobody would guess that he hadn't gotten as much as ten minutes' sleep last night, and he would have plenty of time to make up for it after work.

The first order of business had been to check his schedule. He liked that things changed from day to day. One of the side benefits of working in his field. Of course, he'd chosen his profession wisely and had known all along that variation would be a big perk. Too bad he hadn't given an equal amount of thought to the drudgery side, which was what he found himself stuck with this morning.

Before he could be assigned any fieldwork, the powers that be had demanded reports from yesterday's adventures in wonderland. He would have given his eyeteeth to have received the assignments to cover some of the exciting things happening out there right now. He liked to see what the competition was up to. Unfortunately, they had given them to Addy, his counterpart in the office. She, his boss explained, had stayed late yesterday to complete her paperwork, and thus she was already out in the field. Had been out in the field for hours. Bitch.

While he got a number of great assignments, if Addy was around, she got the best ones. She had seniority, he'd give her that much. That was all she had over him. Everybody knew he had the sharper skills, and thus, he should be given the better assignments based on his level of expertise. It wasn't fair that she kept getting the plum ones.

He ground his teeth as his fingers moved over the keyboard. A shitload of petty detail. Of course, he did understand its importance. But why couldn't he simply dictate into a recorder and let some drone do the work? It wasn't the way it worked around here. He and Addy had to create their own reports. No assistants for them. Budget issues, or so came the explanation each time he brought it up.

It took him an hour to plow through the reports, email them off, and then grab his field assignment. He managed to maintain his cool as he walked to his vehicle. Keeping an outward nonchalance took effort. He wanted to speed out of here like a rocket and get back out on the street for some hands-on work. His heart lay in the dirty houses, back alleys, and wooded parks—places where life and death most often clashed.

Addy passed him on the way out. On her way back in, she smiled and waved. "Caught a good one," she said as she passed him in the rear hallway. The bitch actually patted him on the shoulder. "Things are getting interesting around here. I don't remember when it's been this busy."

He smiled though it hurt and wanted to return the favor of physical contact by snapping off the hand that patted his shoulder. How he hated her, but then as she turned to shower him with her brightest fake smile, he noticed how violet her eyes were. Now why hadn't he ever noticed that little detail before? His mood improved instantly as he envisioned a new section for his collection.

Violet.

Chapter Fourteen

"Hi, I'm Alan Goodman." The man who held out his hand to Vi was medium height with a bald head and a stylish goatee and mustache. His eyes were bright blue and intense. She'd glimpsed him once, briefly, though this was the first time they'd actually spoken. He'd been rushing out the first time she'd seen him, and she'd immediately thought him the kind of guy not happy being cooped up in the office—a true investigator who wanted nothing more than to get outside and do what he did best. She'd had great relationships with the investigators in Anchorage and admired the work they did. It took the whole team to accomplish the finest work possible.

"Vi Akiak." She took his hand and shook it. A firm grip. "Really nice to meet you."

"I heard we had a new autopsy assistant, and I'm guessing that's you?" He dropped her hand and studied her face. She thought him a nice-looking man and, at first glance, attractive. As she studied him, however, she detected a hardness that wasn't obvious immediately. She wondered how long he'd been with the ME's office here. In the faces of those in Anchorage who'd worked in the business of death for a long time she had seen something similar. The nature of the beast, so to speak. It changed people regardless of how capable they might be.

"Yes." She smiled. "I'm the new AA."

"Cool." He nodded. "You're the doc-to-be from Anchorage, right?"

"News travels fast." His gaze was so pointed she found it slightly unnerving.

He smiled, and the intensity in his eyes cleared a little. He should smile more often. "It's a small town inside the ME's office here. News doesn't just travel fast. It goes at the speed of light. Glad to have you on board. We needed some quality help around here. When does school start?"

"In a few weeks. I have just enough time to settle into my new home and my new job before insanity descends and life as I know it ends. I'm excited though. I've waited a long time to begin this journey."

"Well, good luck with school, and welcome aboard." He picked up a bag, slung it over his shoulder, and walked toward the door that led to the parking lot. "I'd have loved to talk, but I've got places to go and dead people to see."

Oh my, she thought as the door closed behind him. Bad joke. Then again, working in their particular field often bred a kind of humor no one else could understand. They weren't making light of anyone's death or being disrespectful in any manner. It was, quite simply, a coping mechanism. Given what they were exposed to every single day, if they didn't find ways to manage the emotional impact of what they witnessed, they'd all end up in a psychiatric ward. Personally, she'd been trying to avoid that destination since the first time the dead came to her. Even as a child she'd recognized it wasn't the kind of thing she talked about unless she could trust someone, or doctors of the psychiatric variety would be involved. For her that had equated to her mother and grandmother.

Until yesterday, that is. When she moved here, no one left alive knew what she could do. Now she knew two people who were very much alive and who shared her secret. Incredible, considering she really believed she'd take the secret to her own grave, just as her mother and grandmother had. Two people knew. People she had been acquainted with for less than a week. The first time in her life she'd had to go with blind faith, and it scared the heck out of her. She wasn't very good at trust.

She supposed she'd have to get good at it. Kat and Circe knew. Not only knew but, in Circe's case, shared her unique ability. Any choice she had about trusting had been wiped away last night.

Just as she'd surmised, because she'd found the body, her assignments for the day did not include the young woman exhumed from the clandestine grave. She'd give anything to be in with Dr. Kelsey, and that's what she was thinking as she passed the door to the autopsy suite assigned to him today. The chief AA stood at his side, gloved, masked, and gowned, and Vi gazed in like a six-year-old who'd been told she couldn't go out for recess. She'd started to turn away when a face appeared in the window on the other side of the door.

Anyone else might scream and jump at the instantaneous appearance of a woman's face seemingly out of nowhere. Not Vi. It wasn't the first time, and it wouldn't be the last.

The face peering toward her had no eyes, leading to the question of how the apparition even knew Vi stood in the hallway looking in. Again, she didn't need an answer because it was irrelevant. What difference did it make anyway? She could see the dead, and the dead could sense her, period. Really, it was kind of an oxymoron. The dead had no sight whether their eyes were intact or not, right? It seemed simple enough, yet it wasn't. They found her, which made her think that her grandmother had been spot-on. They needed her, and as much as she'd prefer to be like everyone else, she wasn't. Normal wasn't in her DNA, and if she ever wanted proof of that, she got it when she met her sister.

The ghost on the other side of the glass in the door touched fingers to her face. Vi understood. She'd known it since the first time one of the victims of her mother's killer had come to her. When they found him—and in her heart she was convinced it was a him—they would learn his killing revolved around the eyes. The only question in her mind had always been *why*?

Her time working with the professionals who used science to understand a suspicious or unexplained death had taught her many lessons about the motivations of killers. Most were not particularly difficult to discern. A few, like the serial killer Israel Keyes, captured in Anchorage but who had killed all over the country, had turned out be quite difficult to peg. He made Vi believe in pure evil, just like the one who had taken the woman's life on the other side of that door. That the killer she searched for had a fixation with eyes might explain some of his actions, but it didn't excuse them, and it didn't make him any less evil. She would find him and discover why he became a monster.

"I will stop him," she whispered. "He will pay for what he did to you." The woman on the other side of the glass nodded as if she heard and understood, and then she faded away. On the other side of the door, Dr. Kelsey and his assistant went about their work oblivious to the visitor who'd just left their room.

"Who are you talking to?"

Vi whirled around. The investigator, Alan Goodman, stood next to her again. That she hadn't heard him come up behind her freaked her out a little. "You came back." He'd been leaving when they met in the hallway ten minutes ago. What had brought him back here to stand so near she could smell the clean scent of his soap? His nearness was disconcerting, and she took several steps to the side.

He smiled, and this time his face didn't look softer. This time he appeared insincere. He shrugged. "Needed to grab a box of gloves, restock. My rig was low when I got out there. So, who were you talking to?"

This wasn't the first time someone had come upon her as she conversed with the dead. She fell back on her tried-and-true answer. "Myself. A bad habit."

He patted her shoulder, and she wanted to step away even farther. She didn't like the feel of his touch even through her scrubs. "We all have them, don't we? I have a couple myself." He laughed and dropped his hand to his side. "Well, better grab those gloves and get to work."

As soon as he was out of sight, she let out the breath she'd been holding since the second he touched her and hoped she'd quit trembling by the time she got to work with Dr. Durze.

❖

Kat appreciated Circe's call more than she would ever be able to explain. It made the rest of her day fly by. Everything that had happened over the last couple of days had put her behind at home. She'd always had a dog and knew the responsibility that came with it was a twenty-four-hour, three-hundred-and-sixty-five-day gig.

Dogs could eat and sleep in the house, making their care warm and easy. With a farm and the animals that were part of it, not so much. They had the same care schedule, only it meant slogging outside in heat, rain, snow, and ice to get them fed and watered. After her first year here, she'd at least installed a moving water system for her animals. It was worth the pretty darned big expense not to have to constantly chip ice during the winter months. That had been a royal pain in the ass.

The physical exertion required to feed the animals and muck the stalls gave her exactly what she needed today. Many handlers went through their entire careers without making a grisly find. She'd now experienced two in as many days. A couple of times, tears gathered in her eyes, and she didn't try to stop them. She let the emotions roll through her, grateful for them. Whoever was responsible for what she'd seen was cold and evil. The heat of her tears on her cheeks let her know she existed in a completely different universe from that beast.

While Kat worked, she felt fine, tears aside. After she'd done everything, and had showered and polished off an entire pot of coffee, she realized how rattled she was over the two bodies they'd found. Her mind raced. Her tears had done their job as far as dealing with the emotions that everyone warned her would creep up after locating someone deceased. She had expected her reaction and, really, welcomed it as part of the circle of life.

Sadness she expected. Anger she didn't, and she was undeniably pissed off. If the recoveries in the last two days had been cases of accidental death, she'd be sad but grateful to have had a part in bringing the bodies home. The fact that neither was natural made her mad. Nobody deserved to be murdered and left out there cold and alone. She wanted to do more, except what more could she accomplish? She and Lucy had done their part. Now others needed to step up to find the killers and bring them to justice. People like Vi.

She stood on the porch holding a cup of coffee and surveyed her small kingdom. Both beautiful and self-sustaining, it made her heart happy. It wasn't enough. She smiled, surprised it had taken her this long to figure it out. Sometimes she could be incredibly dense.

Lucy trotted over and leaned against her leg. She reached down and rubbed the top of her head. "You know it too, don't you, girl." Lucy pressed harder.

Was it like this for all people who had sudden epiphanies about their lives? One minute everything appeared peachy, and the next, the peach had gone rotten. After last night, she wouldn't be able to trot around and pretend everything was okay. She had to contribute more, and worse, she wanted to.

Just as Vi found her calling in her mission to avenge her mother's death, Kat figured she'd moved past the point where she had to step up. Circe and Vi both had a secret weapon, and now she needed to find her own superpower. Circe and Vi were making a difference in the world while Kat hung out here, hiding like a scared little kid.

No more. She was done with that program. Unlike Vi, she wasn't doctor material. Circe, married to a cop, had resources that made her a powerful force. Kat was a farmer, a dog handler, and one kick-ass computer nerd. She might have walked away from the corporate world, but that didn't mean she'd lost her skills. She smiled as she thought about what she could do even if a little rusty. Rusty could be fixed.

Kat went to the door of the unused office and swung it open. Dust motes danced in the rays of the sun coming through window, testifying to the level of disuse the poor room had seen since she'd moved in. A disgrace she planned to correct. In fact, a giant surge of energy made her straighten her shoulders and flex her fingers. The last time she'd felt this excited about getting her hands on a computer was a distant memory. At one time she'd been energized and excited to use her mad skills, with plenty of big corporations ready and willing to pay her well to use those skills on their behalf. How thrilling it had been in the beginning. As time had passed, her enthusiasm had waned, and her profession became drudgery instead of a calling. Today her calling came screaming back.

She sat down in front of her computer and tapped her fingers on the desk. First things first. A plan needed to be formulated. She might have stepped away for a good long while, but that didn't mean she'd forgotten her tendencies, both good and bad. If she didn't lay things out to start with, everything could go sideways in a hurry. Research fascinated her in a way that became addictive. Too easy to get sidetracked, and then before she knew it, she'd be down a rabbit hole that had nothing to do with her original goal. Before she laid her hands on her keyboard, she planned to have a solid game plan in mind, if not detailed out in black and white.

She flexed her fingers and then let them drop to the keyboard. Something like joy washed over her, and she was off into the lure of a world she'd tried to ignore for years. She'd been working for quite a while and loving the feel of the keys on her fingertips, when she heard a knock at her door. She snapped her head up, shocked to see it was six thirty, and outside the window, daylight had faded into twilight. At the front door Lucy barked wildly, and it wasn't her stranger-danger version. The bark telegraphed her "my friend is here and you need to let her in" version.

"Shit," she muttered as she saved what she'd been working on, and only then did she push away from the desk. The moment she stood her body let her know exactly how long it had been since she'd worked like this. Her shoulders were on fire and her neck stiff. She rolled her head to shake out the kinks as she walked to the front door. Given the time, it had to be Vi. After all, she had invited her for dinner, which wasn't anywhere near prepared, or even thought of for that matter. Oh yeah, she was some kind of host.

She wasn't wrong about it being Vi, as she could see her through the glass. Lucy kept jumping at the doorknob as if she could open the door. If she had a different kind of doorknob, she probably could. Kat opened the door and said, "Hey."

Vi looked tired, and that wasn't unexpected. She'd gotten only a few hours of sleep on Kat's sofa before spending eight hours on her feet in the medical examiner's office. At least Kat had been able to work sitting in her chair the majority of the day, and that gave her an advantage when it came to battling fatigue.

Vi sighed and said, "Hi." Even that single word made her sound weary. Lucy jumped at her with enthusiasm.

Kat opened the door wider. "Come on in and sit down before you fall down."

"I look that bad?"

"Bad? No. I'm more inclined to say you look like you've put in a full day."

"Fair enough, and yes, I did." Vi cocked her head and studied Kat. "I interrupted something."

"Yeah." She might as well be honest. "In a good way, though. I got my head into a project and lost total track of time. Lucy didn't even come in insisting that I get up and feed her or the other animals. Here's the deal. You were invited over to dinner by a total loser who has absolutely nothing ready and has to do chores before I can think about turning on the stove."

"We can make it another night."

"Not a chance. I might be a loser, but I'm a loser who follows through." She smiled and liked that Vi returned a smile of her own, even if weak.

"Okay. Truthfully, I'm starving but too tired to feed myself."

She mentally inventoried her freezer and came up with a plan. "Great. Now tell me how you feel about a glass of cabernet, warmed-up spaghetti, and garlic bread."

"Sounds heavenly."

"Give me twenty minutes to feed the crew, and then I'll get ours ready. We can eat in the living room, where we can put our feet up and relax. Grab a seat, and I'll get you a glass of wine to tide you over while I'm out feeding. After that, the beauty of modern technology and a kick-ass microwave will have dinner ready in ten minutes."

"What can I do to help?"

"Tell me you don't think I'm the worst host on the planet."

"Not even close." Her smile had lost some of its weariness.

❖

Despite the painful and boring start to the work day, the rest of it buzzed right along, and the Seeker was surprised when he looked at the clock on the dashboard and realized the time had arrived to wrap it up and go home. That was the kind of day he liked—good work and interesting cases, nobody bugging him, and the effects of a sleepless night nil. All of it combined to create a win in his book. It proved how the universe worked in concert with him.

He really did need to go home now and sleep. While his intelligence and his physical stamina were unmatched, he also couldn't deny that last night had been stressful in many ways. Rest would go a long way toward keeping him at his peak. A hot shower and his comfortable bed were definitely calling his name. The draw to drive directly home weighed heavy.

But the draw to gaze upon his collection held far more power. In the car headlights, tiny drops of rain resembled sparkling crystals. Beautiful and alluring, they confirmed the correctness of his decision. The rain came slowly, more like a gentle mist than a storm. He didn't need to turn on his wipers, the drops on his windshield too lovely to wipe away. Moderate to heavy traffic, not surprising for prime time on a weeknight, didn't bother him or slow him down. He blended in with the thousands of other commuters going about their day-to-day routines. Faces were held straight ahead, and no one paid attention to him as he moved from lane to lane to get ahead of the other cars. All were intent on their own drive home.

The turn-off he watched for wasn't well marked, not that it needed to be for him to locate it. If his eyes were closed, he could still make the turn with perfect precision. The drive used to be immaculate, with sealed asphalt and beautiful trimmed shrubs lining the full length on both sides. These days the cracked asphalt paled, due to sun damage and neglect. Weeds pushed through the cracks as the only living inhabitants. The shrubs the old man had screamed at gardeners about on what seemed at the time like a weekly basis were overgrown and ugly. No more rounded, deep-green perfection. These days they were ragged and pale green, with spots of yellow where branches were dead or dying. It made him smile. If the old guy still walked among the living and breathing, the sight of this driveway would put him into a cerebral coma, and to the Seeker that was just plain funny. He'd pay a lot to see the look on his father's face if he were in the car with him right now.

Sneaking into the place wasn't an issue because the public records were quite clear who remained as titled owner of the property. His father had never owned this mini estate. The house and the several acres that surrounded it had belonged to his mother and her family. Good old Dad liked to let people think it belonged to him because that's the kind of guy he was. Big man around town. Big man in Washington. Everything in the universe revolved around him. The Seeker and his mother had been well-schooled props and nothing more.

"How well did that work out for you, *Dad*?" he muttered as he pulled up and put the car in park. The rain was starting to intensify, so he raced for the garage door. No need to go into the house with the dusty furniture and the still, musty air. Once a year or so he made the trek inside to assure himself that nothing had been disturbed. He didn't like it in there. Too many memories. At the same time, it remained important to him that no one breach the locked doors and windows. The mausoleum must stand exactly as he left it.

The garage was different. It had always been his safe zone, and he liked it here. So many places to hide, his favorite being the rafters that soared over the garage floor. No run-of-the-mill concrete for his father. Far too ordinary for a man of his grand esteem. Their garage had pristine white walls and a black-and-white tiled floor. Nicer than the majority of homes he'd been in over the course of his life, and that included the two-car space of the house he actually lived in.

Even with a memory as exceptional as his, he'd lost count of the number of nights he'd slept on the hard plywood that made up the deck of the storage space. A small hatch in the finished ceiling gave him access to the space, and he'd felt safe in the compact area. His mother used to put Christmas decorations up there, and the boxes of antique ornaments and miniature colored lights were still stacked in the corners, their cardboard boxes brittle from age.

After his mother's death, no one had ever touched the Christmas decorations again. At least not as far as his father knew anyway. In the darkness as he had hidden to avoid the zealot, the Seeker would often take out the ornaments and remember the good times when he and his mother would decorate the huge tree that each year they would pick out together. Not all of his childhood memories were bad. A few brought warmth.

That wasn't quite true. Many memories brought him warmth because he had begun to recognize early on that he did not fit in with everyone else. It was more than the realization of his superior intelligence. Most of his teachers too, for that matter. He'd finally understood the full purpose of his life from the moment he'd stood at his mother's deathbed, yet signs had been there since his grade-school days. Maturity had given him the context he'd needed to put it all together.

In front of the tall black freezer sitting against the back wall, he ran his hand over the door before inserting his key into the lock. Cool air verging on cold hit him in the face, and he breathed it in deeply. He didn't want his treasures to freeze but rather to stay cool and beautiful, and thus he kept the temperature in the freezer higher than one would normally. This new appliance tested perfect for his needs, and it brought him a great deal of pleasure. Plenty of room, a perfect temperature system, and best of all a solid lock, just in case.

As he studied the colorful array, he mentally rearranged the collection to accommodate the newest section he would soon add. When he had it all worked out in his head, he closed and locked the door. The future spread out before him bright and shiny. It was good to be him.

Glancing down at his watch, he sighed. He'd been here long enough. Time to retreat to his own bedroom and rest up. He paused at a metal shelving unit that had black messenger bags lined up in neat rows. Each one looked exactly the same, by design. The idea had come to him years ago, and it had been a good one. From the shelf second from the top he selected a bag and slung it over a shoulder. It wasn't necessary to look inside. The weight of it assured him that everything he'd placed in it before setting it on the shelf remained at the ready.

After he turned his car around, he drove back down the driveway and toward the street without switching his lights on. He wasn't one of those people who left the headlights on the automatic setting. He wanted control of all aspects of life, including the functions of his vehicle. Given the current time, better to go out like a ghost. Though neighbors might have noticed him drive in, he doubted it. At rush hour 99 percent focused only on getting home. Along this street, enough time had elapsed for dinner to be over and relaxation to have set in. Lights driving away from his family home could very well gain unwanted attention. He had every right to be on this property, but that didn't mean he wished anyone to know of his presence here.

Before he drove all the way home, he made one quick stop. It took less than five minutes to hide the bag beneath a pile of firewood stacked next to a house, the address of which he'd grabbed before he left the office.

Chapter Fifteen

Surprised to find Kat unprepared after she'd made such a point of inviting her over for dinner, Vi tried not to let her amazement show. She'd been looking forward to the time with her. After her encounter with the dead woman's spirit this morning, she'd taken on her own duties with intense concentration. She'd needed to focus on her responsibilities and not let her mind wander toward Kat, now back from the barn and in the kitchen rattling dishes.

Keeping her mind off Kat had been a tall request this morning. When she'd left here, she'd felt warm all over and happier than she had in eons. She'd been smiling, at least until the woman appeared to her, and then it changed things up a bit. Something about the spirits she'd seen since she'd arrived here stuck with her. A message lay hidden in their appearances to her, and she wasn't deciphering what they tried to convey. That bothered her a lot. Vi knew she was smart, and that wasn't bragging. She'd never have made the cut for medical school if she wasn't. It was what it was. That said, she didn't feel so smart right at the moment. People were depending on her. They might be people who had passed into another realm, but they were people just the same, and they deserved her attention. Perhaps the dead needed justice and closure even more than the living did. Speaking for herself, closure was overrated. It didn't really happen. If her mother were ever to come to her, the message she would receive would be exactly that.

So why couldn't she put the puzzle pieces together? What was she missing? A better question might be why was she missing it? Or why had she missed it all these years? As much time as she'd put into trying to discover who really killed her mother, she should have solved the mystery by now. Should. Should. Should. What an awful word.

Time for a mindset change. No more *should haves*. From here forward her mantra would be that she *was* going to find the killer, and she had a hunch whoever it turned out to be would be the same person killing the people who had ended up on the tables here in Spokane. Whatever it took, she would make it happen. Only then could she move forward in life, like her mother would tell her to do if she could.

"Voilà." Kat handed her a warm plate piled with spaghetti and a big slice of garlic bread. The glass of wine she'd given her before going out to tend the animals and that now sat on the end table remained three-quarters full. "I know it's kind of lame, but it's warm and filling."

Lame was about the last thing it was to Vi. Her stomach growled as the fragrant scent of the sauce floated up in the air. "It looks fantastic and smells even better. You have no idea how hungry I am." Despite everything over the last few days that for anyone else might banish the appetite, she was starving, and the food on this plate smelled heavenly.

They ate quietly for a few minutes, and Vi felt more relaxed and comfortable than she had in ages. More and more she sensed that the decision to give up her life in Alaska and pursue her dream to be a doctor had been the right one. It all felt good, the appearances of the ghosts aside. No, even that felt appropriate. Her grandmother's words on the porch that first night resonated with her. She was needed, and she had to take that fact to heart.

"So," Kat said after setting her plate aside and taking a sip of her wine. "I don't know how you felt about last night, but for me? It was a kick in the ass, and I don't mean that in the ha-ha-wasn't-that-fun way."

That intro made Vi put her plate aside as well. To give her something to hold on to, she took her own glass of wine—deep red with a faint fruity smell that wafted up into the air. She took a moment to breathe in the lovely aroma before asking, "What do you mean?"

Kat took a deep breath and blew it out slowly. "Here's the deal. Embarrassing as it sounds, this," she waved an arm in the air, "has been my hidey-hole since I bought it, or more accurately, since my dad bought it for me."

"Your father bought this for you?"

Kat looked at her and nodded. "When someone wins a multi-million-dollar lottery, a guy like my dad uses the money to make the dreams of his loved ones come true. I always wanted a small farm with a few acres of land, some interesting animals, and a beautiful view. Dad found it for me."

"That's an incredible thing for him to have done."

"He was an incredible guy, the best, and I miss him terribly."

"What do you mean you've been hiding here? Doesn't seem that way to me. You have a rental, I've seen you with at least one friend, Circe, you're part of an amazing search-and-rescue team, and you've been incredibly welcoming to me."

"All true enough. Just not all of it. Trust me, Vi, I've developed an embarrassing hermit-like personality since I set up out here. I've used this place to shield myself from the rest of the world, and with all the work involved to keep it going, as well as its self-sustaining properties, it's given me a fantastic excuse not to have to engage. Yeah, I train regularly with the team, but that's about it."

"Why?" Kat made her curious. Her first impression had been of a warm and welcoming woman with a lovely home and a fascinating dog. Hermit was the last thing she would have ever thought.

"That's the million-dollar question. You'd think someone broke my heart or I felt like I had nothing to offer the world. Neither is true. I think I was tired and wanted to escape. The plan worked like a charm, and the longer I hid here, the easier it became to disengage. The only real outlet I gave myself was the dog team."

"Last night changed things?"

Kat nodded. "Last night and the search before. I don't like what we found. I hate that someone did horrible things to those two people. It wasn't right, and that's what kicked me in the ass. Bringing them home wasn't enough. Not by a long shot."

Vi knew where she was going before she got there. It had been the same for her after her mother's murder. While she knew the lightbulb had turned on when they'd found her mother, it had taken quite a bit more time for the wattage to hit a hundred. "You want to find him."

"Funny you should say 'him'…"

The more Kat had dug, the more convinced she became that a man or men had perpetrated the murders. The singular kept tapping at her brain. This wasn't the work of a couple of people or even a group. One person had killed these people. She couldn't point to anything concrete and say "there" to show why she believed it to be so. That fact didn't change her deep-seated feeling that it was, in fact, one killer.

On the other hand, she had been one heck of an investigator in a former life and knew better than to narrow her field of research. Once upon a time, she'd been a hot commodity in the information-gathering world, and she'd made a whole lot of money exercising her skills. Her experience had taught her that narrowing her focus would set her up for failure, and she didn't like that lesson very much. Not that she avoided the occasional bomb. On the contrary, she'd made many of her greatest leaps forward after some colossal failures. Just the same, she'd rather avoid them and go straight to success.

Before she opened her mouth to start explaining, she told herself to keep it slow. The more into something she got, the faster she talked. At the computer, her fingers would fly across the keyboard at warp speed. It used to drive her parents crazy. More than one girlfriend had found it too annoying to consider making it a permanent part of their lives. No sense in scaring Vi off before they had a chance to really get to know each other. The word "potential" kept whispering to her in the back of her mind, and she didn't want to shut down the possibility of a relationship before she had a chance to see if it might come true.

"Before I became the professional live-off-my-land type, I worked as a computer scientist with a specialty in investigation. I did work for private companies and contracted with federal agencies like the US Attorney's office and Homeland Security. I have a dual degree in information technology and forensic science. People tried to hide things and I found them."

"That's pretty impressive."

Kat would be lying to say she didn't warm at Vi's words. "Thanks, though really, it's just what I do. Or rather what I did. I walked away when Dad gave me this place, and until today I never looked back. I guess you could say I'd burned out."

"Not anymore?"

For the first time since she'd moved here, Kat felt an overwhelming urge to be that investigator again. "Not anymore."

Vi held her gaze. "You want to find this killer."

Kat heard the statement in her words. They were on the same sheet of music. Good. "Yeah, I do. After you left today it hit me that finding him wasn't enough. After I left the real world behind, I did something I've always wanted to but never had the time, and that was search-and-rescue. Lucy and I worked together to make it happen, and we have. As a consequence, I've been telling myself for a long time that being active in SAR fed my soul and fulfilled a duty to my community. It served as my rationalization for allowing myself to hide here."

Vi gave her a small smile. "I get it. In a morbid way I've done the same thing with my job in the ME's office. I didn't want to deal with life in a meaningful way, and I used my mother's death and my quest for truth to rationalize my actions. Nobody had to ask me twice to do back-to-back shifts. I could have spent twenty-four hours in the autopsy suites. Making a difference, I'd tell myself. I never admitted I used it to hide away from the world."

"Then you get it."

"Yes, I do."

"Earlier today I dusted off my poor, neglected computer and put my much-out-of-practice brain to work." Her words were starting to speed up, and she couldn't help herself. The thrill of doing something after being dormant for way too long excited her. The fact that Vi got what she was trying to explain without actually having to go into detail was like water poured on a dying plant.

"I like it."

"You don't think I'm a weirdo for wanting to track this bastard down? For not leaving it in the hands of law enforcement?"

"Not even a little bit."

"Thank God, because I was kind of worried about myself."

"What you're doing is critical."

"Really?" This woman was so a keeper.

"Yes, and I'll tell you why. The ghost of the woman we found last night came to me at the ME's office today."

The Seeker tapped the steering wheel. He sat there in the car long enough that the overhead light in his garage went off, unable to get his mind off the new section in his collection. Walking away and leaving the spot empty felt like going out to dinner without pants. It simply wasn't acceptable, and the wrongness of it beat against his soul.

Everything was in place, and all that was left for him to do was be patient and allow the timing to be perfect. The pressure he'd felt lately to act with such little time between cases baffled him. It had the feel of someone putting a hand on his back and pushing him into a strong wind. For years he'd practiced a methodical precision that served him well. He'd done his work, gathered his critical knowledge, and increased the power that now filled him to the brim. He'd done it all without anyone catching a clue. No reason anything should be different now.

He dropped his head to the steering wheel and closed his eyes. With each deep breath he willed himself to relax. The faint scent of old grass and fertilizer wafted in through the open car window. The usual scents for a normal garage. All the trappings of a regular guy who mowed his lawn every week, kept his grass healthy and green, thus making him an appreciated neighbor. He longed for a far different scent—hot, metallic, and so much more satisfying.

"Get out of the car, you fool." His words were soft but firm. The self-talk didn't work. They were empty words that contained no pep and certainly no motivation. He couldn't go inside, eat his dinner in front of the television, and pretend to be satisfied. None of it was even remotely okay. His mind screamed at him to act and to do it now. Waiting was wrong. Perhaps it had been the right thing to do in the past. But not now. The rules were changing.

The Seeker turned the key in the ignition and brought the car back to life. His soul hungered. His collection lacked. A couple of hours, that's all he'd need, and then he'd come home and sleep. It would be enough to calm the disquiet inside him.

Her house occupied a prime spot on a nice street on the South Hill. Earlier when he'd driven by to drop off the bag, he hadn't been surprised to discover where she lived. For over a century the who's who of the city had called the South Hill home. Beautiful testaments to the skill of the early architects populated streets all the way up to High Drive, where million-dollar homes were lined up like soldiers. Given her treatment in such a cutthroat business, it all fell into place. No wonder she got all the plum assignments. Ability didn't have a thing to do with it. Come from the right family in the right neighborhood in this city, and you didn't have to have knowledge and skills to move ahead over those who did.

Given his father's propensity toward status, it always surprised him that they hadn't lived on one of these streets. Then again, his father liked to keep his personal life under wraps. It wouldn't do well for his reelection campaigns if anyone got a whiff of what a narcissist did in the privacy of his own home. Their beautiful home on the other side of the city had been surrounded by plenty of land and, more important, privacy. His father had taken to his mother's inherited estate like a fish to water. If he himself had ever considered a move to this part of the city, he'd put it aside once he realized his mother's home would be perfect for his needs.

Now the Seeker sat under old-growth trees and watched the house. The lights in the small craftsman were on in what had to be the front room. Sadly, the blinds were closed, and he couldn't see inside. Despite the lack of a clear view, he still hadn't wasted his time by coming here. Back in his car, he watched the activity up and down the street for three hours. He'd meant to stay for only a couple of hours, but once he hit the two-hour mark, he didn't reach for the key on the chain dangling from the ignition.

When the lights went out in her front room, he finally turned the key, and the car came to life. Unhurriedly, he drove away and returned home. This time after he put the car in park and closed the garage, he opened the door and got out. The weariness of a night without sleep caught up with him, and he swore his feet suddenly weighed fifty pounds apiece. His body was sending him a message impossible to ignore; time to sleep. Before he could even consider hitting his bed, he took a jar from an opened case on the shelf in the garage and set it on the kitchen counter. Shiny and new, the glass glittered in the rays of the overhead light. No label was necessary. It never was.

He turned off the kitchen light and walked in darkness to his bedroom. He didn't bother to remove his clothes. Sleep took him fully dressed as he sprawled sideways across the single bed. He dreamed of blond hair and violet eyes.

Chapter Sixteen

Vi woke up buoyant. The fact that she'd slept for seven hours was nothing short of incredible. The last time she'd slept that long was a vague memory. As she stood beneath the warm water in her shower, she marveled again about last night. It hadn't been a bit like she'd been expecting when she'd knocked on Kat's door.

She liked Kat—pretty plain and pretty simple. When they'd met, she'd thought her interesting and engaging. She'd seen firsthand her skills as a dog handler, and the farm was clear evidence of her success in that arena. Kat had even shown her some of her hand-dyed and spun yarn. She'd been impressed. After last night, she added brilliant to the mix. She'd had no idea about Kat's skill as a computer whiz. How could one woman do so many things and do them all so well?

The other amazing thing: for the first time since her grandmother had died, Vi didn't feel alone. That she was great company was only part of it. Kat's interest in getting to the truth made her feel like she was part of a team. The light kiss when she left to go back to her house hadn't hurt either. It had taken her by surprise in a very good way, and she had no regrets about not pulling away.

When her phone had rung five minutes ago and Dr. Kelsey asked her to come in early, she didn't hesitate to say yes. For whatever reason, Dr. Kelsey was also taking a personal interest in the cases that were identical to her mother's. He'd told her he wanted to talk with her before the start of the workday, and her feeling of being part of a team grew even deeper. Eagerness to hear what he had to say pushed her to hurry and not be late. They were to meet in his office in an hour and a half, and she intended to be there at least a few minutes early.

She made it to the parking lot in her best time yet. She was getting the commute down to a science. At the back door, she waved her keycard over the pad and waited for the click. When she heard the distinctive sound, she pushed the door open and went inside. All was quiet as she put her things into her locker, tucked her hair into a cap, and walked to the coolers. She stood with her fingers on the handle, wondering if she should go in. Her earlier-than-planned arrival provided her an unexpected window of opportunity, and it would be foolish to waste it. The air lock made a whooshing sound when she opened the door to step inside, the cold brushing through her scrubs like they were made of tissue paper. The chill she felt in her bones had nothing to do with the cold.

"All right," she whispered. "I'm here. Tell me how I can help."

The murder victims brought to the ME's office over the last couple of days were still here. None had yet been released. At least one would be, later today, so it was now or never.

She closed her eyes and said again, "Tell me. I need your help. I don't understand what you need me to do." She'd never reached out before. The dead had come to her, not vice versa. It came to her on the drive that perhaps it was time for a new approach.

When she opened her eyes, they stood in front of her: one young, blond, and handsome, and one old with shoulders bent, her face wrinkled in a way that showed she smiled a lot. The final one was a lovely woman who couldn't have been more than twenty-five when she'd been put into the ground. She saw them not as they were now, with empty eye sockets and sutured Y-incisions. She saw them as they had been before the monster crossed their paths. Ethereal. They'd soon be gone. It was that way when they came to her like this. Restoration preceded their ascension, which never failed to make her feel somehow better.

Holding hands as if in life they'd been the best of friends, they passed through the door and into the hallway. Opening the door, Vi silently followed. This was actually a first. Of all the spirits who'd come to her, not a single one had led her on a hunt. They went down the hallway, turning to look at her before they disappeared into the supply room. They'd gone through a closed door. She opened it and stepped inside. They stood side by side in front of a shelf, no longer holding hands.

"What are you trying to tell me?" Supplies didn't make sense. How would that help her find their killer? They turned and stared at her as if willing her to pay attention and then turned back to the shelf.

Slowly, first the man held up his hand and pointed with his index finger, and then both of the women did the same.

She walked over to the shelf and stared at the spot they pointed to. Gloves, shoe covers, evidence bags, and specimen jars. All brand-new and in opened boxes. Rows neatly organized and inventoried. Nothing ominous.

"What?" she asked again. "What am I supposed to see here?"

They continued to point as if she hadn't said a word or they couldn't hear her. She blew out a breath and considered the supplies stacked neatly on the shelves. First she picked up a box of gloves and studied it. Size small, powderless, color blue. She put it back on the shelf, noting that it held sections organized for small, medium, and large. Nothing unusual. Same with the shoe covers and evidence bags.

"What?" she asked again. Nothing here made sense. They turned their heads in unison and stared at her, eyes intent, lips not moving.

Not knowing what else to do, she continued her inventory of the items stacked on the shelves. Her fingers grazed the top of the nearest box of specimen jars. As they did, a jolt raced up her arm. "What the hell." She snatched her hand away as she turned to look at her guides. Could this be what they wanted her to see? They were gone.

Kat woke up with a smile. Oh, dear God, she'd actually kissed Vi, and it had been one of those moments out of character and totally right at the same time. The fact that Vi didn't pull away or run away made her smile grow. She stretched her arms over her head and relived the moment. Sometimes taking a risk brought great rewards. It would have been even better if Vi had stayed so they could wake up in the same room again. Yeah, she got that might be pushing things a bit, but she didn't care. She'd liked seeing her face first thing in the morning.

She got through her morning chores quickly and with lightness she'd been missing of late. Until now she hadn't even realized she'd been going through the motions rather than enjoying her lifestyle. Funny how one kiss brought everything into clarity.

Back at the house she cleaned up and then headed to her office. Like yesterday, excitement filled her as she touched the keyboard. She could hardly wait to get started.

As they'd sat in her living room last night and talked, Vi had shared a great deal of information about her mother's murder. Kat had wanted to know more about the murders here in order to try to piece together their relevance to the Alaska cases. At the same time, she understood the sensitive nature of Vi's job with the county. She was a professional, which meant she couldn't divulge details from open, ongoing investigations. Kat didn't push, even though she really wanted to.

In some ways, she didn't need to. Everyone had strengths, whether they acknowledged them or not. She'd learned that Circe and Vi shared a quite unexpected one. She hadn't exactly wrapped her head around that one yet. Computers were Kat's thing. Oh, how she could make them sing. She'd been able to do it since she was a kid. Used to drive her parents crazy when she'd take their desktop apart and put it back together. She could still do it, and did on occasion, when she couldn't get an off-the-shelf computer to perform as she wanted. Both a practical and a creative outlet for her. A little like building her own robot.

This morning she'd spent two hours researching before an idea struck that could help her refine her data. She knew one person pretty well who had experience tracking down a serial killer, and now was the time to pick her brain. Time to call Diana Erni, a seasoned detective with the Spokane Police Department and Circe's wife. Together, Diana, Circe, and Zelda had stopped an active serial killer who turned out to be the unbalanced stalker of Diana's partner. The huge scandal had rocked the city, not to mention freaking out her partner.

Spokane had already been put on the map by another prolific serial killer, and the last thing anyone wanted was for it to happen again. For a second time evil had touched the city, and it left a wound reminiscent of a cigarette burn on tender flesh. It scared her that, once more, darkness threatened.

What kind of beacon did the city put out that could bring yet another evil soul into a community for the most part populated by giving and open souls? People said hello on the streets. They helped strangers. They volunteered their time to help their community, expecting nothing in return. This was a good place to live, so why did it feel like the city had a giant target on it?

The last few days made her wonder about everything. She and Lucy trained to locate the dead, whether they passed due to natural or unnatural causes. Any time of the day or night they responded to calls to do what they were capable of. Law-enforcement situations were no different. They did their job and left the rest up to the professionals. The details didn't matter, and she never questioned any of the circumstances surrounding a search.

Until now, that is. Her view of everything had morphed during the last few days. Things looked and felt different to her today, and she was reacting accordingly. She didn't plan to tell anyone she knew that she and Lucy had found two murder victims and now planned to take the search further. No turning it over to the law-enforcement professionals and walking away. Nope. Not even close. Today she planned to move from step one, finding the victim, to step two, finding the killer. Instead of searching with her nose and her eyes, like Lucy did, she'd use her own brain.

The only problem? She could do only so much, and a smart woman knew when to call in help. When the help came with mad skills, she wanted to tap into it right this second. She made the call, excitement making her hand shake. A minute later she put the phone back down, disappointed by delay. Diana, currently teaching a class at the academy, couldn't swing by until evening. She felt better when she gave the news a little spin. The wait meant Circe could probably come too, and her kind of help could be useful as well.

With that thought, she grabbed her phone and sent a text message. She planned to tap into the power in numbers.

❖

After sleeping peacefully through the night, the Seeker had gone into work feeling great. Another day, another dollar to put toward his work. Goodness rained down around him.

Things got even better shortly after he stepped inside. A sudden and unexpected departure in the sheriff's department crime-scene investigation unit had opened up a promotion for him. The rules said the position had to be made available to everyone both inside and outside of the department. Nobody else in the county had his skills, education, and years of experience, which meant the job would be his regardless of an open recruitment. Addy included. Oh, she'd want the job and assume the final selection would go to her. How she would hate him being promoted over her. That made it even sweeter.

The realization that in a couple of weeks he'd be right in the mix on the front lines made him almost giddy. That the bitch had up and left was an incredible stroke of luck. She'd always been high and mighty. While he had a particular dislike of her, he didn't believe anyone around here cared for her either. They all liked him. This job announcement was therefore a formality and nothing more. It belonged to him, period.

The only thing that marred an otherwise wonderful day had arrived in the form of the new gal. She came across nice enough and, at least on the surface, seemed pretty sharp. What he found disturbing was seeing her all cozied up to the boss like they were long-lost friends. When he got in, the two of them sat all chummy, their heads close together over a pile of paperwork and drinking coffee. That was messed up. If the chief wanted to discuss anything, he was right here, just like he'd been for years. And it wasn't like he'd been a shiny newbie when he'd come on board either. He'd arrived at this office with a wealth of knowledge and experience that they'd been taking advantage of since the day he walked through the door. It should have been him sitting next to the boss, not some new bitch.

His professionalism came through, and he managed to shake off the annoyance. He told himself he read more into the situation than really existed. She was new, and the boss was helping her settle in. That's all. Their closeness had no effect on him, or his upcoming promotion, because she wasn't a threat. No one in the office could threaten him. Not Addy. Not the new girl. Not anyone.

He shook off the annoyance and logged onto his computer. Before checking the schedule, he pulled up his resume and updated it to have it at the ready in order to be the first one submitted when the official job announcement came out. After he read through the completed document, he breathed out a contented sigh.

Addy had her head down when he passed her workstation. No doubt she worked on her own resume update hoping she would be the first choice for promotion. He wanted to stop and tell her not to bother. Not only would she never best him professionally, but she also wasn't going to be around long enough to try. He thought of her beautiful eyes as he made his way down the hallway, unable to keep the smile from his face. The vision of them kept him motivated throughout the day.

As soon as five o'clock hit, he headed out to the parking lot. He drove straight home without any detours. At this time yesterday he'd been wound up so tight he almost exploded. Only his self-control had kept him from falling apart and doing something potentially dangerous.

All things needed to happen in their own time, and the violet section wasn't quite ready to be completed. The timing wasn't perfect yet. He'd know when it was and would be prepared to act. Everything was at the ready.

Violet was going to be a perfect addition.

Chapter Seventeen

Between the spirits taking Vi on a fact-finding mission she still didn't quite understand, and her one-on-one with Dr. Kelsey, the day started off with a bang. By concentrating on her work and not allowing her personal crusade to sidetrack her, she got through the day without any additional hiccups.

Sort of. There was the kiss. She'd think about it at the most inopportune times, and the memory would make her smile and grow warm. Definitely a good thing that most of the day she wore a mask, so nobody appeared to notice her grinning or the color that filled her cheeks. Insanity. No other name for it. Her plan to work and go to school and call it good appeared to be getting more and more derailed with each passing day. Not that she intended to forgo either of her responsibilities. It just seemed like a third major element had entered the picture.

Once school actually started, it would get better, and she'd return to her solid focus on it and work. The last few days were just a short diversion while she was settling into her house and her job. The pressure of school would get her squared away pretty quick, particularly considering she'd move from day shift to evening. Being on day shift now gave her a chance to learn policies and procedures, as well as get to know the rest of the staff. In just a few days she'd had a chance to meet most everyone. So far the ME's office seemed to be a good fit for her, which was great, considering how long she'd be in school. She hoped she'd be able to keep working there until her residency days.

When she grabbed her phone out of her locker, she noticed a text from Kat. Warmth flooded her again, and she touched her lips as she read, reliving the kiss. They wouldn't be alone tonight, and she could accept that. Even without the possibility of more kisses, she looked forward to any time spent with Kat. She would also have a little more time to get to know her sister better and a sister-in-law whom she had yet to meet. Funny how a week ago she'd had no living relatives left, and suddenly she'd found herself with all sorts of family. Even a father she would have to work up the courage to meet. All in good time though. A woman could reconcile with this much information only so fast. She'd start with a sister and a sister-in-law, then work her way up to a father. Circe's reassurances that she'd like him were great and all, but after a lifetime of feeling abandoned, it would take a fair amount of time to change those feelings. In her heart, pain still lingered for that little girl who never had anyone to take her to the father-daughter dances.

Kat and Lucy met her at the front door, Kat with a tall glass of iced tea and Lucy with an excited bark. She didn't realize until this moment how much she had missed coming home to someone, and she found that she really liked having a dog waiting for her. Talk about unconditional love. She could get used to that. She gave Lucy a quick hug and took the tea from Kat. "Thank you."

"Come on, come on. We've been waiting for you." Kat's words were fast and excited.

Pretty nice to have an enthusiastic greeting too. "Sorry. I got out of the office late."

"No worries. You're here now, and that's all that matters. We've got lots to talk about." Kat spoke fast as she headed toward the kitchen. Vi followed.

In the kitchen, Circe sat at the table, along with a tall, slim, athletic woman with dark eyes and hair. Had to be the detective, Diana. Not a big leap. She had cop written all over her, and Vi had worked with enough of them to recognize the look. Only the very best undercover agents ever pulled off not appearing like a cop, and she'd met a couple that had fooled her and, fortunately, the criminals they worked to stop. Diana clearly wasn't into undercover work.

"Diana, this is Vi. Vi, Detective Diana Erni, Spokane PD, and also Circe's wife."

Vi held out her hand and Diana grabbed it, her grip firm and confident. She liked that. "Nice to meet you. I've heard a lot from Circe. Welcome to the family." She smiled, and the intense-cop persona disappeared. Not hard to see why Circe had fallen for her. Beautiful, smart, and good with a gun? What was not to like?

"Sit." Kat pulled out a chair for her. "We'll catch you up."

"Have I missed much?"

"Oh, only a serial killer." Kat sat next to her and put an arm around her shoulders.

Kat was excited Vi had finally joined them. She'd been so eager for her to get here that she'd wanted to go stand at the end of the driveway or, more likely, pace. Circe and Diana had pulled up an hour earlier, and the things they'd mapped out so far were amazing. All the pieces were clicking together, and once again Spokane appeared to be looking at the work of a serial killer.

The craziest part of all: Kat and Lucy had been involved with the discovery of the bodies of two of his victims. Nothing official had yet been released about an active serial killer, only the insight of the four people sitting around her kitchen table who knew it to be true. Some might say they were stupid to believe they could make a call like that, given their civilian status. They weren't law enforcement.

Actually, that wasn't quite correct. Diana was a homicide detective and had some finely honed skills that gave her an impressive level of expertise. That didn't negate what Circe, Kat, and their dogs could do. They weren't paid for their work, but they were as professional as Diana. Then there was Vi. If she wasn't a total professional, then Kat didn't know who could be called one. So, bottom line, they were a pretty damned skilled crew, and if they said serial killer, then people should sit up and listen.

"Let me bring you up to speed."

Vi nodded as she sipped from the glass of iced tea. Kat should have pulled out something with more substance, like the twelve-year-old scotch up in the cupboard. However, she wanted everyone crystal clear before she dulled anyone's brain cells with alcohol. They were talking some serious shit.

Her friend, Xander, a specialist in criminal defense, had always maintained that looking into the minds of the truly evil changed the viewer. When she'd started training as an HRD handler, he'd warned her again that though her intentions were the best, like bringing home those who perished through natural causes, her work would also bring her face-to-face with evil like she'd never seen before. His warnings hadn't deterred her. Working with Lucy like this had been the best thing that ever happened to her, and that made it easy to discount Xander's counsel.

But a couple of nights ago, Xander's long-ago words had echoed in her ears. He'd been right, damn him. In a mere second, experience had changed her, and it continued to as they dug deeper and deeper into what was happening around them. Not all of it appeared to be bad. Evil had displayed itself in an uncompromising way, yet it had also spurred her forward. A direction and purpose in life that she'd been missing for years became as clear as a lighted airplane runway. She knew what she needed to do and, with the help of some great people, was figuring out pretty quickly how to do it.

"I found patterns." It was as simple as that. Once she'd started with the basics of what she'd seen, she'd been able to capture a crap load of information that she'd used to search throughout the country. The world really. In the end, she compiled enough to make a map.

"She emailed the patterns to me." Diana tapped the top of the tablet she'd brought with her.

"Patterns?" Vi stared at Diana. "Can you explain, please? It's pretty clear I need to catch up with the rest of you."

Kat was impressed by the look and sound of Vi. She'd been pleasant and lovely since the moment they met, even given the strangeness of everything, but right now Kat thought she could see the doctor she would one day become. An exciting insight, and by the expression on Circe's face, she thought so too. Once this was all over, it would be interesting to see the two women connect as sisters.

"You started it." This time Circe spoke. "Your mother's murder gave us ground zero."

"She was his first?" Vi didn't seem to be buying that possibility, and Kat thought she understood. The killer had been too skilled and organized to have been brand-new.

Diana shrugged. "Maybe, maybe not. Probably not. The thing is, for us she was ground zero. We have more detailed information, thanks to you, and it gave us the building blocks. I used what you have, what Kat uncovered, and the resources I have available to construct a picture, and I have to tell you it's a hell of an image. Unless we're wrong…"

"We're not wrong." Kat had no doubt at all. She had the marks on the maps, copies of the homicide reports, and a slew of missing-person reports. The picture it painted was dire. She might have taken some time off, but by the time Circe and Diana had arrived at the house, the pile of data she'd uncovered proved she'd lost nothing. The investigator she thought she'd left behind had come out of hiding.

Diana nodded toward Kat. "Agreed, but as I was saying, unless we turn out to be wrong, and I don't believe we are, this guy's been killing for years."

The Seeker stepped out of the shower and dried off. He reached in and took the two razors from the shelf and threw them into the trash. Every time he shaved, he destroyed at least two and sometimes three. The result was well worth the cost of replacing razors. Silk was the only word that came to mind when he ran his hands over his skin. He smiled at his own little secret that he kept tucked away beneath long-sleeved shirts and pants. He never wore anything else, for obvious reasons. What people didn't know wouldn't hurt them. A trite saying, yet one that rang oh so true, at least when it came to him.

In his bedroom he slipped on the black shirt and pants he'd earlier laid out on his bed. His socks were also black, as were his shoes. The dark-warrior look appealed to him, and if he could get over the one bit of vanity that stuck with him, he'd shave his face as well as his body. The only hair he could still grow on his head graced his face; thus it became sacred to him. So far, he hadn't been able to overcome the hurdle of vanity, despite knowing that he ran a risk by having any hair at all on his body. Besides, if he shaved, he'd look way too much like his father, and that would never do. Anything that would distance himself was worth some amount of risk.

After he dressed, he left his house as though he intended to do nothing more than drive to the grocery store. The neighbors, if anyone happened to be looking out their windows, wouldn't give him a second thought, except maybe the dumb redhead on the corner. For some reason the single mom of three seemed to have latched onto him as potential husband number three and daddy to her kids. He'd done everything he could to discourage her. From all indications, she wasn't bright enough to take his not-very-subtle hints. He knew of a permanent solution to stopping her intrusion, only it wasn't a wise one. He didn't want to take a chance on killing someone this close to home. Only one had been worth that big a gamble. He'd played a winning hand on that one too, however, wasn't about to try it again.

The windows at the redhead menace's house were dark as he drove by, and he sent up a little prayer of thanks to the universe. One of the snotty-nosed brats probably had a basketball game or Scouts or some other plebeian hobby that had never been available to him during his childhood. According to his father's logic, if an activity didn't involve prayers, it didn't involve him. Daddy's rules.

Clouds rolled in as he drove, and the weather pattern pleased him. The darkness resembled a stage curtain designed to block out every bit of light. That provided a definite advantage for what he had in store tonight. Three blocks away from his destination, he parked under a low-hanging tree, its branches forming a natural garage. In all black, he blended in with the night as he walked casually down the street in the direction he'd just driven. No need to hurry. Besides not wanting to draw attention, he loved how a slow stroll allowed the anticipation to build. This intoxicating feeling was better than any of the artificial substances people liked to use for a sensory rush, and his came via natural sources.

When he'd dropped the messenger bag off on his first trip here, he'd taken a quick but thorough scan of the nearby area, as always. That's how he'd noticed a lovely, thick lilac bush that would provide excellent cover, along with a perfect view of the house. He'd be able to see the precise moment when the lights went out, and that's what happened now. She stayed up later than he would have expected, given her propensity to brag about her healthy lifestyle that included plenty of exercise and at least seven to eight hours of sleep each night.

"Me thinks thou doth protest too much," he whispered and smiled. As he'd suspected for a very long time, she was full of shit. If she was an athlete, he was the pope.

He waited another half an hour because he'd discovered quite by accident some years ago that if his victims were deep in sleep when he made his presence known, the fun factor skyrocketed. The shock on their faces became a priceless memory he could tuck away. It kicked the adrenaline up even higher than sneaking into their houses did.

First things first, however. All the pieces had to be in place to make his plan work. He retrieved the bag from where he had hidden it behind the woodpile. From inside, he pulled out a pair of industrial-strength, powder-free, nitrile gloves and slipped them on. Then he headed to the back door and shook his head when he saw it. Really? Given where she worked, a flimsy door handle that he could pop in a heartbeat appeared to be the best she could come up with for security? He felt embarrassed for her but delighted for himself. It took maybe a minute to pick the lock. One learned all sorts of useful skills over the course of a career. He used this particular expertise over and over again.

He checked the wall just inside the door and once more shook his head. Now he really was embarrassed for her. No alarm panel, meaning no alarm system in the house. A woman living alone with nothing to alert her about a breach of her doors and windows? Sloppy or arrogant because of the neighborhood she lived in. Either way it showed poor judgment on her part, and he didn't feel bad for her given what was about to happen. She would be getting what she deserved for being not only stupid but a huge bitch. What did dear old Dad used to say? "You reap what you sow." He should know.

The house reflected her true self: boring. White walls, dark furniture, kitchen countertops with not a single item on them. It reminded him an awful lot of his childhood home. "Cleanliness is next to Godliness" had been another of the old man's favorite sayings. Glad he never had to hear that again or any of the other nauseating kernels of wisdom no one ever asked for.

He swept the kitchen with his gaze and confirmed that it would provide the best work area for his plans. The open floor space in the back of the house meant that anyone passing on the street would be unable to see in. Perfect for his needs. His bag contained a neatly folded piece of thick plastic large enough for an average-sized person, which he took out and spread on the linoleum tile. Another surprise given where she lived. He would have expected a trendy ceramic-tile floor. Did she not care, or was she simply too cheap to update?

Next he pulled out the small case that held his tools—new, sharp, and ready to be used—and set them out in a precise order. The final items, two syringes loaded and ready for administration, were also in their own little zippered case. One he laid next to the tools and one he kept in his hand as he made his way to the bedroom, where he stopped and heard soft snores wafting through the open door. It figured she would be a snorer. She probably didn't even know she had that abhorrent habit, and that thought made him smile as he stepped through the open door and into the bedroom.

"Honey," he said softly. "I'm home."

Chapter Eighteen

Vi listened to Diana and Kat with growing horror. She'd recognized the common threads between the victims that had been brought to the ME's office here and her mother's murder. She wasn't expecting to discover that the homicides weren't isolated to Alaska and Washington. They had indeed stumbled upon a pattern that so far no one else had picked up. Excitement that they had filled her, tempered by disappointment that law enforcement hadn't.

Now she threw even more details into the mix. "Let me share with you what Dr. Kelsey and I discussed this morning." She described his belief that the cause and manner of death for the victims brought to their office for autopsy were identical to those of her mother. He'd already compared what he'd found against the reports he'd received from Dr. Yarno about three other victims recovered outside of Anchorage—in Fairbanks, Valdez, and Kenai. She knew about the one in Fairbanks, as the man in prison for her mother's murder had also been convicted for that one. She didn't know about Valdez and Kenai.

She'd often wondered if more had occurred, and now she knew. Aurora, Colorado; Lompoc, California; and Johnson, Missouri. Diana and Kat were able to uncover those locations in less than a full day's work. She felt certain they'd find more. An interesting side note on those locations—all had military bases. This discovery gave them another avenue for research.

"It's official then. We have a serial killer we've got to stop." Kat looked at Diana.

She held up a hand. "Nothing official yet. This is all off the books for the moment."

Vi didn't understand. To her it was quite clear. She'd been waiting for this moment for years, and she didn't want to wait any longer. "Why off the books? We know what we're up against, so why shouldn't we bring in the police? Maybe even the FBI, given the locations across the country. They can't argue with the information we've uncovered."

Circe answered. "Back up the pony. Think about it, Vi. Do you really want to explain how we knew about the bodies?" She paused as if to let the question sink in. "You might, but I don't."

All right, so she did get the point Circe tried to make, and no, she didn't care to make public their little family secret. Still, doing nothing wasn't an option either. Explanations could be tailored to exclude what others didn't need to know.

"Bodies?" This time Kat spoke. "I, personally, don't see the problem, and Vi's right. You two psychics were in on only one, so you have nothing to explain. I vote for taking this to the FBI."

Vi leaned solidly in the same direction. She'd never been able to get this kind of buy-in from anyone in law enforcement, and she was beyond excited to kick it into high gear. She wouldn't hesitate to bring in the FBI, DEA, ICE, or any other organization with initials that gave them broad authority.

The abashed look on Circe's face told a different story. "Ah, here's the deal, Kat. I knew about the one you found the other day. I saw her, which is why Zelda and I showed up when we did in your search area. It wasn't an accident."

Kat looked crushed, and Vi wanted to rush over and hug her. "You mean it wasn't a legitimate find for me and Lucy?"

Circe beat her to it by jumping up and wrapping her arms around Kat. "It was absolutely a find. You two located the body without any help from me and Zelda. We were on our way in because of what I'd seen, but you'd already done the work by the time we got there. What's really important is that he was found, and you did that."

Kat nodded and her expression cleared. Vi wasn't convinced she totally bought into Circe's reassurances, but enough to get her back on track. "If you don't think it's time to take this to the FBI, how do we deal with it? How do we know what to look for beyond what we've already found?"

Should she bring up what had happened this morning? All the women in this room knew about what she could do—what Circe could do as well—so she doubted any of them would consider her crazy. She summoned the courage to share. "Two of the victims came to me this morning."

Circe dropped her arm from around Kat and turned to stare at Vi. "What did you see?"

Strange as it sounded, it felt incredible to have someone listen to her and ask questions about her interactions with the dead as if it were the most normal thing in the world. Talk about a breath of fresh air.

She shook off her amazement. "They took me to the supply room."

Kat tilted her head and studied Vi. "That's weird. Why the supply room?"

"I wish I knew. I mean I sort of got a hint about all the stuff stored in there. I'm just not fully understanding exactly what they wanted me to see at this point. The puzzle pieces aren't quite together yet."

"Walk us through it," Circe urged her. "Maybe we'll pick up on something you missed."

A good idea, Vi thought. Sometimes it took a village, and this might just be one of those times. She inhaled deeply, then told them about the trip down the hallway, the shelves of supplies, and how when she picked up the box of specimen jars, they disappeared. "The jars." It didn't fully hit her until after she related the events out loud. "It's the jars."

"Yes, definitely." Circe agreed. "Listening to you, that's how I interpret it as well. We need to figure out how those jars play into all this. They have to be important, or the spirits wouldn't have taken you to them."

"Hey," Kat said. "I might not be the great mind the rest of you are, but think about it. All of the victims were missing their eyes, right?"

Diana nodded. "Yes. Every one of them."

"They were never recovered, also right?"

"Correct again." Diana's eyes were narrowing, and Vi suddenly realized where Kat's line of thought was headed. She felt like a dimwit for not picking it up this morning. Now that she was tuned to the right wavelength, it became crystal clear.

Vi grabbed Kat's hand. "You're brilliant. He took the eyes as specimens."

Kat nodded. "And he put them in," say it with me, ladies, and they did, "specimen jars."

❖

Kat's adrenaline raced. The four of them were pounding down a path certain to take them to the person wreaking death and destruction on innocent people in her city. She hadn't felt this alive in a very long time, and all of it thanks to Vi. Beautiful, smart, psychic Vi. In just a few days, it had become impossible to imagine her world without her bright light in it.

They sat around her table talking about murder and, in particular, a serial killer. It was about the last thing she could have imagined doing, yet it felt right. In truth, it felt critical, as though they were on a mission they couldn't stop even if they wanted to. No one around this table seemed to have even the slightest desire to stop until the man was behind bars. The universe had brought them together for this purpose.

This was seriously badass. On another level, quite concerning. How had the system with all the resources available to it failed to pick up on the signs they'd put together in such a short time? She said as much to Diana, a long-time member of said system.

"You know." Diana responded without a hint of resentment. "We have some dynamic people in law enforcement all over the country, all over the world really, and they do a bang-up job the majority of the time. I like to think I do too, and that I've tried my best to keep the people of my community safe."

Circe squeezed Diana's hand. "We know you have, and we appreciate what you do every day. In all the time I've known you, above and beyond is the name of your game. This isn't about you."

Diana kissed the side of her head. "Thanks. I know you all have my back, and I appreciate that. I also know you're not pointing fingers at me. All of that aside, you have to understand that good police work always has a caveat. It's complicated, it's detailed, and in this case, the killer is just plain good. Sometimes the best efforts still fall short. Nobody's fault. It's just the tragic reality of my business."

"I don't get it. If he's so good that nobody's caught on, why is he suddenly leaving bodies out to be found?" Kat thought about the young man she and Lucy had discovered, and a shiver darted through her.

"Good question, and based on everything we've come up with so far, I'd say he's unraveling."

"Why now? From everything we're pulling together, it looks like this guy has been working undetected for years." All Kat knew about killers came from what she watched on television, and she was prone to take that information with a grain of salt. While she'd followed the trail of bad people on numerous occasions, none of them had been murderers. This was out of her wheelhouse, so she wanted to hear a theory right straight from an expert's mouth.

Diana shrugged. "It's usually a combination of the thrill of the kill along with something in their lives that has set the spiral in motion. In the beginning they're able to control themselves, but as time goes on, that self-moderation fades away. That's when the vast majority of them get sloppy and ultimately caught."

It still wasn't making sense to Kat. "I don't get why no one has picked up on this pattern before. I mean, it's right there if someone had taken the time to dig in and look."

Diana was nodding. "True enough, and you're not wrong. Everything is a matter of the right pieces falling into place at the right time. In this instance, it's evidently taken years. That's just the way it goes sometimes."

While she didn't like it, what Diana said made sense. It also gave Kat the chills. "That's fucked up."

Diana patted Kat's hand. "Welcome to my world."

❖

Happiness rolled through the Seeker. Tonight had been fun, and his collection had just taken a new and most pleasing turn. If he'd known that increasing the volume of his work would have led to this type of satisfaction, he'd have bumped up his frequency a lot sooner.

Besides, around here, nobody was smart enough to catch on to what he worked so diligently to accomplish. His service to his country had allowed him to move throughout the country and add to his collection from coast to coast, border to border, and that had been the beginning of the thrills. As he grew older and more skilled, he'd realized he didn't have to move around just to do what he needed to. By the time of his honorable discharge, he'd figured out how to create a life for himself in one place while accomplishing his important work at various locations. When he became tied down and couldn't travel, a place like this provided him with thousands of potential subjects. No matter what, he could do what he needed to do regardless of his physical location.

He smiled, thinking about the red flag he'd begun waving of late. Off and on throughout the years he'd left little love notes for the cops, something to get their minds working and their frustration levels skyrocketing. He was confident responsibility for more than one prescription of medication for high blood pressure came directly from his work. To read the reports in the newspapers and the pleas for assistance and listen to the broadcasts from the grieving families provided him with endless entertainment. A good psychiatrist might say that he lacked empathy, but he'd call that bull. He preferred to think of it as payback is a bitch. Where was the empathy when he'd been under siege? Who shed tears for him when his back was covered with bruises?

He stood over her now, all his tools tucked back into the black bag and the jar safe and sound in his pocket. Which way to go? Did he hide her away as another of his private secrets or leave one more present for the already severely baffled police? Either way he chose, it would turn out to be a win for him, so it really boiled down to which one would yield the highest degree of fun.

Not much of a choice. Some of the glow had worn off the secrets. He'd been doing it that way successfully for such a long time now that it lacked the thrill he preferred to feel in his work. Granted, the secrets had their own appeal in that he could always visit them and remember. Then again, when they were discovered and taken away, so too was his ability to be with them. He'd just lost one, and how long before he lost others? It made sense to opt for immediate gratification and not risk another eventual loss. As he wrapped her in the thick plastic, his thoughts were already on the impending lead topic for tomorrow morning's news.

He opened the door to her garage right off the kitchen. Inside, her four-door, bright-red Ford was parked with the keys in the ignition. How thoughtful of her to make it so convenient for him. She must have known the importance of having her car at the ready. At least she could do something right.

In life she'd been tiny but obnoxious. Death brought silence from still lips, though she weighed more than he would have imagined. Still, he found it easy enough to get her into the trunk, heavy or not. The plastic crunched as he tucked it around her, and a bit of blood dripped out the corner. Not that he cared much if her blood leaked into the carpet. It wasn't his car, and it wasn't like she'd be using it again. Forensically they'd never link it back to him either.

By the time he backed out of the garage, it had grown very dark outside. A cloud cover blotted out the stars. The moon, a dull orb high in the night sky, didn't give off much light. Until he'd driven down the block and made it clear of her closest neighbors, he didn't turn on the lights.

"Where to go?" he pondered out loud. "Do you have any preferences?" He made the comment over his shoulder and laughed. "No? All right then. I have an idea I think you'll appreciate."

Chapter Nineteen

Vi came into the office feeling more alive than she had in years. To be more accurate, she'd never felt like this before. By ten last night, the foursome had a fully developed game plan. Even though she hadn't been assigned to the case, Diana would be point because none of them could argue her status as the only true official in the group. They might not be bringing in any law enforcement beyond Diana at this time, but they still planned to respect standard protocol in their own way. The rest of them would use their specialties to see what information they could glean.

When Kat and Lucy walked Vi back to her house after Diana and Circe left, the scene had become almost romantic. It morphed into assuredly romantic when Kat kissed her. She couldn't deny that she was attracted to Kat and was glad Kat was strong enough to make the first move. Vi wasn't. She might be bright and capable of making it through medical school, but when it came to personal relationships, she sucked. Even if she liked someone, she'd rarely take the initiative. Too much risk involved. Too scary.

Kat wasn't scary, and despite their short time together, the attraction felt solid and deep. She'd never been around anyone who made her pulse race like she'd just finished a 10k road race. She'd also never met anyone who took her obsession with finding her mother's killer in stride. In fact, it was more than that. In Kat's case, she jumped right into the obsession pool with her. She'd be foolish not to want to embrace someone like that.

The night crew was wrapping up when she sat down in front of her computer before her work day began. She tapped the keys with a light touch, somewhat lost on how to get to the information she wanted to mine. If she read the spirits right, they were directing her to focus on the specimen jars. Everyone agreed last night, as well, that her inclination seemed to be right on.

Except the programs she could access didn't have anything to do with procurement. It wasn't her field and never had been. She would have no reason to have been granted access to anything dealing with purchasing for the ME's office. Still, she tried several different avenues before giving up. Instead of continuing to spin her wheels, Vi got up and walked to the supply room. In front of the shelf holding the jars, she stopped and stared. As far as she could see, they weren't unusual or unique. She picked up one of the cases and studied the manufacturer information. Nothing catchy there either. What did they want her to see?

"Good morning."

The greeting startled Vi so much she almost dropped the box of jars. "Oh my, you scared me." She put the box back on the shelf but not before making a mental note of the information printed on the bottom of the box. It might not mean anything to her, but she planned to run it by the rest later tonight.

Vi had met Sharman Reid, the office manager and procurement officer, on her first day. From what others had told her, Sharman also happened to be the keeper of the secrets, as she'd been here longer than anyone else, the two MEs included. After twenty-eight years, Sharman was on a forty-two-day countdown to retirement. They'd immediately hit it off when introduced. Sharman was a member of the Blackfeet Nation while Vi was Yupik. In many ways, they were kindred souls, and it made Vi sad to think they'd get to work together for less than two months.

"Sorry." Sharman smiled. "Didn't mean to startle you. Did you need something? I can help you find whatever you're looking for. I know this room like the back of my hand."

What could she say that would make sense? Not much, without a detailed explanation that she couldn't give her. "Wondering about the jars you use here."

Sharman studied her intently. Her dark eyes seemed to take in everything, spoken and unspoken. "I think there's more to the story than what kind of jars we use."

It would be easy to lie, except she liked Sharman, and besides, she had a hunch she'd hear the lie in her words a hundred miles away. She decided to go for the truth, or at least partial truth. "There is, but right now I need to keep it close to the vest. I'm sorry."

For a moment, Sharman studied her face, and then nodded. "Good enough. Tell me when you can. Maybe I can help."

Relief washed over her. She knew she liked this woman. "I will." She turned and started to leave.

"So, about the jars." Sharman stood next to the shelf, tapping one of the boxes.

Vi stopped and stared at her tapping fingers. Probably too much to hope that Sharman might have some helpful information she could share. She asked anyway. "Anything unusual about them?"

Sharman tapped the top of one of the boxes again. "No, not so much about the jars themselves. The fact that some of them have gone missing, well, that's what I'd call unusual."

Her heart kicked up. "What do you mean missing?"

"I not only order all this." She waved her hands to encompass the entire room. "I inventory as well. This is my little kingdom, if you will. I know what's here, what should be, and what's not."

"Meaning?" She actually got where Sharman was going with this but wanted to hear her say it.

"Meaning that off and on I've noticed that our inventory of jars is light when compared against our actual usage. In simple terms, day-to-day consumption and inventory levels aren't matching up."

"Someone's taking them."

"That's my educated guess. An occasional supply item being carted home isn't unusual, and nobody gets their panties in a twist about a pad of paper or a pen or two walking out the door. Swiping specimen jars is weird, and once I realized what was happening, I started watching. My recent inventories show that the number of them missing is increasing. For a long time, it's been four or five jars at a time. In my last audit, a whole case went MIA."

Excitement started to build in her chest. "Did you find out who's carting them off?"

"No." Her heart sank, and it must have shown on her face. Sharman smiled and winked. "Not at first anyway. I have now."

❖

Kat flew through her morning chores with a speed that amazed her. Usually she took more time, savoring the company of her animals, the fresh air, and the physical exertion of the work that left her feeling invigorated. Today, it wasn't her body she wanted to push in exercise;

it was her mind. Eagerness to get into her office and start working made her move like a madwoman.

Lucy was having none of it. They hadn't been out training for a week, and for a working dog, that equated to an eternity. Lucy needed to do some work, and she wasn't about to give her a moment's peace if she tried to sit down at her computer first. Kat knew better than to even try. As much as she wanted to get her hands on the keyboard, running a few problems with Lucy actually did sound like fun. Besides, fresh air and movement would do them both a lot of good. Clear the mind, keep the body fit.

"Okay," she told the prancing dog as she opened the back door on her truck. "Load up."

Kat and Lucy were in Deer Park at a great recreational area about twenty-five miles north of Spokane when her cell phone rang. They were on the way back to the truck after spending a good sixty minutes on a training she'd set up for Lucy. It had been a difficult one that required Lucy to really work it through. She always enjoyed watching Lucy perform and studying her as she figured the puzzle out. Ultimately, Lucy's determination won the day, or the morning rather, and she received a reward for her good job. The hour it took them to complete the problem proved to be exactly what Lucy needed, and she was cheerfully trotting back to the car when the phone went off.

It was Vi, which surprised her. Pleased her as well. They seemed to be finding a rhythm both as neighbors and as budding friends. Friends that appeared to be leaning toward benefits, she thought as warmth flooded through her.

"Hey, what's up?" She didn't have to be told that once Vi stepped inside the ME's office, she went into unshakable professional mode. In the short time they'd known each other, Kat had already figured out her impeccable code. A personal life would not intrude on her work, and Kat respected that level of dedication.

Working on the farm, she became more open to interruption and conversation. She never minded if someone called her in the middle of mucking out the barn. In the field with Lucy, however, everything changed. She had to focus on their mission and, even more importantly, on her dog. Lucy had certain tells that let Kat know if she was in a scent pool. If she looked away or allowed her attention to her dog to wander, she could easily miss one of them and blow right by something important.

Fortunately, Lucy excelled at her job, and even if Kat did miss something, Lucy had a way of bringing her back. The only fly in the ointment, so to speak, was that if a handler wasn't careful, they could pull a dog off scent, every handler's worst nightmare. If her phone rang when they were working, she ignored it. Besides, wasn't that what voice mail had been created for? Vi seemed to have the same sentiment about her work. The handwriting was already large on the wall; she was going to be all kinds of impressive as a doctor.

She opened the back door of her truck, and Lucy jumped up onto the seat or, as Kat thought of it, her throne. From the crew cab, she sat high enough that she had a three-hundred-sixty-degree view, and Lucy loved it. God forbid anything ever happened to this rig. Lucy would be crushed. She got in behind the wheel and hit the button that linked the phone to the onboard system allowing her hands-free access to her cell.

"I need you to do some digging." Vi's quiet voice came across the truck's speakers. She had the sense the lowered tone was intentional. She didn't want anyone around her to hear their conversation. Curious.

Kat turned the ignition and the truck engine started. She pulled out of the parking lot and onto the road that would lead them back to the highway. "Absolutely. Lucy and I are on the way home as we speak."

"This is kind of off the beaten track, but I think we need to follow up. I want you to find out whatever you can about an investigator here."

"Seriously? One of your coworkers?" Just the thought blew her mind. No way could the person they sought be an insider, though her logic might be skewed. The killer that had been stopped around here not that long ago had been a respected cop. If it happened once, it could sure as hell happen again. She supposed when it came to evil, it was an equal-opportunity employer.

"I can't go into the details here. Too many people around me, and I don't really want to make this public."

"No need to explain. Tell me who, and by the time you get home tonight, I'll have his grade-school report cards." It felt incredible to be needed.

"Great." She gave her a name. "It might turn out to be nothing."

The hairs on the back of Kat's neck stood up even though she didn't recognize the name. "It might turn out to be exactly what we're looking for."

"That's what I'm afraid of."

❖

The Seeker paced his living room. Finally home, he could at last express the feelings he'd been forced to bottle up all day. He'd started the day upbeat and optimistic. His world appeared perfect. His opinion changed quickly. Something seemed off, and he could feel it as intensely as he felt the cold of a snowstorm.

Disturbing signs had been revealed to him within minutes of arriving at the office, such as the glances and comments never directed at him before. He'd been operating in his workplace without extra scrutiny from the day he arrived. He expected as much, given that he'd come to the organization with experience, knowledge, and impeccable references. With his background, he could have taken a position in any of the biggest offices in the country. That he chose to come home and use his considerable skills in Spokane was an undeniable coup for them.

He thought over the day, and while he'd like to be able to pinpoint the source of his unease, no one did anything overt. More that he noticed a couple of his coworkers paying undue attention in areas they wouldn't in the normal course of day-to-day business. When he approached them, albeit casually, as if he was simply curious, their whispered conversation stopped. He wasn't stupid. Clearly, they hadn't wanted him to hear whatever they were talking about.

All day long he told himself their unusual interest could have been unrelated to his activities. After all, they were two women who might have similar interests and were friends, even if one of them was the office's newest employee. Could he be making more out of the abrupt silence than there really was? Of course he could. Neither of them treated him any differently, and their faces didn't display anything that made him think they were uncomfortable with his presence.

Still, it unsettled him, and the unease stayed with him all day. Despite doing his normal exemplary job on his assignments, he'd been dwelling on his early morning encounter since the moment it occurred. No matter how he rationalized what he saw, he believed they'd been talking about him. He didn't like it, and he wanted to know the substance of their whispered conversation.

This was a most inopportune time for things to start going sideways. The choice he'd made lately to taunt law enforcement was, as far as he was concerned, still not an issue. They were as baffled now as ever, and he enjoyed the opportunity to watch them run around trying to figure out the identity of the big bad wolf. His only misstep, a minor one, came in mixing his profession with his personal calling. While it would be easy to make excuses for why he'd had to do it, he couldn't.

The decision had all been his and based on the thrill factor. Taking things from right underneath their noses had amused him. Still amused him, and part of the joy came in the form of pushing the envelope as much as he could.

He stopped pacing and stared out the big picture window, the focal point of the living room. It brought in golden sunshine during the day and soothing darkness during the night. Outside, the sun started to dip low, and soon night would fall, ushering in what he liked to refer to as hunting time. Not this night, however, and for two main reasons. He'd done a fine job last night, and it had filled his soul as well as brought his collection to a new level of completeness. Also he didn't have a plan. He hadn't decided on his next experiment yet, and maybe the time had come to take his work on the road again. In any event, he'd think about it and decide how to proceed. In the meantime, he needed to shake off the unsettling interaction this morning and put it into perspective. From here on out he would forgo playing the game at work. It had been fun while it lasted.

Now that he had it all squared away in his head, he could settle down for the evening and start to consider his future plans. With his feet up on the coffee table, he leaned back in the comfortable sofa and relaxed. He smiled, and as he did, a brilliant plan began to form in his mind. Why he hadn't thought of this long ago? Suddenly he felt as though someone had hit him over the head with a baseball bat. His feet dropped to the floor, and he stood upright as if someone had yanked him up by the hair. He suddenly understood why that interaction with his coworkers had stuck like glue to him all day, and it had nothing to do with the conversation they didn't want him to hear.

It had everything to do with their eyes. One pair had been simply interesting, and he recognized the other pair.

Chapter Twenty

Vi found her job fascinating. Not a big mystery why most people would do anything to avoid working in a world where death existed front and center. What she and others like her did wasn't for the weak of mind and spirit. For her it was different. The dead needed her. She could be their voice, and even though she'd never asked for this role, she took it seriously. If she'd had a choice, she'd have chosen not to be the one they came to, yet she also realized she'd probably still be in exactly this place. Natural death held sadness, and for those left behind, it took a piece of their heart each and every time. When death arrived in a way not so natural, it took more than a piece of the heart. Instead, it often shattered the lives of those who remained in the land of the living. Some found ways to survive, like Vi had done, while others never did. Taking innocent lives wasn't right, and it wasn't fair, just like with her mother. That injustice compelled her to do whatever she could to make it right.

Her mother's death had showed her the way, although as each year passed, she'd begun to believe that she'd have ended up here anyway. The universe gifted each person with a calling whether they heeded it or not. She had taken hold of hers and run with it. Because of her choice to listen to the will of the universe, she'd made a difference in the lives of many families. Someday she hoped her work would make a difference in her own life as well.

Following this path in life wasn't always easy. She wanted to share what she'd seen, to be able to talk with someone throughout the day so she had help putting the pieces together. Just the little bit of companionship she'd found in Kat, Circe, and Diana made her greedy. She wanted it all and to know what it was like to be an open book. A lifetime of secrets became a heavy burden.

It would be nice to believe that, at some point, she could share everything with someone special, to be open and seen as a whole person. A little hope grew inside her, especially now, because she was no longer alone, not in her secrets and not as a person without a family.

All these thoughts tumbled through her mind as she drove home, and before she knew it, she had pulled up in front of her house, wondering how it had gotten so late. The day had buzzed by, and they'd been, according to Dr. Kelsey, unusually busy. None of them left before six, and the ME's office officially closed at five. Hungry and tired, she'd never be able to sleep until she had a chance to talk to Kat. After their conversation this morning, she could hardly wait to hear what she'd found.

All the new women in her life made her head spin a little. Just thinking about Kat made her smile. Circe came as a huge surprise and a not unpleasant one. After the initial shock, she anticipated the days to come and learning what it was like to have a sister, especially one that shared her gift. Kat presented the wild card, and she brought an even more exciting element to the mix than finding out she had a sister. Though she'd had girlfriends in the past, for the first time she could easily drop everything just to spend time with her without feeling guilty. The fact that she was bright and active and interesting made it even better. No, she absolutely did not have time for any of this, and it didn't matter an iota.

After she'd showered and changed into comfortable knock-around clothes, she figured the best thing to do would be to grab a bite to eat and then get some sleep. Instead, she slipped on her shoes and headed down the driveway. Sleep was overrated anyway. Lucy met her head-on before she got more than twenty feet from her front door.

"How you doing, girl?" She reached down and rubbed the top of her head. Lucy leaned into her, and warmth spread through Vi. She really liked this dog. She really liked this dog's partner, and a broad smile spread across her face as she stepped up onto the front porch and knocked on the door. Only then did she notice that no lights were on. Outside, the daylight faded enough that Kat would have needed to turn on at least one light.

"Where is she, girl?" Lucy ran from the porch and around the side of the house, stopping to turn and look at Vi as if to say "are you coming?" She followed, watching as Lucy disappeared through the dog door mounted in the back door.

Lucy popped her head out a few seconds later and stared at her expectantly. Apparently, she wanted Vi to join her. "Ah, no, sweet girl. I'm not following you through that thing, even if I could fit."

For at least thirty seconds she stood staring at the house and wondering where Kat had gotten off to. A trickle of fear rippled through her, but it didn't make sense. For all she knew, Kat might have simply run to the store. Yet the uneasy feeling in her gut told her the simple explanation probably wasn't the correct one.

She pulled her phone out of her pocket and scrolled through her contacts until she reached Kat's number. She hit the button and put the phone to her ear. The call went immediately to voice mail.

"Shit, shit, shit." Kat crouched in the corner of the closet and whispered to herself. How in the fuck did she talk herself into this literal corner? When did she decide to become some kind of super detective? Her super-sleuth skills were of the cyber variety. Breaking and entering private homes wasn't on her résumé. Until today, that is. Perhaps it had been a bad idea to leave her unsupervised with an unsolved murder mystery.

No argument about that at the moment. Here she sat in some guy's closet cowering like a frightened mouse, wondering how in the hell she would be able to get out of this mess. Earlier, she'd thought it such a smart idea to come over here and let herself in. At first she intended to just look around outside and get a feel for the guy. See what kind of house and neighborhood he lived in? A person could learn a lot about somebody just by taking the pulse of their environment.

She hadn't intended to break into the house. That had sort of happened organically. It worked too. She'd actually picked a fricking lock! Dumb luck and nothing more. She'd never be able to do it again.

A good PI would have brought gloves along, so clearly she wasn't a good one. Wiping away her prints as she went along and being careful to do it well would have to suffice. Not that she touched much because there wasn't much to touch. Talk about a neat freak. The place was almost sterile. Houses like this always gave her the creeps and made her wonder about the kind of people whose homes were perpetually spotless. She preferred to truly live in her home, and a little clutter, a little dust, a dirty dish in the sink not only didn't bother

her, they made her feel cozy. People who lived like this were not, in her book, actually living. A person couldn't experience real life if they worried about a speck of dust or a towel hung askew. Besides, it was just plain weird.

She'd been almost done with her perusal when a car pulled up. The window from his office gave her a clear view of the driveway. Darn. She'd just needed ten more minutes in the last room. It had been as tidy as the rest of the house, with not so much as a single piece of paper loose on the desk. His computer was a desktop model with a large, wide, flat monitor and one of the popular ergonomic keyboards she hated. If she could have had those ten minutes, she'd have been able to hack into his hard drive and see what secrets it held. Instead, she'd been forced to run for cover, and the closet near the front door turned out to be the best she could come up with before he let himself into the house.

Huddled there and trying not to make a sound, she listened to him pace back and forth and mutter to himself. Unless something earthshattering resided on his computer, after she'd gone through the rest of the house, she'd been ready to think they were heading down the wrong path. What she heard now made her think differently. This guy sounded off in a totally creepy way.

It would be a whole lot better if she could crack the door and hear his words clearly, or if instead of muttering he would talk louder, but no. He had to pace and mutter. Each time he moved away, she lost his words completely. When he neared, she'd catch bits and pieces. From what she could gather, he worried about somebody interrupting his work and was pissed off too, from the sound of his voice. She was trying to make sense of it when his pacing and words abruptly stopped.

"Oh, shit," she muttered again. *Please don't let him open the closet.* She hadn't left a single trace of her presence in the house, she hoped. He wouldn't know she hunkered down in here, yet if he decided he needed a jacket, he'd find her. If he was the killer, Circe and Zelda would find her body displayed like Jesus on the cross somewhere out in the woods, with her eyes gone. The mere thought made her stomach roll hard enough that she almost threw up beneath the raincoat, camo jacket, and hoodies.

Her hope for salvation soared when a door slammed and a moment later a car engine came to life. Could she be lucky enough to have him leave? *Thank you, God.* As much as she wanted to run right this second, she waited just to make sure. No sense risking discovery this close to escape. As she waited, her phone vibrated in her pocket, and she sent up another prayer of thanks that she'd thought to turn off the ringer. She didn't even pull it out of her pocket to look at the display, afraid the light it would generate might give away her hiding place.

After five minutes, she cracked the door, grateful for the darkness. "Thank you, God." This time she said the prayer out loud.

She stood, her legs protesting after the long squat beneath the coats. When the tingling in her legs subsided, she turned toward the back of the house and the rear door that would let her leave the same way she'd gotten in. As she passed the office, she paused in the still-open doorway. Again the thought flitted through her mind that ten minutes and she'd have all she needed. The keyboard beckoned to her, and her fingers flexed at her sides. Good sense screamed at her to move her ass and get out of this house. Temptation packed a powerful punch. She opted for good sense.

Kat let herself out the back door, making sure the door clicked behind her. The darkness that had fallen while she hid came as a comfort. She didn't breathe freely until she sat back inside her car with the doors locked.

The Seeker badged himself into the office. Easy enough to do, even at night. Staff remained here at all times. The nature of the beast, so to speak. It also wasn't that unusual for him to be here at odd hours. Like the majority of the staff, he worked a normal eight-to-five schedule. A small staff worked the swing and graveyard shifts. Occasionally, he would help out, so coming and going late at night or in the wee hours wouldn't raise an alarm. He banked on that.

"Hey, Joe." He greeted the swing-shift supervisor as he headed toward his workstation.

"I didn't know you were working tonight?" Joe leaned back in his chair as he looked up.

The Seeker shook his head. "No, man. Not working, but I forgot my wallet, of all things. Got all the way home before I noticed. Figured since I had to come get it, I'd finish the report I left hanging earlier."

"Sorry, dude. Sucks when you have to come back downtown."

He shrugged and smiled. "Not the first time. Won't be the last."

"I hear ya." Joe leaned forward again and returned his concentration to his computer. Like everyone around here when they were wrapped up in a project, he tuned out the Seeker as if he had never been there.

Perfect. Joe wouldn't bother him again. He sat down in front of his own computer and logged on. It took him less than five minutes to get into the HR program and find what he needed. He wasn't a hacker and didn't have the ability to crack password-protected programs. What he did possess held more power: charm. All he'd had to do to get the password was to entrance the young HR tech, Patty. Not that she gave it to him outright. She might be young, but she had the kind of ethics this place demanded. No, he'd been able to gain her trust enough that she allowed him into her personal space. With his quick mind, it took one time of watching over her shoulder as she logged in to decipher her password. That password worked like magic right now.

He jotted down the info he'd been seeking, folded the piece of paper, and stuffed it into his front pocket. He logged off his computer and stood. As he walked out, he held up his wallet so Joe could see it. "See you, man." Joe waved a hand without looking up. Show a person what they expected to see, and no questions were asked. Once more he proved how much a master he could be when it came to the craft of making people see what he wanted them to.

The biggest hurdle at the moment? His own desire to push forward. He wanted to race out to the old homestead and grab one of his ready-packed black bags with the shiny tools and prefilled syringes. He wanted to do his work right this second. It wasn't the time, and even though he knew it, he hated it. Of course, that it took effort meant it would be all the more satisfying when he could finally go out, and he had the self-discipline to wait until the right time presented itself. Not that it would take long. Twenty-four hours. Forty-eight at the most. The anticipation would kill him just as it would feed his joy. The one he had planned would be as exciting as the first one. Maybe more so, because it would bring a new dimension to his work that he'd never considered before. He could hardly wait, but wait he would.

The second he walked back into the house he stopped and looked around. Something felt off. The same feeling he'd had when his two coworkers abruptly stopped talking washed over him now. Slowly he walked through, turning on lights as he went and scanning each room. Nothing appeared out of place. All seemed to be as he left it. As he always left it.

Satisfied that his home was undisturbed, he wrote off the feeling as a side effect of the anticipation building for his next great work. As he sat down in front of his computer and began to sketch out the details of his next grand plan, warmth flowed through him, and any lingering unease melted away.

Chapter Twenty-one

Vi stood on the porch with her cell phone on speaker. "Is it like her to be gone this time of day?" Vi asked Circe. It seemed to her that Lucy expected dinner, and the fact that Kat had left her here didn't feel right. They might have only known each other a short time, but in that time she'd already picked up on the incredible bond between the woman and her dog. Then there were the other animals on the farm. She wouldn't bail on any of them. Something seemed definitely wrong here.

"Maybe she ran a quick errand?" Circe appeared to be thinking along the same lines as Vi had been when she first got here.

"I've been here over an hour. She hasn't fed Lucy or any of the other animals. I checked." She'd felt bad for the livestock when she realized feeding hadn't happened, but she was no farmgirl and, without specific directions, didn't have a clue what to do. At the same time, she couldn't just leave them, and so she'd done her best to feed everyone, even Lucy, after she'd taken her back to her place and given her some chicken left over from her lunch. Kat would have to double-check her efforts when she got back. *If* she got back, a little voice whispered in the back of her head. She shook her head. She refused to think that way.

Lucy leaned into her legs, and her depressing thoughts vanished. She reached down and ran her free hand over her head.

"Okay. You're right. That doesn't sound like Kat," Circe said.

"Something's wrong."

"I'm getting the same feeling. Hang tight there. Diana and I are on the way."

"Thank you." She ended the call and looked down, dismayed to see her battery had dropped to 3 percent. Damn, what if Kat tried to call?

Rather than wait outside as her phone died completely and she risked missing a call, she ran back to her house, where she'd left the charger on the kitchen counter. Lucy trotted with her, and Vi had the feeling that Lucy didn't want to be left alone. Fine with her. She didn't particularly feel like being alone either.

Immediately after she plugged the phone into the charger and saw the little lightning bolt, she punched the redial button for Kat. Just as it had done earlier, the phone rang once and then went to voice mail. That made her worry more. Kat would answer if just out running errands, right? Well, except for the law that prohibited the use of cell phones in the car without a hands-free device. She knew Kat had that technology because she'd used it this morning when Vi had called her. That would make it perfectly legal to take a call even while driving. What that meant? She should be answering her phone.

She didn't like to feel helpless. That feeling had been driving her obsession with finding her mother's true killer for years. The drive to do something pushed her now to discover Kat's whereabouts. Maybe she was blowing this all out of proportion. Or possibly her unsettled feeling was right on, and that's precisely why she'd wasted no time in calling Circe and Diana.

Gratitude filled her when she saw headlights swing into the driveway. From her house they were hard to see, but she'd been watching for them. They'd gotten here quicker than she would have thought, and gratitude filled her. She ran out the door and toward Kat's house, Lucy behind her at first and then overtaking her. As she got closer, it surprised her to see Kat's vehicle, not Circe and Diana's. A surge of relief flooded her as she picked up speed. Lucy beat her to Kat. She jumped and barked even though Kat still sat behind the wheel. It was the first time she'd seen Lucy act like that, and she realized the dog had been as worried as her human companion.

"Where were you?" She realized she was yelling and that someone would have to be deaf to miss the panic in her voice. What a good way to show Kat she was a calm, sane individual.

Kat almost flew out of the car. "That was fucking crazy." If Kat was thrown off by Vi's panic, she didn't let on.

Vi ran to Kat and threw her arms around her. Her heart beat like a drum, and she breathed hard and rapidly. "Are you hurt? What happened? Where were you?"

Kat hugged her back with a brittle laugh. "I'm fine. Really. Come on." She wiggled out of Vi's embrace and took her hand. "I have to feed the animals, and then I'll tell you everything. You are not going to believe what I did this afternoon."

Vi stepped back. "Everyone's fed, including some snacks for Lucy. Tell me now."

The way Vi ran to her and wrapped her in a warm embrace thrilled Kat. She could have stayed in her arms for hours. But Lucy and the rest of the crew wouldn't be pleased if she did. As excited as she'd been about her B&E adventure, she'd raced back here, worried for her animals. To find out Vi had taken care of them touched her heart. This woman kept getting better and better. Kat didn't neglect her charges.

And she didn't hide in closets of houses she broke into either. Breaking and entering wasn't a good plan under any circumstances. Doubly not a good plan with Diana as a close friend. Diana could take friendship only so far, and felony was a line in the sand that Kat knew she wouldn't cross.

It must be a day for firsts. Kind of like pulling up and finding herself in the warm embrace of a woman who made her shudder all over. If she had that kind of reaction with a simple hug, what would it be like to make love to her? Someday she hoped she'd have the chance to find out.

Right now, while the majority of her herd had been fed, she still had a hungry dog to attend to. Snacks might have been good enough to tide Lucy over, but her dog did have her dinner standards. Vi followed her into the house and waited quietly while she prepared Lucy's dinner. She made it extra yummy tonight by adding some cut-up roast beef and a little gravy. Lucy deserved the treat.

The whole time Kat worked, she could feel Vi's eyes on her. She didn't mind and she didn't blame her. She had a whole lot of explaining to do and, now that she was safe in her own home, was anxious to share her adventure into PI land. Lights flashing through the window made her step into the living room and glance out the big front window.

"What are Circe and Diana doing here?" Diana's unmarked but unmistakable cop car had just pulled up in front of the house.

"Oh, oops. That would be my fault. I called them."

"You called Circe? I mean that's cool and all, given you're sisters. I'm a little surprised though. I guess I thought you hadn't had much time to get comfortable with that relationship yet."

Vi shrugged. "You're right on that score. It's still weirding me out that I have a sister and a father, for that matter. That's not why I called her. You missing had me a lot more scared than uncomfortable about reaching out."

"Missing? I wasn't missing." That thought hadn't occurred to her. It wasn't like she'd been gone for days. She'd definitely been up to a bit of mischief, but missing? Not even close.

Now Vi put her hands on her hips and met Kat's eyes. "You might have known that. I didn't. When I got home and you weren't here, the animals weren't fed, and Lucy was pacing, I got scared. Lucy was here alone and kept trying to get me to crawl inside through the dog door. Clearly she was upset. It was more than the animals too. Your house was dark, and you didn't answer your phone. I tried you several times, and it went straight to voice mail."

That explained the couple of times her phone had vibrated. It occurred to her now that she hadn't turned her ringer back on or looked at the missed calls after she snuck out of the house. Once she got out of there, she'd just wanted to get home. Looking at it from Vi's perspective, she could understand. "Okay. You're right. If I'd been in your shoes, I'd have thought the same thing."

"So where were you?" It appeared that Vi's patience had hit its limit.

She couldn't help it. She smiled. Diana most assuredly wouldn't when she spilled. "Ah, well, you know the guy you asked me to check out?"

Vi nodded. "Yes, of course."

"I kind of broke into his house."

❖

The Seeker pushed back from his desk and thought about the plan he'd just drawn up. Everything about it screamed perfect, and the thought of what he would do next thrilled him.

He'd believed the inclusion of the new violet section the biggest high he'd had in a while, and now he knew he'd been way off base.

Expanding beyond the basic color selections was the right direction, yet it wasn't the only direction. Many more prospects existed out there, and today the universe had shown him that fact.

He didn't want to wait. No matter how hard he tried to self-talk himself into slowing down, he failed. As far as he was concerned, he was on a roll, and he intended to go with it. Despite the body count piling up, nobody had the slightest clue that he was responsible for all of it. No reason to believe things would change. He believed himself better than ever and had nothing to worry about.

The lure of discovering the progeny of a very special one here in the city filled him to overflowing with excitement. Too much to ignore. He had to have her, and he had to have her now. Screw waiting. By God, he would go for it. He grabbed the info he'd sent to the printer from the tray and then turned off the light in his office. He'd felt odd when he'd first walked into the house, as if somehow things weren't right. As he'd worked at his computer, watched his videos, and made his plans, that unsettling feeling that his space had been invaded faded. Everything fell into the familiar routine, which made him a happy man.

"Take that, old man," he said as he stomped a foot on the hardwood floor. While at least a hundred square feet smaller, this office was a carbon copy of his father's home office, right down to the stupid expensive floor. His father would hate that he'd copied it, and that's one of the reasons it gave him joy whenever he worked in here. "Showed you, didn't I?"

Anticipation spurred him to movement, and he wished he'd gone with his instinct earlier to run out and pick up a bag. That oversight meant he'd have to take the time to drive out and retrieve the things he'd need from his father's old house. In a way the detour worked. He did his best work late nights or early mornings, as the case might be. By the time he picked up the bag and drove out to the address on the paper he'd tossed onto the passenger seat, the timing would be just about right.

When he got near the driveway of his family home, he once again turned off his headlights. He'd go in like a ghost and out like one, which made him chuckle when he thought about how many he'd turned into ghosts.

When he parked in the driveway and got out of the car, he'd intended to grab one of the packed black messenger bags and leave immediately. Get right to work. Best intentions and all that dribble. Once he neared his collection, the draw became irresistible. He couldn't ignore his compulsion to stop, unlock the freezer door, and open it wide. Cold air slapped his cheeks, and he breathed in deeply. The kaleidoscope of colors filled him with indescribable joy. This setup was a stroke of genius on his part. Never before had he enjoyed his collection like this, and to witness its growth amazed him.

After five minutes of drinking in the view, as much as he hated to do it, he closed and locked the door. A glance at his watch confirmed the time had arrived to grab his bag and go. Time to take things full circle, and that thought made him smile. He headed for his car, intending to leave right away, when he changed his mind. He dropped the bag into the passenger seat first and then walked to the back door of the house. With the key he always had with him, he unlocked the door and stepped inside.

He rarely went into what he thought of as the prison of his childhood. The only bright spot the house held for him was the knowledge that his destiny had been born inside these walls. Once inside his father's office with the dusty Brazilian teak floor, he stopped in the middle of the room. Just standing in the opulence made the scars on his back ache and his knees throb. It always happened the moment he stepped foot inside the lavish office that had been his father's undisputed personal kingdom. While his mother lay dying in her bed upstairs, women would come to him here, the doors locked behind them, their cries and moans making him cover his ears with his hands.

In this room his father had met with all the rich and powerful supporters who made sure he kept his seat in the Senate so he could represent their ultraconservative agenda. He often wondered if they beat their wives and children too. If they turned their backs on modern medicine because God would heal the sick. If they held their marriage vows in such little regard. Not that he had a problem with conservatives in general. Or liberals, for that matter. Each group had its good points and its bad ones. He had a problem with the kind of men and women like his father who used their God and their power to hurt and destroy others. They were monsters, and he took pride in the fact that he'd been able to stop at least one of them.

If the world knew of his work, he had no doubt that in certain circles he too would be referred to as a monster. They'd be wrong. He was nothing like his father or his good buddies. His labor had a higher purpose. The joy he took in it came simply as a by-product of doing what others were afraid to. Of pushing the accepted boundaries in the pursuit of knowledge. Of hearing the whispered words of gods and going forward with them.

No, he wasn't a monster. Far from it.

Chapter Twenty-two

Vi shook her head. She couldn't believe what she'd just heard. "You're kidding me, right? Tell me you did not break into his house." True, she'd called Kat this morning and asked her to do a little sleuthing on one of her new coworkers. But she'd simply intended for Kat to use her uber computer skills to mine the web and see what she could find on the surface. That was all.

Kat gave her a lopsided smile as she shook her head. "That would be a no, I kid you not. I really did let myself into his house."

"How?" If he turned out to be the guy they were looking for, Kat had put herself in serious danger. Her stomach lurched.

"Oh, you know, a friend who happens to be a former juvenile delinquent with a penchant for picking locks and who may have shown me how to pick said locks one night when we had a few too many beers."

"You did not." She didn't want to believe Kat would do something that dumb, yet something in the tone of her voice told her otherwise.

"Did, and for my first attempt I have to say I'm a regular Houdini."

Her worst fear confirmed. She really did do something that dumb. "Oh, dear God, Kat. That's a felony."

She shrugged. "Yeah, I suppose it is."

"You suppose?"

Kat tilted her head toward the front door. "I think we better go let them in, and I'll tell all of you what I did and what I found."

The two women coming up the front steps presented another problem. Or one of them did anyway. "You're not serious? Diana is a cop. She'll have to arrest you. You broke into someone's house."

That remark stopped Kat, and a strange look crossed her face.

"Uh. Didn't really think that through. Maybe I can give her what I know as a hypothetical. We could maybe not mention the felony part."

"You're walking a fine line." Vi had been around enough law enforcement to know what would fly and what wouldn't. Like so many cops, she'd heard it all. She'd seen it all. Well, except for this situation. This would be the first time she'd been around a computer genius turned farmer who broke into a suspect's house because she'd learned how to pick locks while drunk. Not that he was an official suspect. More like a potential suspect.

"Wouldn't be the first time. Can't be in my line of business without balancing on a tightrope now and again. I'll make it okay, I swear."

Vi put her hands on Kat's shoulders and looked her in the eyes. "This is different, and you know it. I will not have you going to jail because of me."

She liked the smile that crossed Kat's face. It almost made her want to forget being angry with her. "That's the sweetest thing anyone's ever said to me."

Vi shook her head and couldn't help but laugh. Being firm with Kat took a lot more effort than she would have imagined. "Clearly you need to get out more."

"I'll work on it. Might need a little help." She winked and bumped Vi with a shoulder before going to the front door. "Better get this over with. Putting it off won't make it any better."

Vi wasn't quite so sure. She felt responsible. If she hadn't called Kat with the suspect's name and her suspicions, she never would have gone over to his house and taken an unnecessary risk. She would be more careful in the future. On the other hand, Kat's drive and enthusiasm had an intoxicating quality. She'd taken charge of her life and made the kind of changes Vi would be petrified to do. That is, if she wanted to change. Her path had been solid in her heart and soul for so long that the thought of not following through made her almost ill.

That didn't mean she didn't appreciate Kat's impressive courage and determination. She saw a question that needed an answer, and she charged forward to find one. Felony be damned.

Vi put a hand on her arm before she opened the door. "Are you sure? I haven't known Diana long, but I have a feeling she won't take this well."

Kat shrugged. "What's she gonna do? Arrest me?"

Vi looked at her and nodded. She wasn't smiling any longer. "Exactly."

❖

Kat didn't disagree with Vi's observations. Despite her flippant attitude, Diana might very possibly slap her ass in jail for her B&E episode. The down and dirty of it was, she'd broken the law, and it didn't matter that her pursuit held a higher purpose. Diana probably had a pair of handcuffs with her name on them.

She refused to let on to Vi that she had any anxiety about what she'd done and its potential consequences. Besides, denial was a very powerful force. All she had to do was hang on to the denial that Diana would go all five-oh on her, and it would be fine. No harm. No foul.

Circe didn't let Kat even open her mouth. "Where have you been? You've had us all worried. What a terrible thing to do to poor Vi. Keep that up, and she'll race right back to Alaska."

Kat looked at Vi and then back to Circe. "I've already apologized profusely to Vi. Now, I'll apologize to you. Sorry."

Circe made a sound and shook her head. "You don't sound very sorry, but I'll take it. Now where the hell have you been? Given we drove all the way out here, you owe us an explanation."

Kat shrugged and gave them her best noncommittal look. "Nowhere important."

"Bull. You and I both know you'd never leave Lucy hanging come dinnertime unless the world just fell apart. Did the world fall apart?" Circe's hands were on her hips. Diana stood behind her staring intensely into Kat's eyes. For a detective accustomed to interrogating people, she let her wife take the lead on this one, and Kat was glad. Easier to deal with her familiar teammate than an experienced interrogator.

"Well..."

Vi stepped up and put a hand on her shoulder. "You need to tell them, Kat. All of it."

She liked the feel of Vi's hand on her shoulder, and she covered it with her own. Yeah, that felt good. Kat just wasn't sure she needed to tell Circe and Diana about all her afternoon's activities. A nice abbreviated version would surely due. "Vi called me this morning with a little bit of a lead."

"What?" Diana's head snapped around, and she stared at Vi, hard. "Why didn't you share that information with me? I thought we agreed last night that we were all in the loop at all times."

Vi looked a little sheepish. "It was nothing concrete. Just something that came up at work about specimen jars. I figured Kat could do some initial footwork, and then we'd all talk about it tonight."

Kat jumped in to take the pressure off Vi. She'd known Diana long enough to have been around her when she shifted into cop mode. Vi hadn't, and she felt responsible for putting her in the direct line of fire now. "I was supposed to call and let you know because Vi was at work. My magic fingers and I got caught up, and I forgot to." She waggled her fingers in the air. "Then I figured we could share everything with you tonight. I mean, we're only talking a few hours."

Diana still didn't look happy. "Suppose I buy that line, which, just for the record, I really don't. Where were you, and why did Vi have to call us in?"

"Well." She looked away. "That."

"Yes, that."

Vi's hand dropped from her shoulder. Instead of putting distance between them as Kat got close to confession time, Vi took her hand in hers. "Tell her," Vi said.

She might have sounded all brave and tough before, but now that she was face-to-face with Diana, her face stern and a gun at her belt, brave and tough went right out the window. Now she felt more like the little kid who got caught shoplifting a candy bar and the store owners were about to call the parents.

"Spit it out, Kat." This time Circe spoke.

Oh, what the hell. "Okay. Okay. Here's how it went down. After I did my computer sleuthing, I decided to do some hands-on work."

"What do you mean, hands-on work?" Diana's hand rested on her gun, her fingers tapping.

Kat looked down at the floor. "I kind of let myself into his house."

"Tell me you went in through an unlocked door."

She looked down at her feet. "Sure, unlocked." *After I picked it.*

Diana threw her hands up in the air. "Sonofabitch. I don't want to know any more." She turned and walked out of the room. Or maybe more like stomped out of there.

Now Kat did feel terrible. As she'd been driving home, she'd been pretty proud of herself for being all private-investigator-like with cool lock-picking skills. When face-to-face with a pissed-off detective, she found that pride wasn't the emotion that coursed through her now. She looked pleadingly at Circe. "I know it was wrong. I get that and I'm sorry." She paused and couldn't help the smile that twitched at the corners of her mouth as she met Circe's eyes. "You want to know what I found?"

Circe glanced at the kitchen where Diana had retreated, and her eyes lit up. "Hell, yes."

❖

The familiar glow intensified as the Seeker drove out of the city and toward the outskirts, where the houses thinned and the properties were measured in acres, not feet. The nicest thing about the wide spread of homes was the privacy. No need to change locations, no need to be concerned about noise.

Often, he'd felt that the fates had conspired against him when they brought him into the world as *his* child. Other times, it seemed fortuitous. He had first learned about drugs that could be used to subdue at one of his father's pressing-the-flesh events. The who's who of society in eastern Washington would fill their mausoleum of a home, stand around with drinks, and brag about themselves. One particular recurring guest had been a doctor who bragged about what he'd slip into the drinks of unsuspecting attractive women. The colorful doctor's boasts about his sexual exploits didn't much impress the Seeker. He had, however, been very interested in the drugs he'd used to accomplish his trysts. A few drinks and the good old doc had been more than happy to share his vast knowledge with a willing student.

The recipe proved most successful for the doctor and, initially, for the Seeker as well. As his own knowledge and experience grew, he tested and refined his version of the cocktail until it worked far more effectively for his purposes. He smiled now, thinking of the pompous bastard who finally got his dick caught in a wringer. He'd used his drugs on the wrong woman, and she'd had him brought up on charges. Kind of a gutsy move in that day, but she would have none of it. Once she'd come forward and his behavior became public knowledge, the doctor with the wandering dick went down in a blaze not so glorious. He might have felt better about his fall from grace had he known of the impression he'd made on the preteen with brains and a mission.

The night grew darker as he drove along the semi-rural roads. In this area with no street lights, numbers on the mailboxes were difficult to make out. Hard but not impossible, particularly when on a mission as critical as his. Tonight would be one of his best. It amazed him that he'd never thought to work generational before. The potential power he would be able to capture in that scenario went beyond mind-boggling. His thoughts were already spinning on where to take it next. So many possibilities and all of them thrilling.

Everyone had some family, whether they were close either emotionally or geographically. With a little work, he could make those familial connections all over the country. His work would grow like a well-tended crop, and the varied locations spread across a continent would make any chance of discovery impossible. Perfect in every way.

Even this one. The work he'd done in the immediate area of late was admittedly out of the ordinary for him. To be safe, he should gear it down, except that with his skill level he didn't really believe it necessary. Nobody would figure out his identity, and teasing law enforcement proved to be the kind of fun he would be hard-pressed to give up.

Tonight would be his last local one. He promised. Then he'd go back to his normal style and work in other areas throughout the country, as well as Canada. He did pride himself on being international. He might even give Mexico a try. Sunshine, palm trees, and blue ocean. Definitely going to make a visit to Mexico.

Once he had his newest piece of the collection, he'd return to researching his next trip. What he had planned for tonight would be big enough to keep him satisfied for a long time, or at least long enough to get some scheduled time off for R&R. Missoula was a nice place to visit this time of year. Did anyone have relatives in Montana? The thought of researching that possibility made him happy.

The Seeker hummed as he drove, squinting to read the numbers on the mailboxes. When he noticed the address he searched for highlighted in the beam of his headlights, he slowed. "Yes."

The driveway was so long, he could barely see the house from the road. Instead of driving down it, he decided to turn the car around and get back on the main road. About two hundred feet north, he found a spot on the shoulder wide enough that he could park there without catching attention. Given he hadn't seen another car in a while, nobody would notice anyway.

From the back seat he grabbed the black bag and slung it over his shoulder. Showtime. In his dark clothes, all he had to do was walk along the fences that bordered the driveway. The shadows swallowed him as if he were part of them, and in a way he was. This adventure promised to be fantastic. At least that's what he was thinking until he saw the cop car parked in front of the house. What the fuck?

Just seeing that car made him mad enough to wish he'd brought a gun. He'd go in shooting and kill anyone and everyone inside. How dare they be here? How dare they spoil his night. His project. His destiny.

At the sound of voices, he dropped behind a prickly fire bush wide enough and tall enough to provide cover. Two women walked out the door laughing. Laughing? That didn't make sense. If they were expecting him, they should be afraid and most certainly not chuckling like a bunch of schoolgirls. The cops knew of his work and possessed an intimate knowledge of his capabilities.

Behind the two who stepped out onto the porch followed two other women: One he didn't know. One he did.

"Damn, damn, damn," he whispered under his breath. This complicated things. The first two women were making their way to the cop car, though not very quickly. Their leisurely movements could work to his advantage. If he could get back to his car without being noticed, he'd be gone without anyone being the wiser He was far enough away and the shadows were so deep, he doubted any of them would notice.

Not one of the foursome did, except for some goddamn goats that decided to scream like little kids and run as he made his way past the small enclosure. By the time he reached his car, he was breathing hard and wondering if flashing lights would be racing down the driveway any second. When they didn't, it surprised him. Then again, maybe the goats did that kind of stuff all the time so no one paid any attention. He'd go with that.

As much as he wanted to stay and finish what he'd started, he had to admit defeat. Not defeat exactly, more like postponement. Tonight was out. Tomorrow was a different story.

Chapter Twenty-Three

Vi was surprised at how well Diana took Kat's news, which was to say she basically stuck her fingers in her ears and muttered "la la la la." For a cop she found that unexpected and pretty impressive. Circe was a different story. Like Vi, she'd been anxious to hear all about her adventure, in minute detail, and once Kat got going, she rolled. When she finished relating the story, it boiled down to a pretty big nothing. For the risk she'd taken breaking into a house, the payoff was nil. She hadn't found anything to help them identify the killer.

Yet Kat's words came faster and faster as she got into her story, and the glow on her face made her even more attractive. After Kat wound her story down, Circe yelled toward the kitchen, and Diana finally came back into the room. Then Vi shared what she'd learned from Sharman. Kat added the details of her computer search, leaving out the breaking and entering now that they were all back in the room together. Diana promised to do some searching of her own and said she'd let them know what she could.

As much as Vi was beginning to enjoy being around her newfound sister, when Circe and Diana left, she felt good. Not because they made her uncomfortable but because then just the two of them had some privacy. Diana left with a scowl and a stern warning not to do anything else stupid. Vi had no problem heeding that warning. With Kat it remained to be seen. Her new friend seemed to be contemplating a shift in careers from small farmer to private investigator. Given her work today, it really wasn't a stretch. Not that she'd tell Kat, but she wasn't half bad at it.

After the taillights of Diana's car disappeared, Kat whirled and smiled. "Wanna drink?"

Vi smiled back and nodded. Why not? "Sure."

"What's your poison? Wine? Beer? Something with more of a punch?"

"Actually, I could go for a beer."

"You got it."

While she waited, Vi sat on the sofa and rubbed Lucy's ears. Strangely enough, Lucy had stuck very close since she'd come and gotten her earlier. The dog had seemed as worried about Kat as she had been, and now they were kindred souls comforting each other. She would be lying to say she wasn't becoming quite attached to Lucy… and her partner. Funny how things could change so quickly. Given what had happened to her mother, this turn of events shouldn't come as a big surprise. She'd learned early how fast life could change.

Kat returned and handed her an ice-cold IPA. "Come on." She waved her toward the office. "We have some work to do."

Vi wasn't sure she felt up to anything else. It had been a long and eventful day. Throw in the stress of Kat's disappearance and her brain was fried. "Haven't you done enough today?"

Kat winked. "Oh, my darling, Vi, I'm just getting started."

"Diana won't be happy with you."

She tapped the side of her head with one finger. "Hey, I'm only using my brain this time. She can't get mad at me for that."

Vi stood up and followed her down the hall. Kat had a point. They couldn't get into too much trouble checking information via the internet. At least she hoped they couldn't.

In her office, Kat pulled another chair close to the one she used. "Sit." Vi sat. "Here's what I think we do next."

"Do tell." She took a pull on the beer. It was cold and biting. She liked it.

"Remember how I told you earlier that our guy has an interesting history. Prominent family. Mom dies. Dad goes missing. Junior ends up going career military. Twenty years in."

"Got it, and I agree it's interesting, but it doesn't really mean he's our guy. You found absolutely nothing in his house that would indicate he's done anything illegal or, more to the point, in this case, evil."

"True enough, but stay with me. Here's what I'm thinking. I dug around in his background using my preternatural computer skills, which are astonishingly good, by the way, thanks for asking. I didn't realize how much I missed this kind of stuff until you asked me to break them out of cold storage."

"Glad I could help. Wish it had been for something less distasteful." She still liked the way Kat had really come alive the last couple of days. She'd liked her before. She liked her better now.

Kat turned and looked at her, and the expression in her eyes made Vi's heart flutter. "If I can help in any way to bring down the man who killed your mother, I will do it. This sonofabitch has to be stopped, and it looks to me like the cops are sucking a hinny. Just don't tell Diana I said that."

"I won't, I promise, and thank you." She put a hand on Kat's. "Really, thank you."

Kat nodded and whirled back around to the computer. "So here's my thought process. I checked out Junior, and you know what we've found so far, which is pretty much squat. Now I think it's time to check out his dear old mom and dad."

"I thought you said they were dead."

"Mom confirmed dead. Dad, oddly enough, has been missing for decades and is presumed dead. Doesn't that seem odd to you?" She didn't wait for Vi to answer. "Let's see what we can find out about them, and maybe it will tell us a little more about Junior, and why after all these years he hasn't bothered to go through the motions to declare his daddy dead."

She liked the way Kat was thinking.

Two hours and two beers later, Vi leaned back in her chair and shook her head. "You, Kat, have some serious skills."

Kat held up her hands and spread her fingers wide. They ached a touch, a good kind of ache. What they'd managed to pull up thus far possessed a fascinating quality. Politics, power, and intrigue. All the required elements for a good made-for-TV movie. "So, looking at this, wouldn't you think that after all this time, pretty much anybody would transfer an asset that valuable into his or her own name?"

Kat was talking about the massive home on acreage they had found, still in the name of his dead mother. Like any piece of property these days, the computer search yielded not only the property-assessment records listing the titled owner but also actual pictures of the property. It was big, expensive, and not quite as well-maintained as some of the neighbors' estates, as if testifying to the fact its primary owner remained MIA, according to the county records.

"I would tend to agree. She's been gone since he was a kid. Even if it passed to his father, by now the title should be in his name."

"Makes you wonder why our boy hasn't done that yet. How many hoops did you have to jump through after your mother and grandmother passed away?"

"Too many, but it had to be done. I never even considered leaving things hanging. Maybe he's hoping his father will return?"

The whole missing-father thing made for some pretty bizarre reading. Considering his prominence, she found it curious they'd never solved the case. Then again, why should she be surprised, given what had happened in the case of Vi's mother. At least here they hadn't put an innocent man in jail for something he hadn't done. "Or knows he won't and he wants a place to hide away."

"That's an intriguing idea. Could be. We'll have to pass this info along to Diana. She can go deeper with it."

"Yeah. I'll do that." Kat reached for her cell and then laid it back down. "I think maybe tomorrow. She might not appreciate a midnight call."

Vi jumped up. "Midnight? Crap. I need to get to bed. I have to work in the morning."

"You've worked every day since you got here."

Vi nodded. "I know, and it's been a lot, but with the murders, it's been all hands on deck, and I feel like I have to be there."

Kat put a hand on her arm, her fingers warm. "I understand, but please don't go."

Vi shook her head. "I really need to. We can discuss this in more detail tomorrow, after I get home."

"I don't want to work anymore tonight." Kat hated herself for the desperation that echoed in her voice. She'd hate herself more if she let this moment pass in silence. "Please," Kat said softly. "Stay."

For what felt like an eternity, Vi looked at her and said nothing. When Kat was about to give up, Vi nodded. "Okay."

Her hands were trembling when Kat took them in hers. She led her out of the office and down to her bedroom—a nice room, with a large bed covered by a dark-blue comforter. She said a silent thank you that she'd actually made the bed this morning.

Vi turned to face Kat, making the first move. She put her hands on her cheeks and leaned in to kiss her. It started soft. It didn't stay that way. A fire that had been building since the moment she'd stepped through the front door and had seen Vi's beautiful face burst into a conflagration she couldn't control. Her own hands touched and caressed.

She didn't recall taking off her clothes, but here she was naked and stretched out on the bed next to Vi. They didn't bother to remove the comforter. Vi's touch against her bare skin was enough to drive her wild. Her kisses were hot and intoxicating.

No words were necessary. Everything existed in the contact, skin to skin. Their bodies found a rhythm soothing and thrilling at the same time. Each touch created a wave of excitement that brought her nearer and nearer to the edge. Each kiss made her want more.

Vi's hands, palms down, smoothed down her legs, and she arched her back in response. So close. Oh, dear God, she'd never felt anything like this before. She'd never wanted another woman like this before.

"You're so beautiful," Vi whispered in her ear. "Every inch of you." Her fingers brushed down her body from her nipples to her abdomen and finally to the spot between her legs that made her groan. Her lips met Vi's in a long, deep kiss that set everything on fire.

The world melted around Kat as her orgasm took her away on waves of pleasure. Nothing else mattered except the woman in her arms, and in her bed.

The Seeker became so despondent over the failed mission that he couldn't bring himself to return home. It would be too quiet and lonely. He'd never failed before, and he didn't relish the feeling. This one would have been very special too, and it hurt him to be denied what he was due.

Instead, he turned and followed the familiar path to his past, his boyhood home. Being there helped him remember where he'd come from and what had molded him into the master he had become. It also helped soothe him when he felt disquieted. There where pain had hardened him and God had abandoned him, he found a strange sort of solace. It reminded him that when the world darkened and the forces appeared to conspire against him, patience would rule the day, and in the end, he would come out triumphant.

Shielded from prying eyes by fences, trees, and shrubs, he nonetheless liked to operate on the side of caution. Instead of flipping on the interior lights, he chose the soft glow of candlelight. In his father's office, he lined votives on the desktop and along the mantel of the fireplace. Their flickering light gave the room a homey ambience that made him shake his head. His father had never been the kind of person anyone with a clue would have described as homey.

He'd carried in the unused case from the car and set it down on the top of the desk. That he'd been denied the opportunity to use the contents tonight made him sad. He could think of only one thing to ease his disquiet: touch his tools. The feel of them against his fingers would be so much better than doing nothing. He opened the case and first pulled out the neatly folded plastic sheet. In the middle of the floor he spread it out and smoothed it with his hands, the plastic soft and pliable. At one edge he lined up the two filled syringes, two brand-new scalpels, a pair of latex gloves, a bottle of alcohol, and the empty specimen jar he'd carried in his pocket.

He stood back and surveyed his work, expecting a rush of feeling to begin. Nothing happened. Even this beautiful display didn't soothe his soul tonight. The tried-and-true fell flat. Then a thought occurred to him that made him smile. He got up, pulled his special key from his pocket, and went out to the garage.

To make his vision come to life, it took more trips than he thought. At last he completed his task. Along the mantel, in front of the votives, on the side tables and the low table positioned in front of the sofa, his precious collection brought beauty to a room once marked by ugliness. Now as he stood staring at the fruits of his labors, pleasure filled his heart. He couldn't put into words the incredible joy of the soul that each jar represented.

His mind, body, and soul quieted at last. This was what he needed to bring him back to center. He would be able to rest at last. No need to go home either. He lay down in the middle of the plastic sheet, his legs together and his arms spread wide. Peace settled over the Seeker, and he was smiling as he drifted into dreamless sleep.

Chapter Twenty-four

The smile on Vi's face when she walked into the ME's office the next morning had nothing to do with work and everything to do with last night. She hadn't felt this good in forever. Maybe never. Something about Kat was infectious, even in the face of the horrible things they'd encountered. She exuded hope, which Vi had needed for a really long time.

The hope came multilayered too, a surprising and unexpected twist. Her heart felt lighter, her anticipation for the beginning of her new life much deeper, and a certainty that she would finally succeed in finding the person who killed her mother solid. The latter was no longer a question of "if" in her mind. Now it was "when."

Dr. Kelsey came flying through the door with a scowl. This was the first time she'd seen such an expression on his face. So far he'd come across as an exceptionally skilled pathologist who did his work with dedication and pride while also maintaining a genial and collegial manner. The darkness on his face bothered her for reasons she couldn't define.

"Is everything all right?" she asked him.

He shook his head. "I don't know what the hell is going on around here. First Addy doesn't show up for work yesterday, and nobody seems to know where she is. Now Alan is late, and he's not answering his phone either. Both my lead investigators are gone. The body of a young local newscaster has just been discovered, and I've got the night guy on his way. If we get more than one, I don't know what we'll do. It's not like it's something just anybody can step in and take over. This is a disaster, and it feels like all hell is breaking loose out there."

Her mind whirled. Alan wasn't here. She had to call Kat and

let her know. Before she could retreat to her workstation though, Dr. Kelsey put a hand on her arm. "Come to my office for a few minutes."

He sounded so serious, and given his already agitated mood, she wondered if he'd found out about her digging into Alan's background and planned to fire her. She didn't think she'd messed up anything else to date, and both MEs had been verbally supportive. It would be an awful, if not a fatal error, to be fired in the very field she was going to medical school to specialize in. She followed him to his office, her stomach in knots and her mind racing.

"Have a seat." Dr. Kelsey sat in his big ergonomic chair. He shuffled around the few papers on his desk as if looking for an elusive report. He finally stopped and looked up at her. "You were right."

"I was right?" She had so many things going through her mind, she was having trouble sorting through them to find the thread to this conversation.

"About the similarities between your mother's murder and the murders here. About all of it."

The pieces fell into place. She wasn't getting fired. She wanted to scream, *I knew it*. Instead, she simply said, "Thank you for letting me know."

"It's worse than we thought. First, the method of murder is not just similar. It's identical. Second, after going over this with a couple of detectives whom I consider several of the finest investigators in the county, they took your suspicions and our findings and went even deeper. It is turning out to be a very ugly picture."

The bad feeling got worse. "And?"

"And whoever this guy is, he's been killing all over the country. We have yet another bona fide serial killer, who has apparently been at work for years."

Vindication of her theories should have felt better than it did. But people had died, and to hear it from Dr. Kelsey, lots of people had died. That his findings were matching up to what they'd uncovered should have helped too. Somehow it didn't. It didn't feel good to be right. In fact it felt terrible.

"Don't worry." Dr. Kelsey must have picked up on the sadness the news brought her. "We'll get him this time. Nobody's turning a blind eye anymore, and the technology that's evolved over the last couple of years means this guy will get caught. His reign of terror is about to end."

She wanted to believe him. She didn't.

"Thank you again for letting me know." She stood up. "Anything else you need from me?"

He shook his head. "Unless you're a field investigator?" He shot her a hopeful look.

"Sorry. Fieldwork is definitely not my specialty."

"It was worth a try."

She left his office, trying not to run. She had to contact Kat. Back at her workstation, she called Kat's cell phone, which went directly to voice mail. Not again. Vi didn't even look at the assignment sheet for the day. She grabbed her keys and ran for the parking lot.

Kat understood all about choices. Sometimes she made good ones, like when she walked away to begin life again on the farm her father had purchased. Sometimes it didn't work out at all, like when she'd decided to go all in with Meg. Talk about making a bad choice. Meg had cheated on her, lied to her, and if that wasn't enough, she'd left without a word and taken their dog. She could have handled all of Meg's bullshit, if not for the dog. She loved that dog.

Then came the problem of Scooter. His obsession with her had made life miserable for almost a year. If not for the stalking laws in this state, things could have turned out very differently. With Scooter now a free man, it could all start again. She didn't believe for a moment he'd walked out of jail a reformed man. Yet now she knew how to handle him and had people who would watch her back. If he came back with the same old behavior, she would deal with him. Period.

If Kat had tended to let betrayal or dangerous obsession blacken her soul, things would be very different right now, and she'd have missed out on something wonderful. She got chills just thinking about last night, glad she'd decided to take a chance.

Now she was making another choice that had the potential to be a bad one. She knew it and had made it anyway. This PI bug had bitten her squarely in the middle of her ass, and she didn't want to resist this compulsion. Shame on her.

When Diana got wind of what she planned to do, she'd be straight-up furious. That reality didn't stop Kat from driving to the address she and Vi had dug up last night before their sojourn to the bedroom. She'd been thinking about it since she got up, and at least in her mind, it was worth a look-see.

Once she found the fancy sign with the street address on it, she eyed the driveway for a moment and then thought better of pulling in. The house wasn't visible from the street, and thus she had no way of knowing if anyone else was around. She might be doing something decidedly unwise, but she wasn't stupid.

The driveway surprised her. In one of the most expensive areas in Spokane County, from the street all looked as she would expect from a high-end piece of real estate. The farther in she walked, the more it changed from tidy to shaggy. Broken tree branches were hanging. Shrubs were overgrown and crowding what once was a long, wide drive. Weeds and wildflowers sprouted between cracks in the patterned concrete. If not for the broken vegetation she spotted down the length of the driveway, she'd think no one had been here in years.

Her keen observation skills were point-on when she neared the house and spotted the car parked in front of a garage that appeared to be big enough for at least six vehicles. The doors were down, and she didn't spot anyone outside. Kat stood in the shadows for a good five minutes and debated whether to go forward. The house looked ignored and uninhabited. It was a beautiful home, yet it seemed sad. Her mind screamed for her to turn and go home. Her heart whispered for her to go for it. The intrigue was too much to ignore. Go for it won.

If someone waited inside, and she had a feeling someone might, stealth would be prudent. Good thing she hadn't brought Lucy with her. Lucy was incredible at her job. Subtle, however, wasn't in her job description. Unlike Lucy, Kat could do low, slow, and quiet, and that's exactly what she did to get close. The whole time she remained on alert for sounds of another human being. She heard nothing, even when she stood at the back entry.

Despite all good intentions not to, Kat prepared to try her lock-picking skills again. If she did it once, she could do it again. She didn't need to. The doorknob turned easily for her. Wasn't that handy? Fear made her briefly consider giving it up. That would be the prudent thing to do. Then again, she was here with a conveniently unlocked door. She wasn't breaking and entering this time, so what was the harm? She stepped inside.

The door led into a well-appointed but decidedly large kitchen. Judging from the neighborhood, she would have expected the latest and greatest in everything. That wasn't what she saw here. The empty room didn't appear to have a single item that even suggested new and modern. The first word that came to mind: dated. Unless she was totally off base, no one had made so much as a piece of toast in here for a very long time.

Rather than charging around, she paused and listened. Still no sounds that would let her know she wasn't alone. Could she be the only one here? Maybe he used the driveway to store an unneeded automobile? Maybe only a caretaker came around every now and again. That sounded dumb even to her. If he did use the place to store a car, he had a great big garage out there. No need to leave it parked in the driveway. And no lawn guy drove a car like that. It told her one important thing: she needed to be quiet and careful.

When she didn't hear sounds of footsteps or movements, she walked silently across the kitchen and into the hallway. Not a quick or easy trip, given the size of the kitchen, the hallways and the whole frickin' house for that matter. She peeked into doorways as she inched down the hall. Like the kitchen, the rooms were tidy, without the slightest hint of recent occupation. At least until she reached a massive office across from a living room that featured a giant crucifix as its centerpiece. Somebody had a pretty clear religious bent.

She stopped in the doorway of the office and stared. "What the fuck?"

The Seeker hadn't slept so well in years. This house had been a symbol of pain, lies, and hatred for the majority of his life. As a child, his nights were long and fitful. He'd never known when he would be pulled from beneath the comforter and dragged down the stairs to the living room, where the ornate cross graced the wall above the fireplace mantel. Long before he reached adolescence, he'd learned that "sleep with one eye open" was not just a saying.

When he'd awakened on the floor of the office, he realized how far he'd come and, strangely, how much he'd become like the old man—a guy who presented a certain image to the outside world and in private morphed into someone completely different. Yet he became better than his father in every way, and the truth of that revelation enabled his restorative slumber. The failure of his mission last night had disappointed him. In the light of day, he felt as though everything was as it should be. It was all coming together. He could see it all now with an inspiring clarity. Last night had not been a failure. Instead it had been part of the journey to where he stood right now.

In the bathroom upstairs, he ran cold water and splashed it on his face. The reflection in the mirror amazed him. He saw traces of his father—the set of his jaw and the shape of his head. His eyes were different. They were his mother's…before.

A sound made him stand up. Did he just hear the door? Did he fail to latch it last night and now the wind had pushed it open? Maybe or maybe not. He would not simply dismiss it. Not the time to take chances. He moved silently out of the bathroom and into the hallway. That skill had saved him more than once, and now he made his way to the staircase without making a single floorboard squeak.

The sound that had broken into his reverie wasn't the wind shoving the door open, and the proof of it came in the form of a woman who might have thought she moved through his house without making noise. On that score, she'd be wrong. He knew every moan and creak this house made, despite the long years away. Those kinds of things had a way of staying with a person.

From where he stopped, he could see her clearly as she stood in the office doorway but unfortunately couldn't hear what she'd just said. Given the room she'd now stepped into, he could very well imagine what her comment might have been, and it made him smile. How convenient that everything had been put into place. He just wished he had the syringe in his hand. Oh, well, he'd make do. He'd been doing that his whole life.

She didn't hear him as he entered the office. Light on his feet was his trademark even in a house he didn't know quite this well. She stood staring down at his tools, as if trying to figure out what they were for. She didn't have to wonder. He'd educate her on that soon enough.

He stood a mere arm's length from her, and if she'd been truly alert, she'd be able to hear his excited breath. "Beautiful, aren't they?"

She screamed and jumped back as if she'd just experienced an electric shock. Exactly the move he'd been anticipating and hoping for. Not much of a challenge to take her down. She turned out to be scrappy, he'd give her props for that. Too bad for her that she was too small and he was too big. A whole lot more experience also gave him a huge advantage. She wasn't a match for him, and if she'd realized that, she never would have stepped foot inside this house. This home invader had not done her homework.

Once he had her subdued, tied up, and on a chair, he had a chance to take a good look at her. The face that looked back at him came as a surprise. "Well, I'll be damned. Now, missy, if I pull the gag out of your mouth, you promise not to scream? We need to get to know each other a little better. Promise you'll be a good girl?"

Her eyes were blazing, a sort of "if looks could kill" expression, and he knew she would fight him if given even the slightest opportunity. Then her face softened, and she nodded. He pulled the cloth from her mouth, even though he didn't really believe she would behave. She coughed as she spit out, "You're him."

"Oh, him? As in the Seeker. Or at least that's how I think of myself. Of course I am. If I'm not mistaken, that's who you came here looking for, wasn't it?"

"Seeker. That's fucked up. You're no seeker. You're a monster."

He walked around her, touching her hair as he went past, and meandered toward his lineup of tools that had become scattered during the scuffle. That would never do. "I beg to differ with you. I don't kill."

"Seriously? How fucked up are you? Ask those bodies down at the ME's office if you're a killer. Pretty sure you'll get a different answer."

He straightened his things and, when satisfied, picked up one of the syringes and studied it as if he'd never seen it before. He liked the color of the cocktail it held. He liked even better how it worked once that liquid found its way into an unwilling vein. "It's all in your perspective. You see a killer. I see a Seeker. I've been one since the day I captured my mother's soul."

"You killed your mother?" Her voice rose in a quite unpleasing way. This back-and-forth had been fun for a minute or two. Now it was getting on his nerves. He held up the syringe and pushed the plunger until a golden drop trickled from the needle head.

He looked over at her with her wild eyes and full lips turned down into a frown. "Of course I didn't kill my mother. Cancer did that. I just learned the truth from her, and it has carried forward in my work. She gave me a priceless gift with her final breath, and I'm quite grateful for it. My precious mother was a wonderful woman who didn't deserve what happened to her."

"Your father. What happened to him?"

"Well, well, well, apparently you have done a bit of homework. You and your little friends, I presume."

"You know who I am?" The fear that came into her voice made the conversation more fun. He liked it when they were scared.

"Not your name, exactly, but I know who your friends are. A cop and an ME's assistant named Vi."

Her gaze darted around the room before coming back to settle on his face. "Don't get too cocky. They all know who you are. Did you kill your father too? Is that why he disappeared?"

He shrugged and laughed. This game really was fun. "I'll tell you a little secret while we get ready."

"Ready for what?"

"You'll see." He walked around behind her and pressed the needle into her neck. God, he liked how it felt when he pushed that plunger and felt the muscles beneath his hands tense. Nothing like it. His cocktail didn't take long to achieve the desired effects. He untied her hands and legs while at the same time keeping her from sliding like a rag to the floor. He didn't want his things messed up again after he'd just gotten them all put back into order. Instead, he guided her to the plastic, making sure to position her just so. "Here's my secret. Dear old Dad didn't exactly disappear. You see, darling, he never left the house."

Even with the drugs coursing through her and immobilizing her body, her mind worked. The beauty of the old doc's magic formula. She understood everything, and it showed in her eyes. She had such pretty eyes.

He put his mouth close to her ear and whispered, "Yes, that's right." He pressed a kiss to her ear, almost laughing as he did. "Daddy is right below you, taking what some so coarsely refer to as a dirt nap. He was my very first, you know. I got better after that." He leaned away from her and looked down at his organized tools. He picked up a shiny scalpel. "Would you like me to tell you the whole story before we begin?"

He leaned close to her face this time and peered into her eyes. "Oh, I think that's a yes. Here goes." He got up and pulled the chair next to the tarp. With the knife still in his hand, the Seeker started to tell her of his great work. The look in her eyes was divine.

Chapter Twenty-five

The urgency that compelled Vi to drive back home was unlike anything she'd ever experienced before. She broke every speed limit between the ME's office and the house and sent up a thanks that she didn't get pulled over in the process. Her tires scattered gravel at the front of Kat's home as she screeched to a stop.

Not a big surprise to see her grandmother on the porch since every sense she possessed had gone on high alert. What did surprise her was to see her mother and, between them, very much in the flesh, Lucy. For a couple of seconds, she just stared at the trio because she'd realized with a start that Lucy saw them too.

She shook off the shock and bounded up the steps. "What?" She faced the apparitions, and the one very alive dog, and waited. Her family had come for a reason, and she didn't have time to play a guessing game. For once in her life she prayed for straight and clear. She doubted she'd get it, and she didn't.

As before, her grandmother had only one thing to say. "She needs you."

"No shit." In life she'd never spoken to her grandmother like that. She wasn't overly proud of herself for doing it in death. The point was, if spirits were going to come to her, then they could damn well be helpful, and cryptic wasn't. Her mother, who'd never appeared to her before, reached up and touched her eyes. She didn't speak, but then again, no one ever did except for her grandmother.

"I know, Mom. I know it's him. I know. Now, help me find him."

In a flash they disappeared. She looked down at Lucy. "I don't suppose you can help? Did they tell you anything?" As if understanding, Lucy turned and raced toward the back of the house and her dog door. Vi blew out a breath. "Not this again."

Lucy wasn't giving up. She went in and out of the dog door at least half a dozen times in a frenzied loop. "I can't get through there," she said. Lucy didn't even pause. What was it with Lucy and the damn dog door?

Vi looked at it again. No way could she fit through there. It appeared to be big enough for a dog maybe fifty pounds, sixty tops. It most assuredly had not been designed for an adult to slide through. In fact, she thought pretty strongly that it had been designed so that an adult couldn't get through it. Then Lucy did something that made her think differently. On about her eighth round of in-and-out, she leapt up to the doorknob. She did the same leap three times. Could it work? It might be a worth a try.

Vi got down on the ground, reached in through the dog door, and felt up for the doorknob. *Please don't be dead-bolted.* With a whole lot of effort and a shoulder that would most certainly end up bruised, she reached the doorknob and turned the lock. The moment of truth. She stood up and tried it. No deadbolt. Hallelujah. The door opened.

"Kat," she screamed as she ran toward the office where they'd done so much work the night before. "Kat!" She raced to the bedroom. The bed she'd left in a tangled mess earlier in the morning was now smooth and made up. The silence surrounding her told her everything she feared.

Back in the office she looked around. Printouts were spread all over the desk in random piles. She dug through until she found what she'd hoped to uncover. She had a bad, bad feeling that Kat had done precisely what she'd promised she wouldn't. Why did she believe that she'd had her fingers crossed behind her back when she'd made Vi the promise? She raced back out into the car, Lucy on her heels. She opened the passenger door, and Lucy jumped in. In the passenger's seat, Lucy sat upright and staring out the windshield. She looked as tense as Vi felt.

She reached over and ran a hand over her head. The simple gesture, the touch of her fur against Vi's fingertips gave her courage. "Okay, girl. Let's hope we get there before your partner does something really dumb." If she hasn't already, she thought but didn't say out loud. No sense worrying the dog.

❖

Kat had never been so scared. In her mind she screamed as loud as her lungs would allow. Nothing came out of her mouth. The thing was, she couldn't talk. Couldn't move or run or hide. Whatever this fiend had injected into her had made her a mummy as surely as if her body had been wrapped in strips of treated linen. A mummy whose body refused to respond while its mind worked with perfect clarity. She wondered with horror if this was what had happened to all the others, including Vi's mother. If her body worked, she'd have thrown up.

A million things were flying through her mind. Mostly she cursed herself for the overconfidence that had brought her here and the curiosity that had pushed her through the back door when she should have turned away and left, taking it further to the professionals. The worst part came with the certainty she would die here on the floor of a killer's childhood home. All the promise of last night would be lost.

No one knew she'd come here. She hadn't called Vi or Circe or Diana. She hadn't left a note at her house. Nothing would point anyone in the direction of this place, if anyone was even looking. They had no reason to. She worked from home. Sometimes she could go days without talking to anyone. For a long time that had been fine. Now it made her want to sob.

She'd finally met someone who made her feel alive and wanted. Someone who made her want to jump out of bed each morning and see what the new day would bring. After years of avoiding her computer, she was finally thrilled to sit down again and flex her mental muscles, and all of it because of Vi. Since the day she stepped into her life, everything had been better, and each day it became more so.

Now it was all about to end, just because she'd decided she could be a superhero PI. Nothing superhero about her. She was an idiot.

"You are going to be such a prized addition to my collection." He held a wicked-looking scalpel as he circled above her. Because her eyes wouldn't move, she could see him only when he leaned over her. She didn't like what she saw when he did that and wished he'd sit back down in the chair he'd dragged over.

"You see." He bent over her now, and she noticed how his face had changed. He didn't look the same. That scared her most of all. "It's all about the eyes. I've been studying them for years and years." His laugh brought a new wave of nausea.

"My mother showed me the way. Oh, don't you worry now." He patted the top of the head. "Like I told you earlier, I didn't kill her. Oh, did I tell you I saw you and Vi together? I came for a little nocturnal visit last night." This time his laughter was bold and loud. Her stomach rolled again, and she wondered if she would gag and die on her own vomit.

"Unfortunately, the police car parked in your driveway gave me second thoughts. Minor setback, that's all. My plans were to show up again tonight. At least they were until you came to me. Now isn't this fun? I know it is for me. I get to add you to my collection, and then I'm going for the best prize of all. You have no way of knowing that Vi's mother was one of my early cases. Actually, my first non-related project. I learned so much from her, and now I can use all that hard-earned knowledge when I take her daughter. I'm a little disappointed in myself that it took me longer than it should have before I recognized those eyes. When I did, it made my day."

The crazy bastard got a high out of this. She could hear it in his voice and see it in his eyes when he'd stop his pacing and look down at her. Vi had given her Alan's name to research, and it had brought up interesting things like his prominent family, his mother's death from cancer, his father's disappearance. What hadn't fully dropped into place until right now was the piece about Alan's military service. He'd entered the service right after graduation from high school, his father still serving as eastern Washington's golden boy in Congress. He'd gone missing right before Alan had been stationed in Alaska. Vi's mother had been murdered shortly after his deployment to the base there. The pieces of the puzzle clicked together to form a sickening picture.

He droned on, detailing his work as he referred to the gruesome murders, when she heard something. It wasn't Alan. He stood at her feet regaling her with what he clearly believed to be his divine purpose. Despite all his bragging, she knew him to be nothing more than a delusional serial killer.

There it was again. Given the rest of her sense were dulled, her hearing remained acute, and she definitely heard something that hadn't been there before. Could she dare to hope someone had come after her? A darker thought intruded on the momentary ray of hope. What if he wasn't doing this alone?

"Well, those are the highlights. I wanted you to understand the higher purpose of what I do. I don't want you going to the great beyond believing that I'm some kind of freak, because I'm not. What I do is important, and you're going to help me further my knowledge. You are going to be part of the higher purpose. Isn't that wonderful? Your soul will stay with me right here." He patted his chest. "And those pretty eyes of yours, well, let's just say they'll have a new home as well."

Now he lowered himself to his knees next to her head so close she could feel the fabric of his slacks against her cheek. He leaned over her face, and she could smell his acrid breath. The scalpel looked huge as he waved it back and forth. When he set it down, relief almost made her cry. "First things first." He picked up a small roll of duct tape. Her relief vanished as he taped her eyelids to her forehead and she understood why.

Oh my. Could this get any more fun? He'd been a little pissed off when he'd first realized this woman had stumbled onto his private domain and his secret. Then it had all changed in a heartbeat when he decided to make her part of the process. In fact, it was turning into something really entertaining, particularly considering where he had her spread out. He would be able to complete his work with Daddy so close beneath her. Talk about poetic justice.

Despite the fact his cocktail had done its work and immobilized her, emotions were rolling off her like waves, exactly the way he liked it. Her mind continued on full alert, and she understood everything he said to her. That part made this all the more satisfying. At the same time, he didn't want any of his subjects to believe him to be a garden-variety murderer. He'd seen plenty of those in his career both in the military and as a civilian. No way would he be lumped in with any of those bastards. They were mere killers.

He'd given her the history lesson, so she understood where she fit in. He had even tried to make her understand that he'd be capturing her soul while also adding her contribution to his collection. She got the latter when he taped her eyelids to her forehead. Staying tidy was a high priority for him, as was being clean and neat. The signs of a true professional.

For a few seconds he studied her face. Yes. Time for the second cocktail. This step always made for a moment of great satisfaction. Like that day all those years ago when he'd stood next to his mother's bed, her hand clinging to his with surprising strength. Of course he'd realized later on that she'd had a mission too and she'd been showing him the way. Even as she'd been dying, his mother had been a messenger, the one true person in his life, and he'd be eternally grateful for the way she'd shown him destiny.

Now the time had come to wrap up this project. To linger over her, as much as he might want to, didn't figure into his plans. He still had another mission to complete today. The thrill of adding both mother and daughter to his collection filled him with almost orgasmic excitement. Just the thought brought joy, not to mention that he'd never done two in one day. The higher peaks he would reach before the sun set today went beyond incredible.

He held up the syringe and smiled at the liquid that filled it. Once administered, it would work relatively fast. At the same time, it stayed slow enough that he could enjoy the journey from life to release. That's what he waited for with such anticipation. The final release that brought their souls home. He had perfected his method of providing that over years, and now the journey moved smoothly and flawlessly. His smile stretched his face as he leaned close to her ear.

"Let's do this."

Chapter Twenty-six

Vi saw Kat's car parked down the block from the address she'd come here searching for, and the sight of it made her stomach roll. She'd hoped against hope after she'd left the house that Kat hadn't repeated her amateur investigation work at the second address they'd uncovered. Her hopes had just been hit with a giant bucket of ice water.

Not expecting a different result than her previous attempts, she tried Kat's phone one more time. It went directly to voice mail again. "Damn you, Kat." Before she stuffed the phone into her pocket, she sent Circe a text to tell her where she'd located Kat's car. Why hadn't she put Diana's number in her phone last night instead of writing it on a piece of paper that was God knows where right now? She hoped Circe could get the message to Diana ASAP. This situation called for law enforcement, not a dog handler or a med student.

She left her car parked behind Kat's and started down the street, checking each of the mailboxes as she went. Lucy stayed close. No collective mailbox station in this neighborhood. Each and every driveway was capped by a single box with a single address. When she reached the one she looked for, she picked up speed as she ran down it. The air felt thick as it pressed against her skin. The spirits were here, even if she couldn't see them. If she had any doubts about Alan being the one they were searching for, they were firmly laid to rest. The closer she came to the house, the more the air thickened in a way that wasn't natural. This was not going to be good. She had a hunch Lucy felt it too, as she never moved more than three feet away from Vi.

A car sat parked in the driveway. Impossible to know if it was his. Equally impossible to believe it wasn't. She jumped when she felt the touch of fingers on her cheek. The voice in her ear said in an urgent whisper, "Hurry."

Tears blurred her vision as she recognized the voice. "Okay, Mom. I'm hurrying."

She wiped away the tears with the back of her hand as she sprinted toward the massive front door with the elaborate pillars and gabled overhang. It was the first time she'd heard her mother's voice since the morning she'd left their home, never to return. "I'm hurrying." She kept wiping away the tears and telling herself to knock it off. She'd have time enough to cry later.

The front door proved to be locked. Big surprise there. Nobody in their right mind would leave a house like this unsecured. She almost laughed. The guy they were looking for was most assuredly not in his right mind.

Where to go from here? This place was huge, and she ran around toward the back, trying to find another entrance. In the rear, she discovered a door to the kitchen not only unlocked but open a crack. Before she stepped through it, she stopped and listened. In some distant room, she could hear a voice, a man's voice, and the words she heard sent ice down her spine.

"Do no harm, my ass," she muttered under her breath as she entered the kitchen. "Before she took more than a step inside, she turned to Lucy. "Stay," she commanded her. Lucy sat. "I'll be back," she promised as she quietly pulled the door shut. While she appreciated Lucy being with her, she worried that she might alert him to their presence, and for reasons she couldn't explain, she believed that would not go down well.

The first thing she spied once she got inside the big kitchen was a teakettle on the stove. It looked heavy, and that was good enough. It had to be, because that's all there appeared to be, and she wasn't going to take the time to try to find something better.

She followed the sound of the man's voice, and when she looked in through the open doorway to an office, she almost dropped the kettle. *Dear, sweet Jesus.* A scream rose in her throat. Alan leaned over Kat, who was lying on a sheet of plastic like Jesus on the cross. She didn't understand why Kat wasn't trying to get away. He held a needle mere inches from her arm, just about to plunge it into her flesh. Everything about the room, about Kat, about Alan telegraphed wrong in ways she couldn't quite categorize. She didn't have time to try to figure out why either.

"No!" She raced forward and swung the kettle as hard as she could. It connected with Alan's head, and he toppled over sideways.

He bellowed in rage and kicked his legs. She could tell he'd been stunned by the blow but held onto consciousness. Around him stood her mother and the victims from the ME's office, as well as others she didn't recognize. Her mother's gaze connected with hers, and she gave Vi a little nod. She didn't need to hear her voice again; she knew what she needed to do.

Vi pulled back her arm and once more swung the teakettle. It connected with his head. This time he didn't kick, scream, or move.

"Well." Diana's voice came from the doorway at the same time Lucy raced in to begin licking Kat's face. "I guess you didn't need me after all."

Kat's eyes fluttered open. Jesus, she felt awful. Her eyes hurt, her stomach rolled, and everything ached. For a second she wondered if she'd tied one on. Then, as her eyes focused, she realized she wasn't at home, and it all came back to her in a frightening rush.

She lay in a hospital bed. The lights were low, the sky dark outside the window. On the other side of the door, the sounds were muted, undoubtedly nurses going about their duties as the patients slept. A white blanket was pulled up almost to her chin. She shifted and groaned. Her whole body ached as though she'd been beaten.

"You're awake."

Kat turned her head to see Vi sitting in a chair. "Yeah, and to be honest I'm not all that sure I'm happy about it. What the hell did Alan shoot me up with? I feel like I just went twenty rounds with Mike Tyson."

Vi came to the side of the bed and took her hand, pulling it to her lips for a kiss. "We're not sure exactly. Some kind of custom-made date-rape cocktail, but he's not talking. We had to treat you the best we could."

"You didn't kill him?" She remembered Vi coming into the room like a warrior and blindsiding that son of a bitch. She might have been drugged to hell, but she recalled that when Vi hit him, he hadn't gotten back up.

She shook her head. "I'm not a killer. Kind of goes against what I'm trying to be. Knocking the asshole out is another story. Let's just say he's going to have a headache for a good long time."

"Most excellent." She squeezed Vi's hand. "I'm glad you're here.

Are you okay? That whole smacking somebody had to be traumatic for you."

"I'm fine. You're right. Hurting people isn't my thing. Then again, there are exceptions to everything. You worried me more. I came in the ambulance with you here to the hospital. Diana and her crew are at the house now."

"Did you see the eyes?"

Vi's cringe would have been impossible to miss unless she had been rendered totally blind. "Kind of hard not to."

As long as she lived, Kat would never be able to banish the macabre scene in that office, candles flickering as though arranged for a romantic tryst. Instead of romance, the room had been set up as a horror chamber, with the specimen jars that had prompted their inquiry into Alan's history displayed all over the room. Inside were eyes, and though she wasn't a doctor, no one had to tell her they were human eyes. The creep had been killing people and saving their eyes. What kind of monster did something like that?

The truth came out in a whisper. "He almost got mine."

Vi leaned down and kissed her forehead. "No, he didn't. I wouldn't have let that happen."

Brave and comforting words. She knew the truth in her heart. "If you hadn't come when you did…"

"Shhhh, all that matters is that I did. Don't let your mind go to the *might haves* and *should haves*. That way of thinking will drive you crazy."

"Thank you." She squeezed Vi's hand, never more grateful for someone to hold on to.

"Anytime, anywhere. Forever." Vi kissed her again. "I promise."

Tears welled in her eyes at the words. "I don't think I'll try for a PI license," she said with a crooked smile.

Vi laughed. "That's a good plan, because you suck at it."

Epilogue

Vi sat at the kitchen table drinking coffee with Kat while they waited for Circe and Diana. What a whirlwind the last year had turned out to be. She'd come here to become a doctor and, more specifically, a forensic pathologist. Her goal remained still firmly on track. She'd finished her first year of med school and kept her job at the ME's office. After everything that had happened and her part in solving the murders came out, even Dr. Durze afforded her grudging respect.

What she hadn't anticipated came in the form of falling in love with a beautiful, smart, and funny K9 handler-farmer-computer genius. Her personal life had never been this thrilling. In fact, she no longer lived in the little rental, having broken her year-long lease to make a move. It was a very big move. She lived in the big house now and loved waking up every morning next to Kat and, on most mornings, with Lucy licking her face.

Her start of this new life with a new love wasn't the end of the story. The strangest thing of all had been finding out she had a family. After her grandmother had died, she'd been alone and adrift in the world. Though she'd tried to come to grips with the reality that she had to move forward in life on her own, it had been a difficult hurdle to clear.

Now, in the blink of an eye, she was not only not alone in the world, but she also had a whole family at her side. She'd met her father and now had a greater understanding of what had happened all those years ago and the motivators behind the decisions her mother had made. She'd always thought she'd hate the man who left her mother pregnant and alone. Strange how it hadn't turned out that way at all. She liked him a lot and knew in her heart that, over time, she would love him.

Her sister Circe had already captured her heart, and she loved her as much as if they'd known each other forever. Diana proved to be an absolute joy to have as a sister-in-law and Zelda just flat-out amazing. If she could, she'd steal that dog from her sister.

At the sound of Circe's voice, Vi got up and grabbed a couple more mugs. Diana had called earlier to announce a family briefing on the status of Alan's case. The wheels of justice moved slowly, but given the size of this case, it didn't come as a big surprise. After waiting so long to see anything at all happen, she embraced an attitude of gratitude for the of work law enforcement now.

"Thanks," Diana said as Vi handed her the mug full of hot, fresh coffee. Circe kissed her cheek and ruffled her hair. She liked to impress upon Vi her family position as older sister.

"Okay, so here's the latest," Diana said as she sat down. "The FBI have fully taken over. We're out. They're in."

That bit of news didn't shock her. It had become clear pretty quickly that Alan's killings weren't limited to Spokane County. The jars were too numerous. It became federal the moment he stepped across a state line.

"Good." Kat's voice held the bitterness that came from almost being a victim. "I hope they lock the creep up and lose the key."

Diana nodded. "Usually we locals hate it when the feds step in. Not in this case. This guy is one of the smartest serial killers I've ever seen, and if he hadn't started to unravel, we might never have caught him."

"What do you mean, unravel?" Kat took a sip of her coffee.

"He'd been killing maybe one person a year since his father went missing, at least until recently. For whatever reason, he began to go off the rails, which is what got him into trouble. He killed too many people in the same area, and the threads, as you well know, started trailing back to him."

Vi had been thinking about his change in behavior. "I wonder what made him start falling apart."

This time Diana shook her head. "Don't know. This guy is smart, and he played us during our interrogations. It was frustrating as hell, and he knew it. Now he's doing the same thing to the FBI. He thinks he's in charge and is doling out one piece of information at a time. What he doesn't get is that, in the end, they'll kick his ass. He's going to spend the rest of his life in jail unless he gets convicted in a state with the death penalty, and then…"

Vi wasn't sure how she felt about that idea. After losing her mother, she completely understood the eye-for-an-eye philosophy. But since part of her was all doctor, taking a life went against everything she trained for. Better to let others make those kinds of decisions. She would simply be grateful he'd be locked up and never again be a free man, regardless of the ultimate disposition of the cases against him.

"What about what I told you?" Kat asked.

Once Kat had recovered from the drugs he'd injected into her, she'd described how Alan had ranted and bragged about his exploits and his murders, and Vi had shared that information with Diana. It still scared Vi that he'd never told them exactly what he'd put into Kat's veins.

"Your information has been critical despite his reticence, and at least one mystery has been resolved. We found his father's remains beneath the floorboards of his office. Now we have to identify the rest of his victims. We believe he's been killing since his days in the military, which, by the way, is how he encountered your mother. He was stationed in Alaska when he targeted her."

Vi nodded. She'd already put that piece of the puzzle together, even before he confirmed it in his rantings to Kat, and now that they knew who really killed her mother, the machinery had been put in motion to release the man sitting in prison and who everyone now knew was innocent. She didn't have much to feel good about when it came to capturing Alan, but this one thing pleased her.

After Diana finished sharing with them what she could about the ongoing case, Vi got up and pulled a bottle of champagne from the refrigerator. As she did that, Kat grabbed four crystal glasses from the cupboard.

"What's this?" Circe asked.

Vi smiled as she popped the cork. "We have news to share too." She met Kat's gaze, and warmth flooded her. It was a great feeling. She took a breath and said with a giant smile, "We're getting married."

About the Author

Sheri Lewis Wohl grew up in northeast Washington State, and though she always thought she'd move away, never has. Despite traveling throughout the United States, Sheri always finds her way back home. And so she lives, plays, and writes amidst mountains, evergreens, and abundant wildlife.

When not working the day job in federal finance, she writes stories that typically include a bit of the strange and unusual and always a touch of romance. Her novel *Twisted Whispers* was a 2016 Golden Crown Literary Award winner for Paranormal/Horror, and *Twisted Screams* was a finalist for a 2017 Golden Crown Literary Award.

Sheri and her K9 partner, Zoey, are a nationally certified K9 Search & Rescue team. She also likes to participate in local triathlons and puts her acting chops to use every chance she gets. You can catch her in televisions shows such as *Z Nation* and *Grimm*.

Learn more about Sheri at her website www.sherilewiswohl.com, her blog sherilewiswohl.wordpress.com, Twitter: @sherilewiswohl, and Facebook: @SheriLewisWohl.

Books Available From Bold Strokes Books

Blood of the Pack by Jenny Frame. When Alpha of the Scottish pack Kenrick Wulver visits the Wolfgangs, she falls for Zaria Lupa, a wolf on the run. (978-1-63555-431-1)

Cause of Death by Sheri Lewis Wohl. Medical student Vi Akiak and K9 Search and Rescue officer Kate Renard must work together to find a killer before they end up the next targets. In the race for survival, they discover that love may be the biggest risk of all. (978-1-63555-441-0)

Chasing Sunset by Missouri Vaun. Hijinks and mishaps ensue as Iris and Finn set off on a road trip adventure, chasing the sunset, and falling in love along the way. (978-1-63555-454-0)

Double Down by MB Austin. When an unlikely friendship with Spanish pop star Erlea turns deeper, Celeste, in-house physician for the hotel hosting Erlea's show, has a choice to make—run or double down on love. (978-1-63555-423-6)

Party of Three by Sandy Lowe. Three friends are in for a wild night at billionaire heiress Eleanor McGregor's twenty-fifth birthday party. Love, lust, and doing the right thing, even when it hurts, turn the evening into one that will change their lives forever. (978-1-63555-246-1)

Sit. Stay. Love. by Karis Walsh. City girl Alana Brendt and country vet Tegan Evans both know they don't belong together. Only problem is, they're falling in love. (978-1-63555-439-7)

Where the Lies Hide by Renee Roman. As P.I. Camdyn Stark gets closer to solving the case, will her dark secrets and the lies she's buried jeopardize her future with the quietly beautiful Sarah Peters? (978-1-63555-371-0)

Beautiful Dreamer by Melissa Brayden. With love on the line, can Devyn Winters find it in her heart to stay in the small town of Dreamer's Bay, the one place she swore she'd never remain? (978-1-63555-305-5)

Create a Life to Love by Erin Zak. When sixteen-year-old Beth shows up at her birth mother's door, three lives will change forever. (978-1-63555-425-0)

Deadeye by Meredith Doench. Stranded while hunting the serial predator Deadeye, Special Agent Luce Hansen fights for survival while her lover, forensic pathologist Harper Bennett, hunts for clues to Hansen's disappearance along the killer's trail. (978-1-63555-253-9)

Endangered by Michelle Larkin. Shapeshifters Officer Aspen Wolfe and Dr. Tora Madigan fight their growing attraction as they work together to destroy a secret government agency that exterminates their kind. (978-1-63555-377-2)

Incognito by VK Powell. The only thing Evan Spears is focused on is capturing a fleeing murder suspect until wild card Frankie Strong is added to her team and causes chaos on and off the job. (978-1-63555-389-5)

Insult to Injury by Gun Brooke. After losing everything, Gail Owen withdraws to her old farmhouse and finds a destitute young woman, Romi Shepherd, living in a secret room. (978-1-63555-323-9)

Just One Moment by Dena Blake. If you were given the chance to have the love of your life back, could you ignore everything that went wrong and start over again? (978-1-63555-387-1)

Scene of the Crime by MJ Williamz. Cullen Mathew finds herself caught between the woman she thinks she loves but can no longer trust and a beautiful detective she can't stop thinking about who will stop at nothing to find the truth. (978-1-63555-405-2)

Fear of Falling by Georgia Beers. Singer Sophie James is ready to shake up her career, but her new manager, the gorgeous Dana Landon, has other ideas. (978-1-63555-443-4)

Daughter of No One by Sam Ledel. When their worlds are threatened, a princess and a village outcast must overcome their differences and embrace a budding attraction if they want to survive. (978-1-63555-427-4)

Playing with Fire by Lesley Davis. When Takira Lathan and Dante Groves meet at Takira's restaurant, love may find its way onto the menu. (978-1-63555-433-5)

Practice Makes Perfect by Carsen Taite. Meet law school friends Campbell, Abby, and Grace, law partners at Austin's premier boutique legal firm for young, hip entrepreneurs. Legal Affairs: one law firm, three best friends, three chances to fall in love. (978-1-63555-357-4)

The Last Seduction by Ronica Black. When you allow true love to elude you once and you desperately regret it, are you brave enough to grab it when it comes around again? (978-1-63555-211-9)

Wavering Convictions by Erin Dutton. After a traumatic event, Maggie has vowed to regain her strength and independence. So how can Ally be both the woman who makes her feel safe and a constant reminder of the person who took her security away? (978-1-63555-403-8)

A Bird of Sorrow by Shea Godfrey. As Darrius and her lover, Princess Jessa, gather their strength for the coming war, a mysterious spell will reveal the truth of an ancient love. (978-1-63555-009-2)

All the Worlds Between Us by Morgan Lee Miller. High school senior Quinn Hughes discovers that a broken friendship is actually a door propped open for an unexpected romance. (978-1-63555-457-1)

Falling by Kris Bryant. Falling in love isn't part of the plan, but will Shaylie Beck put her heart first and stick around, or tell the damaging truth? (978-1-63555-373-4)

An Intimate Deception by CJ Birch. Flynn County Sheriff Elle Ashley has spent her adult life atoning for her wild youth, but when she finds her ex, Jessie, murdered two weeks before the small town's biggest social event, she comes face-to-face with her past and all her well-kept secrets. (978-1-63555-417-5)

Cash and the Sorority Girl by Ashley Bartlett. Cash Braddock doesn't want to deal with morality, drugs, or people. Unfortunately, she's going to have to. (978-1-63555-310-9)

Secrets in a Small Town by Nicole Stiling. Deputy Chief Mackenzie Blake has one mission: find the person harassing Savannah Castillo and her daughter before they cause real harm. (978-1-63555-436-6)

Stormy Seas by Ali Vali. The high-octane follow-up to the best-selling action-romance *Blue Skies*. (978-1-63555-299-7)

The Road to Madison by Elle Spencer. Can two women who fell in love as girls overcome the hurt caused by the father who tore them apart? (978-1-63555-421-2)

Dangerous Curves by Larkin Rose. When love waits at the finish line, dangerous curves are a risk worth taking. (978-1-63555-353-6)

Love to the Rescue by Radclyffe. Can two people who share a past really be strangers? (978-1-62639-973-0)

Love's Portrait by Anna Larner. When museum curator Molly Goode and benefactor Georgina Wright uncover a portrait's secret, public and private truths are exposed, and their deepening love hangs in the balance. (978-1-63555-057-3)

Model Behavior by MJ Williamz. Can one woman's instability shatter a new couple's dreams of happiness? (978-1-63555-379-6)

Pretending in Paradise by M. Ullrich. When travelwisdom.com assigns PR specialist Caroline Beckett and travel blogger Emma Morgan to cover a hot new couples retreat, they're forced to fake a relationship to secure a reservation. (978-1-63555-399-4)

Recipe for Love by Aurora Rey. Hannah Little doesn't have much use for fancy chefs or fancy restaurants, but when New York City chef Drew Davis comes to town, their attraction just might be a recipe for love. (978-1-63555-367-3)

The House by Eden Darry. After a vicious assault, Sadie, Fin, and their family retreat to a house they think is the perfect place to start over, until they realize not all is as it seems. (978-1-63555-395-6)

Uninvited by Jane C. Esther. When Aerin McLeary's body becomes host for an alien intent on invading Earth, she must work with researcher Olivia Ando to uncover the truth and save humankind. (978-1-63555-282-9)

BOLDSTROKESBOOKS.COM

Looking for your next great read?

Visit BOLDSTROKESBOOKS.COM
to browse our entire catalog of paperbacks, ebooks,
and audiobooks.

Want the first word on what's new?
Visit our website for event info,
author interviews, and blogs.

Subscribe to our free newsletter for sneak peeks,
new releases, plus first notice of promos
and daily bargains.

SIGN UP AT
BOLDSTROKESBOOKS.COM/signup

Quality and Diversity in LGBTQ Literature

Bold Strokes Books is an award-winning publisher
committed to quality and diversity in LGBTQ fiction.

CPSIA information can be obtained
at www.ICGtesting.com
Printed in the USA
LVHW091906120919
630816LV00005B/68/P